THE HILLS ARE STUFFED WITH SWEDISH GIRLS

by

Richard Happer

JonesCat
PUBLISHING

Published by JonesCat Publishing Ltd
PO Box 27134
Edinburgh EH10 9AJ
www.jonescat.com

ISBN 978-0-9562428-0-8

Cover artwork and typesetting by sangsterdesign.co.uk

The Author asserts the moral right to be identified as the author of this work.

For you, Rowan.
We hope you like the view.

KITLIST - FITCH

Tent
Sleeping bag
Roll mat
Stone Roses T-shirt ('What The World Is Waiting For' design)
Levis
Green Flash trainers
Underwear (3 sets – pants and socks)
Cagoule
18 packets Tesco own brand Pasta Shells 'n' Sauce (Tomato & Herb flavour)
Frisbee (with deep rim to double as plate)
Travel scrabble
Moleskine notebook & pencil
iPod with mini speakers and new playlist added – 'Grooving In The Glens'
Toilet bag containing: toothbrush, toothpaste & suntan cream
The Collected Poems of Robert Frost
Men Only Volume 23 issue 5
1 ginger cat (large)
Ray Bans

Tent – Mountain Hardwear Trango 2

Rab 4/5 season Summit 700 sleeping bag (goose down)

Thermarest

Travelpillow

North Face Goretex waterproofs

Goretex gloves

Harris Tweed cap

Walking poles

3 pairs walking trousers (1 with zip-off legs)

1 pair walking boots (Meindl Burma Pros)

6 pairs Bridgedale walking socks

1 pair action sandals

Selection of base layers

6 pairs silk boxer shorts (bought in Singapore)

Fleece

Coleman 2 Burner Dual Fuel Stove

Camping gas

Spare camping gas

2nd spare camping gas

M.S.R. Blacklite Non-stick Gourmet Cookset

Map case with Ordnance Survey maps (sheets 41, 50, 56, 57, 64)

Compass, torch & whistle

1 kilogram Waitrose honey roast ham

2 kilograms Double Gloucester cheese

Packet of 6 pitta breads

8 Waitrose on-the-vine organic plum tomatoes

1 packet bacon (smoked)

1 chorizo sausage

2 packets Waitrose gnocchi

2 packets Waitrose fresh ravioli

1 kilogram Italian risotto rice

Large Tupperware box containing selection of fresh vegetables – carrots, peppers, green beans, onions and mushrooms (porcini)

Small Tupperware box with separate plastic bags containing dried herbs – basil, tarragon, rosemary and garlic cloves

Double-ended plastic salt and pepper pot

Small bottle of olive oil

1 deli pot anchovies

1 deli pot houmous

1 deli pot mixed olives

4 packets of oatcakes

1 bottle mineral water

Plastic vitamin container (full)

Old plastic vitamin container now filled with washing-up liquid

Polythene sandwich bag containing: 2 sponge scourers & 2 Brillo pads

Hipflask of Highland Park whisky (18 year old)

Packet of cigars

First aid kit including triangular bandage

Shaving foam

Razor with 5 spare blades

Contact lenses with solution

Spectacles (Dolce & Gabbana)

Ayurvedic hair oil

Paco Rabanne aftershave

Biography of Audrey Hepburn

Compact mirror

KITLIST - MACRAE

24 condoms
8" hunting knife (with compass and sewing kit in handle)
3 metres para cord
1.5 metres snare wire
6 metres^2 industrial polythene
Black leather boots (steel toecap, 18 hole lacings)
Lightweight green trousers
Canvas army jacket with camouflage pattern
Balaclava (black, woollen)
Headtorch
1 small bag of Mars bars (snack size)
1 large bag of mushrooms (magic)
Plastic film canister containing: 1 paper-wrapped gram of cocaine
and 8 Ecstasy tablets (7 Mitsubishis and 1 flying 'V')
Brut 33 deodorant aerosol
Lucky Snoopy

KITLIST - JONESY

6 pounds of sausages (Fitch to carry)

BambambambamBAM!

"Open up, you ginger mongo!"

Which is how it starts.

With a sigh I lay my latest draft down on my desk. It had to be now. Just when I was thinking of some really cool Death rhymes.

I stand, reknot my dressing gown cord and pad along the long, stone-flagged passage that leads to the front door.

BAMBAMBAMBAMBAM!

"Hurry up, Fitchy-baby, it's adventure time!"

The door is shaking in its frame with his banging. For a second I think about not answering and just hiding. But he'd only break in and do something revolting to me.

I flip the snib and swing the door wide to reveal Alan Macrae standing on the basement steps in the rain, army kitbag in one hand, bottle of vodka in the other, big grin on his face.

Appearance of Macrae: swarthy, unshaven, ramlike.

"Got you a present," he says, thrusting me the bottle. "Top-notch 'ka. Won it from a Georgian tank commander. Dude actually distilled it in his tank's heat exchanger. It's flavoured with gunpowder. I also brought sausages."

"Oh. Wow. Good to see you," I say, slowly taking the bottle. "But you really should call before you–"

"Don't be a cock. Get your Ribena out." And he muscles past me into the dark hall that leads into the depths of the house.

I throw the door shut and catch him in the kitchen. He slings his kitbag into a dusty corner where it clatters into a rack of ancient copper saucepans. One of the pans falls and echoes round the stone hearth.

"Careful! Wentworth is very particular about his–"

"Fuck is this place?" says Macrae. "It's like a fucking tomb in here!"

I look at him properly as he stares round the kitchen. He's deeply tanned. His brown eyes shine with mischief. As he smiles, a few golden grains of sand tumble from the deep creases round his eyes. It may be more than a year since I saw him, but the old fire is still there. He glows in the basement darkness like a miniature sun.

For a second I let the warmth tingle my skin and thrill my bones. It's good to see my old friend-

-then I catch myself and remember the profound danger that this feeling represents. If I'm not careful he'll trap me in the orbit of whatever perverted plan he's obviously cooking up and then I'll never get any work done. Got to be strong with him.

"It may appear neglected, Macrae, but this is a very old house. Original New Town. Wentworth inherited it from his grandmother last year. She hadn't done anything to it in decades. I think she was a bit eccentric-"

"No shit," says Macrae, and he reaches up to a dusty shelf, pulls down a book and reads its title: "'How To Get Good Work From Bad Servants'." And he tosses the book over his shoulder into the sink, where it slides slowly into the stew of unwashed dishes. "What you living in the damn basement for? Ah, glasses."

And he opens the cabinet by the window, picks out a pair of antique crystal goblets, spits in them and wipes the goo off on his camouflage tunic.

"Wentworth doesn't like to go in the upper floors," I reply. "Says there are too many bad memories."

"Spastic rellies walled up in cupboards, that kind of thing?"

He opens the freezer and fishes for an ice cube tray. I take a breath. It's hard, but I must persevere.

"Wentworth has been very kind," I point out. "He opened his door to me at a… low time, and has been very supportive since." But Macrae isn't looking at or listening to me. He's too busy smacking the ice tray over the glasses. A couple of cubes make it in, the rest skitter all over the floor. He leaves them where they lie. "And," I add, "he's not going to take too kindly to you trashing this place. How long were you intending to-?"

"Stop stressing," he replies. "We'll be gone in the morning. On the Macrae Mission you're so desperate for. And what a Mission I have lined up for you!"

Knew it. Be strong…

"Uh, hang on. I don't remember being desperate to go any 'Mission' with you."

"Yep, still got your text." And he reaches into his camouflage jacket and pulls out a sandy, battered mobile. He clicks a couple of buttons and reads from the screen: "'Macrae it's all fucked and I don't know what to do cos me and Judy have split up nine years over just like that how could she do it to me I don't know what I'm going to do with my life it's a fucked fucked fucked fucked fucked fucked fucked fucked situation and there's no way to unfuck it you got to help me'. Where's your Ribena?"

And he starts clattering through our cupboards. A packet of rice tumbles out and spills over the floor. Macrae pushes it under the pan rack with his boot. Damn him.

"Macrae, I wrote that nine months ago!"

"Yeah, well," he shrugs, "took me a while to get some leave. But now I am here, boy, are we going to unfuck your situation! Weirdly, by getting you fucked. Just wait till I tell you the plan – it's the most awesome one ever! Ah, found it."

And he stands up holding a large bottle of Ribena.

"Macrae, it's nice of you of you to finally come and visit, but I sent that text a long time ago when I was upset and, by the sounds of things, a little drunk. I'm fine now."

"Don't act dense because you're not. You know what I mean. Shagging. You can't get over losing a bird until you shag the next one. That's physics. I am here to make that happen."

"Macrae, life is not that simple-"

"Fitchy, here are the facts." He opens the Ribena and pours a couple of wild sloshes into the glasses. Sticky purple juice goes all over the ancient oak table. "You and Judy had a tough time of it for reasons I'm not going to go into, but which were harsh. Damn harsh. So it strung you out and you split up. Understandable. Then you move in here and go a bit mental and lose your job. That's fine too. I'm not judging you."

Why is that the older a friend is, the more annoying they can be? It's like the better you know people, the more ways they find to wind you up. I'm going to have to go on the attack.

"I find it interesting that the man who once nailed his scrotum to a barstool is calling me mental."

He puts the Ribena bottle down in one of the splashes and turns to me.

"Fitchmeister. It's four in the afternoon and you're shuffling about your lair in a dressing gown that doesn't close properly. You need this. Pass me the bottle." And he reaches for the vodka which I still hold.

I can't take it any more. I turn half away and hoist the vodka behind me.

Macrae's eyebrows pile together like a caterpillar carcrash.

"Give me the 'ka, Fitchy."

And he steps menacingly towards me.

"Listen. I can't come with you," I hiss, lifting the bottle back and up over my head. "There are things you don't know-"

"And there's plenty YOU don't know."

Then he quickly dummies left, darts right, grabs my other hand and deftly twists my thumb in a vicious pincer grip until I yelp and squirm enough for him to reach the bottle. He takes it and lets me go. I slump back against the table holding my burning knuckles.

"You see, Fitchy-baby, I have in my noodle a top-secret piece of intel!" Macrae taps his temple and beams at me. "So powerful is this secret that only a handful of men know it." He unscrews the lid of the vodka bottle and throws it in the bin. "And here I am, about to entrust it to you." He pours huge measures of vodka onto the ice and Ribena, picks up the glasses and hands one to me. "If only you will spare me the courtesy of listening for just one friendly minute."

And he cracks his wildest, warmest grin at me and I try to think of something to say but can't. I stop rubbing my hand for a second and accept the drink.

Macrae smiles, hops his backside up onto the kitchen worktop and leans forward.

"Picture this, right," he says, brown eyes shining, "me and the rest of the four-five lads are sitting in a NATO camp in Afghanistan, ten miles up some godforsaken wadi. The dunes all around are rammed with bad men wanting to kill me, bum me and steal my stash, so the only thing to do is talk and I get gassing to this dude from Holland, fucking Nils or something-"

He takes a long slug of his vodbena.

"Mmm, the gunpowder really lifts it. Anyway," he goes on, "he said a pal of his had gone on a walking holiday with a couple of mates in the Scottish Highlands and – well, you remember when we used to do some hills at uni and we always joked that when we got to the top or the next glen or the campsite

13

there'd be some gorgeous European birds there, all lost and sweaty and lovely?"

"I remember," I nod, sitting a little further forward despite myself.

"Okay, so imagine this, right – roasting hot day in July. Nils's pal and his crew are walking along the West Highland Way, crossing the hills outside Crianlarich, knee deep in heather and deer and scenery and all that shit, and they see these girls coming towards them. Lovely blonde girls, from Sweden as it turns out. But these girls right… are fucking topless. Can you just visualise that? Boots, denim shorts, rucksacks, pigtails and big blonde knockers banging about in the sunshine. Isn't that amazing? All this time we were joking and laughing and it's been fucking true – the hills are stuffed with Swedish girls! So. Here's the plan." He looks around like someone might be listening. Then leans in closer. "We take a week off and do The West Highland Way." He thrusts his vodbena towards the ceiling, adding with hushed awe: "Just think. Ninety five miles of hot Scandinavian fanny…"

Then he downs the rest of drink and hops off the worktop.

"Hurry up and finish your vodbena, we got to get you packed."

I sigh.

I'd forgotten how useless mere words are against a rampaging Macrae. You might as well ask a bull with its tail on fire to please stop charging about now. Blunter tactics are required.

"Come through to my bedroom," I say, "there's something I have to show you."

And I turn and lead him into the long, stone-flagged passage.

DIARY ENTRY ENDS

FROM MACRAE'S NOTEBOOK

Macrae's log stardate: TR7-WD40-quattro

Wish I'd got here sooner.

I left the second I got his text but I ran into a spot of bother getting out of Afghanistan. Had to go cross-country on foot for a while before I stole a camel near the Pakistan border. Eventually I manage to swim the Indus then hitch through the Great Thar desert into India and pick up a dodgy passport and some top quality gear in Delhi and hop a flight from there to London.

So I'm off the plane at Heathrow and heading north as soon as I can well as soon as I'd had a ding dong with one of the hosties not for selfish reasons you understand but just to sort out my jetlag so I can be more switched on for Fitchalicious. Because hosties are the only real cure for jetlag you know. It's all about biorhythms right? Well the hosties fly all the time making their biorhythms in tune with the delays so if you shag them then you get tuned up as well. I don't know how it works because I'm not a medical man but I can tell you that by the time I left her flat I was feeling brand fucking new.

Anyway that's not the point. The point is I've bunked on a train up to Edinburgh and gone round to Fitch's gaff and –

– it's worse than I thought.

I knew he'd split up with Judy and moved in with Wentworth and lost his job and stuff. What I didn't know was just how much this would have fucked with his shit.

A five-story Georgian townhouse and Wentworth's got them living in the cellar. It's dark and cold and Fitchy is all pasty and he's not that jizzed about the Swedish girls which is suspicious for a man who hasn't had a ride in nine months and I don't know it's just not right. I've seen my old pal in all sorts of situations genuinely ill with hangovers but not like this.

The kitchen's enough of a hole but then he leads me down this creepy corridor to his bedroom like we're walking into the earth itself and fuck me how to describe this place. Well forget flies and mice I'm telling you there were frigging slugs on the ceiling. Dark mushrooms crowding the corners like youths outside a Falkirk chip shop and wine bottles fighting each other for space.

And then I see the paper.

It's everywhere. Sheets and sheets of it stacked in teetering piles and strewn over the floor and crumpled in the corners. At first I think there are swarms of epileptic spiders crawling all over the pages but then I pick one up and see it's worse than spiders it's POETRY and I feel like I just ate a yak vindaloo.

Now look Fitchy may be a talented poet. He may not. My instincts tend towards the latter but I wouldn't know a good poem from a bad fart so please don't think this is a literary issue. All I know is that he only ever writes them when he's upset. Any time he and Judy had a big rumble or his granny died or he failed a poxy final then he'd pick up his notebook.

And all it ever did was make him worse.

When he should have been drinking and shagging away his troubles he was wallowing in them like a pig in shite.

"Fuck's this?" I say, picking up a page between my finger and thumb and holding it at arm's length.

"That's what I'm telling you!" he hisses. "That's why I can't go anywhere right now."

"What did I tell you about poetry?"

"I know, I know, but that was before. Things are different now. You see, I had an epiphany."

"Eppy-fanny?" I say. "Don't like the sound of that."

"No, an epiphany. A moment of clarity. Deep understanding verging on the religious. You can't ignore that sort of thing."

His eyes are glazed like he's just chugged a tin of Evostick and his dressing gown is falling open again. His ginger cock is waggling in emphasis as he makes his points which is pretty disconcerting I can tell you.

"Fitchy, you need to tell me what happened."

"Okay, but you have to promise you'll believe me, no matter how bizarre it sounds."

"You know full well my promises are worthless."

"Can you at least pretend to promise?" he pleads. "This is important."

He seems to mean it.

I nod.

"Over there," he says, tilting his head. "Careful though. He can be a bit boisterous." And he lifts an arm covered in sctatches and manky bits of sticking plaster and points to the bed.

I follow his finger and notice for the first time that sat on the duvet nesting in paper chaos is the biggest hardest-looking ginger cat I have ever seen in my puff. This creature eyes me briefly then yawns and flips its rear end forward and starts lapping noisily at its arsehole.

"That's a hell of a puss," I say. "Jesus shite, look at the size of his pods. Where d'you get him?"

"That's the start of the mystery," whispers Fitch, eyes wide and hands waving. "He just arrived one day not long after I'd moved in. I'm not sure how he got here and I still don't know how he comes and goes – you see… there's no catflap!"

"He has has own ways," I nod. "Good strategic thinking. Clearly an officer-class feline. Mind you, I'm surprised George let you keep him."

"Oh, he wanted to get rid of him. Tried to get him in a catbox. Jones – that's his name, by the way – took one leisurely swipe and Wentworth was in the Western getting six stitches."

"Hah!" I laugh, "I like this furbag more and more. But what's he got to do with you chucking your career away?"

"He was the one who told me to write the poem."

I stop for a second and stare at my old friend. He's serious.

"I know it sounds a little weird," Fitch goes on, "but I swear it's the truth. That's how he first arrived. I woke up in the middle of the night and there he was, sat on the end of my bed glaring at me. I was scared enough to see a cat I didn't own sitting there, but then his eyes started glowing like they were lit by deep orange flames, as if there was a spirit in him or something. And then he spoke to me. Freaked me out old-style, I can tell you."

I look at Jones. Seems to me like an ordinary ginger tom a bit on the brawny side but nothing obviously supernatural about him. I look back at Fitch and I can't think of a time I've ever seen him more earnest. My massive urge to take the piss out of him is going to have to wait. This needs delicacy.

"Fitchy. That's not a little weird, that's a lot weird. How many days had you been drinking for?"

"No! That's just it, I bloody hadn't!"

"Remember who you're talking to."

"Okay, well maybe I'd had a little Rioja. But nothing heavy duty. And no more than a bottle or two. You do believe me, don't you? You promised you'd try. If you don't believe me I don't know what I'd do."

He looks so ill. Our boy's hanging on by a thread.

"So what did it sound like?"

"You do believe me! Oh, that's fantastic! Well, it's very, very difficult to describe. The closest I can get is like Sean Connery," he says, "if he was miaowing a bit as well as talking."

"Okay-"

"And had a mouse in his mouth."

I stare at him. His dressing gown is falling open again. Damn he has a big bawbag.

"What exactly did he say? I mean, you don't think you could have misunderstood him?"

"Oh no, he was very specific. He said, 'Tom Fitch, I have come here to tell you that you must write an epic poem on the Question Of Death. In iambic tetrameter rhyming abab, a thousand stanzas long. That alone will give you the power to free yourself from this darkness which has descended upon you.'"

I look at my old friend. He is perfectly serious. I don't think I've ever seen a man more in need of my help.

"That is specific," I nod. "Particularly for a cat."

"Which is why I took him so seriously."

I really don't like where this is going. Got to bring him back round.

"But why d'you think he wanted you to write a poem on the Question Of Death?"

"Maybe because Death is the only absolute in life?"

"Not true," I smile, "there's Absolut vodka."

He ignores me.

"You want me to read you a bit?" he coos, eyes starting to roll a bit.

"Uh-"

And before I can stop him he's grabbed a sheaf of paper and started reading:

> Who Is Death?
> And What Does He Think He's Doing?
> An epic poetic answer by Tom Fitch
>
> Who dulls your eyes and blacks your skin?
> Who makes you smell and steals your breath?

Who rots your head and puts maggots in?
The killer of life? Of course, it's Death!

My cat brings Death to little mice
He eats them up with savage purr
It's natural, but not that nice
And leaves but air where once was fur.

Death is nasty, death is grim
The bus of Death is 22
He's there when you don't want him
And never around when you do.

Death! Oh Death! -

"Okay, Fitchy, stop there."

"You like it?"

"I can honestly say it is the most incredible poem I have ever heard."

"Oh, thank you! Wentworth also thinks so. He says when I get it finished he'll pay for it to be published!"

"Close your dressing gown, sit on the bed and take a drink."

I propel him into a sitting position and wait until he's had a good draw of his vodbena. Then I sling my arm round him, draw him tight and say as gently as I can:

"Listen. Fair play, Fitchy. I mean, if I'd been binned by a cracking bird I'd loved for nine years and then a fire-eyed cat who sounded like Sean Connery visited me in the middle of the night and told me that writing a poem would make me feel better, I'd probably give it a go too. Got fuck all to lose at that point, right? And it is definitely a plan. But, here's the crucial thing – is it the best plan? Perhaps a better line of attack would be to go north and rattle some Swedish birds."

He shakes his head.

"Jones said-"

"But did he? Can you be sure heard him right? Big Sean can be hard to understand at the best of times. If he was miaowing and had a face full of rodent as well, who would know what the fuck he was on about? Maybe what he really said was, "Tom Fitch, you must write an epic poem about a Quest For Breasts".

"Is it possible?"

"Probable, I'd say. Look at him. A tomcat with knackers that big is far more likely to be interested in sex than poetry." And I reach into the pocket of my jacket and pull out the packet of sausages I brought. I open it out and offer one raw to Jones. The cat eyes it suspiciously for a second then there's a flash of ginger fur, a glimpse of razor claw and half the sausage is gone. Jones lifts the bit he speared to his mouth and chomps into it.

I pop the other half of the sausage in my own mouth and chew.

"You see? Captain Jones and I understand each other."

"Now you put it like that-"

I put my arm around him and pull him close until he wheezes.

"Fitchy, I know you don't see it, but you're in a very serious situation. Fucking critical in fact. So no more arguments. I'm getting you out of this place tonight. Come on, a nice blonde bouncy Swedish shag will solve all your problems."

"A profound analysis which has somehow been overlooked by all the major schools of psychotherapy," says a voice, and I look round to see George Wentworth standing in the doorway.

Description of Wentworth: tall, saggy, ivory pale; an aristocratic polar bear in a suit.

And from the smug smile on his coupon I know that things are really fucked up.

FROM WENTWORTH'S NOTEBOOK

I must confess (and I am sure that he would hold no unmatched affection for me) that Alan Macrae has never been a human being to whom I have wholly warmed. He is charismatic and has a certain rugged good look about him, undoubtedly; he

20

possesses a fine body, despite persistent abuses of it with intoxicants; he is an active person. But his mind is blunt. His sensitivities are insensitive and he has not the self-awareness to see that these failings mark a quite chasm-like flaw in his character.

Tom, bless him, has the ability to see these shortcomings and not judge them. I do not. Where Tom sees room for improvement to which he offers sympathy and guidance, I observe mere delinquency to which I give little in the way of time and a great deal in the way of distance. Tom puts up with Alan because he has a loving heart, as one might not scold a puppy that, in its affectionate desire to please, had soiled the rug rather than remove itself from your presence for even a second.

But we are puppies no longer.

And with each unannounced visit, Alan has charmed me less, and soiled my metaphorical rug (on one occasion my literal rug) more.

His appearance in our home tonight is doubly irritating. First there is the uncouth presence of the man: a scratching, sniffing, drinking machine that shares raw sausages with the cat. Then there is the issue of what that presence means to Tom.

Alan's arrival could not have come at a worse time for my dear protégé. Tom is finally, after years of wasting his talents teaching infants their ABC, applying his efforts to something worthwhile. (It's not really relevant, but I might here add a personal note that Tom has also been something of a lucky talisman to me: since he moved in I have won every single case I have presented.)

He is also free of Judy; a prodigious millstone finally shaken off. She was a personable enough female, I suppose, but she rarely encouraged his sensitive, poetical side, and seemed to lay a great deal of aggravation at his feet following their little misfortune. Indeed, when they parted in January, I felt no great sadness. It seemed to me that rather than being the end of anything, this was instead a new beginning, for the two of us.

Tom had nowhere to go and no money; I could provide both. He had lost his professional direction: I had the knowledge to act as mentor to a new, more creative endeavour. His companion of nine years had left him feeling lonely; I had known him ten and would step in to keep him company. In short, this was a chance for him to step out of the chains of that relationship and into a new era of civilised co-existence with me, in which he could pursue his artistic goals.

I simply will not let Alan distract him at such a wonderful time. Something must be done. A fly in the ointment may only be an insect, but it still must be removed.

"Good to see you, George," says Macrae, smiling disingenuously and holding out a dirty paw.

I reach over and grudgingly shake.

"You want a vodbena?" he asks.

"No, Alan," I say, "I want an ice cold glass of Moët."

"You won the case?" asks Tom. How typical of him to remember.

"Indeed," I reply, retrieving a bottle of '82 from the scullery. "We must toast the lengthy incarceration of yet another kleptomaniacal undesirable."

"What?" grunts Alan.

"Shoplifter, old smoke. I was advocate for the prosecution and secured a two year reprieve for the good burgers of Dunedin."

"What did he nick?" asks Alan.

"I believe the guilty youth was apprehended in a convenience petrol station with cylindrical snack meats inserted into his coat sleeves."

"You got a guy banged up for nicking Pepperamis from the all-night garage? That's harsh. Maybe he was hungry."

"The fact that he was apprehended while stealing food would suggest that your observation is correct, Alan. But the fact of the case is that he broke the law. He needs to be punished. It really is rather simple."

And I smile at him until he drops his eyes and glares at the floor. Round one to me. Jolly good.

I turn to face Tom.

"And how is my little poetic genius?"

"Well-" Tom starts.

"He needs to get out of this shithole," interrupts Alan. "Into the hills."

Down but not yet out. I smile and take a calming breath.

"Firstly, Alan, that's a rather insulting way to refer to a house that has been in the Wentworth family since it was built in 1820 when, I might add, the great J.M. Barrie lived next door. And secondly, Tom has everything he needs here: space, materials, a roof over his head and, most importanty-" I pause to sip my Moët, "-my support."

"But no fanny," says Alan, lifting his head and staring insolently at me.

"And 'fanny' – as you so charmingly put it – will help the creative process how, precisely?"

Alan is starting to turn puce.

"It's nature, right?! Fields and trees and bonnie lasses bum-naked in burns. Poets and artists are always using that sort of stuff as their inspiration. I'll bet Leonardo Da Doo-da hadn't been sitting around a basement for nine months when he sculpted that lad's cock."

I twirl my goblet, watching the bubbles canon into each other for a moment.

"You know, Alan, the heights of ignorance you have attained simply make my head spin. I presume you are referring to Michelangelo and his sculpture of David. And while I cannot be certain, I can make an expensively educated guess that the creator of the masterwork of the Florentine Renaissance was not inspired by a week's vodka drinking up a sodden Scottish glen."

Alan is beginning to resemble a beetroot.

"Of course he wasn't!" he spits. "But Fitchy might be – beauty is in the eye of the beholder, right?"

"No, actually, that's a common misquotation. Plato in his Symposium talked of beholding beauty with the eye of the mind, but that, I feel, is not the point you are making."

"I don't know anything about that pish," says Alan, "but I do know that this man needs Swedish girls, and soon!"

"Alan, Tom is not going anywhere."

"He bloody is."

"No, he isn't."

"Hang on, the pair of you. Don't I have a say in this?"

"So what do you say?" asks Alan.

Tom looks helplessly between the two of us. He seems so lost, I want to put my arm round him.

But at that precise moment his phone rings.

Tom looks at the screen, then up at us, blue eyes wide and shining.

"It's Judy," he says.

FROM FITCH'S DIARY

I open the basement door to a dense mist of rain. Water pours from the gutters and streams down the steps that take me up to road level. My hair is sopping by the time I get to the top. Not that I mind. There's a bounce in my bones and a flex in my muscles that I haven't felt in a long time.

Judy called me.

I reach the end of Great King Street and turn up the hill, the mist swallowing the tops of the buildings. Car tyres swish on the shining cobbles. The trees in the gardens hunch together against the wet. Their leaves are turning – it's autumn already. A whole summer has been and gone and I haven't seen my girl. The weatherman said it's been the wettest ever. I'd have to agree.

But when she phoned just now it was like that first day of spring when the sun is truly warm on your skin and every creature in the land has a glint in its eye.

The pattering of rain on paper distracts me. I look down. The pages of poem I stuffed in my cagoule pocket are getting damp. Strange thing – I grabbed them just before I left the house. Some odd part of me thought maybe she had somehow heard I was writing and wanted to read it. But now, as I kick through cascading gutters with careless ease, I realise that's stupid. There's only one reason she'd want to call me now. Only one motive behind asking to meet me tonight.

She wants us to get back together.

*

Judy suggested we meet between the art galleries on the Mound. This twisting rib of land rises from the elegant Georgian New Town to the tottering heights of the mediaeval Old. From here there's a broad view of the castle. You can walk down into the gardens or up to the bars of the Royal Mile. And of course there are the art galleries themselves. It's a nice spot.

It's also where we met for our first date – another good sign.

But God, the haar is thick tonight. The streetlights shine nicely in the damp, but the castle is nothing more than a blur. And it's bitter. Ten minutes I've been waiting and I'm starting to shiver. I huddle between the massive Ionic columns of the Scottish National Gallery and hop from foot to foot.

"Hello."

I turn to see Judy and my heart leaps in my chest like a fish in a net.

Most girls are just girls. Nice to look at and chat to, but that's as far as it goes. Some girls, though, have this light about them – it shines from their hair or their legs or the skin above their cleavage. It draws you in, like a moth to a bulb, and you just can't help staring.

Judy is the only girl I ever met who had the light shining from her eyes.

The first time I saw it, she flashed a glance at me on a bus on the way to a field trip at uni, and bombs went off in my head and trousers at the same time. Sexual terrorism – pure and simple. It wasn't that I couldn't think straight, I couldn't think. Nor could I decently get off the bus for a while. When I looked at her face I couldn't tell if her nose was pretty or her chin shapely or anything else. I'd try to work it out while her face was in profile, but then she'd turn to me and flash those eyes and once again I was lost in the glare.

Now she's standing in front of me under a see-through bubble umbrella, yellow wellies on and unruly hair flopping over one ear. But there's something not quite right. The light is still there, but it's like it's turned down a little, or shaded maybe.

"Sorry I'm late," she says.

"No problemo," I reply.

"Really, I shouldn't have kept you waiting." She looks me up and down, as if appraising the weather-worthiness of my clothes. But she doesn't catch my eye. "You look cold."

"I'm fine. Absolutely, completely fine. Takes more than a shower to dampen my spirits!"

And I smile at her. She doesn't smile back, just half turns away, looking out at the mist. She seems nervous – like a kid on the first day of school. Guess that's understandable. She was the one who made me move out all those months ago. It must be hard for her to admit she was wrong. Well, I'll happily help her out.

"You fancy a drink?" I ask. "We could pop to one of the new bars on George Street–"

"Can we just walk for now?" she asks, looking at her wellies.

"Sure."

And she instantly starts up the Mound towards the Old Town.

I flip my hood up and trot after her.

As we rise up the hill, the mist perceptibly thickens. Soon the elegant white streetlamps are nothing more than fuzzy stars.

"So. You getting out much?" she asks. Whis is a strange question. 'How have you been?' might have been better.

"Not for a month or two," I say.

"Oh, Tom," she says, suddenly turning back to me, but still not looking up. "Aren't you seeing any friends?"

Her nerves are making her voice go all high. Despairing almost. Better lighten the mood so she can speak freely.

"Well," I say, "Macrae has pitched up again. He's even madder than normal, if that's possible. It never ceases to amaze me that he defends our nation."

She smiles, but there's something mechanical about the way her lips move.

"That must be nice for you," she says. Again, a weird comment.

"It's a bit stressful actually. He wants to go on another lunatic adventure up north. This one is really insane."

"Sounds like fun!" Judy says, suddenly strangely enthusiastic. "It must be a while since you spent some time together and you used to love going up north."

I stop and turn to her. We've reached the corner of the Royal Mile and we turn the corner by Deacon Brodie's Tavern. I can hear the rain pattering on the cobbles. I say:

"I loved going north with you."

And with a blinding flash the tightness drops away, she smiles completely, the glow is right back behind her sea-blue eyes and I swear I feel nineteen again.

"Remember that time we bunked off uni and hitched to Glen Nevis?" I say.

She nods and smiles and replies:

"We camped in the glen then walked up to the waterfall and…"

"…got our picnic out, then…"

"…you kissed me and…"

"…when we turned round…"

"…a stag had eaten all the food!"

We laugh together. For a second I feel heat in my bones, despite the fog. The memory of that sunny moment is so perfect, so warm, it feels like a different person lived it.

"That was a nice spot," I say.

"A good day," she nods.

We don't say anything for a second.

Suddenly a giggling girl rockets in front of us, smiling boyfriend chasing two paces behind. They duck laughing into the pub's Dickensian glow. Through tiny square windows I watch them tumble to the bar. With the shining beer and flickering fire, the scene is almost impossibly warm and welcoming.

"You sure you don't fancy a drink?" I ask.

"Mind if we walk a little further?" she asks, and her unruly hair flops forward and drops her face into shadow again.

"Course not."

And so we continue up the cobbled hill in silence. After a couple of minutes we reach the esplanade, the broad parade ground below the castle ramparts. Nomally you can see the sheer walls and cannon embrasures picked out cleanly by floodlights. But tonight the castle is a doomed ship, lost in the thickest of fogs.

We walk over to the parapet that lines the edge of the esplanade. From here the rock drops away sharply, before curving out towards the New Town far below. On a clear day we'd be looking out at a peerless view of the city lights, and in the distance the start of the far hills of the north.

Instead we're high on our own foggy plateau, lost above the world.

Judy looks out at the greyness. My fingers pick at wet stone. It's really cold now. More like winter than early autumn.

She still isn't speaking. I'm trying to think of something to say, but my brain is frozen. An age passes. A bloody ice age we stand there.

Then I shiver, once, hard, and the oddest memory drops into my mind. I remember learning how the rock on which I'm standing as well as the valley before me were carved into their current shapes by vast glaciers. And suddenly I see the fog before me parting to reveal not a city, but fields of ice bound by a sea of snow, stretching way beyond the northern horizon. Death as far as the man can see. There must be a verse or two I could write about glaciers-

"There's something I want to say to you, Tom," comes from nowhere.

I turn round. My mind has drifted, but when I see the courage on her face my concentration snaps back.

Her eyes are focused. The little muscles around her mouth strain under the skin.

I can't wait for her to say the words. I'll say nothing for a second then just grab her and run my fingers through her hair and hold her warmth close to me.

She takes a sudden, deep breath.

"Tom," she says, "I've met someone else."

Fog freezes on me. My head spins and my knees snap like icicles.

"We're not really going out yet," she says, "but I wanted to let you know before anything... might... Oh, Tom, I know this is going to be hard, but I have to start living again."

And she stares at me, waiting for me to say something. I stare back at her, but no words come. All I can think about is damn glaciers squashing everything. She goes on:

"These last nine months since she... you know... it's been like I've been in hiberation or something. Course, I knew it was going to be hard when I made you move out, just not how hard. And I still had to do it. You were so quiet and rational about everything that had happened, and I was furious. Furious at nature, at life, at God... I thought kicking you out might shock you into saying something. But you just went. I wanted you to call, but month after month passed and you didn't and I knew that you, somehow, had truly moved on. Then I knew that I had to as well."

Judy stares at me for a long time. Only one eye is visible behind her curtain of hair, but I can clearly see a tear forming in it.

"Don't you have anything to say? Are you upset? Angry? Please, I want to talk to you about this! Do you feel anything at all!?"

"I've been writing a poem," I say, and start to reach inside my sopping cagoule.

"Tom, what is wrong with you?!" she yells. "You're like a... ghost!" And she presses her fingers hard, once, on my chest, as if to check that I am real.

Then she takes a step back. Delicate ribbons of mist curl between us.

A sob lurches in her throat. She chokes it back.

"Goodbye Tom," she says simply.

And she turns and runs and in a second the mist swallows her.

"Bye, Judy," I whisper, but she's already out of earshot.

I turn back to the parapet and stare out at the swirling greyness where the city used to be.

And that's when I realise that my vision is not a dream, but a view of an approaching reality. At some point in the future the glaciers will come again to cover this city. That's a geological certainty. We know the climate is going to change – well, what if the filthy summer was a sign the change is coming? What if this very moment is the start of it all? It has to begin sometime, why not right now?

And what will be left of us when the ice comes again? What will exist to let people in some further future know that we were once here? To show that there was Life and Beauty and Love and Death and people who appreciated all of it?

I reach into my soaking anorak and pull out my pages. They suddenly seem very thin and fragile. And they don't have the answers to any of my questions.

But now I know why I really brought them.

I lean right over the edge of the parapet and let my creation flutter to the invisible rocks below.

★

"Pack your bags, you muscle-bound mongo!"

Damp from the shower and wearing nothing but a tea-towel, Macrae lounges regally on the sofa. I don't know how he does it – all these years, all the abuse, and there's still not an ounce of fat on his torso. He'd look like a Roman sculpture if he weren't eating sausages with his fingers.

"Huh?" he gawps.

"We're off!" I cry. "Those hills are stuffed with Swedish girls and someone has to help them with their pigtails!"

"You fucking dancer!" shouts Macrae and leaps off the sofa to hug me. Sausages get air. Jones springs after them.

Wentworth pads into the room, his pale bear face drooping.

"What's going on, Tom?" he wails, his voice a few tones higher than normal.

"We're off on the West Highland Way, George."

"You're going to leave me here on my own?"

"No, because you're coming too!" And I slap him heartily on the back.

Macrae's face freezes. He and Wentworth look at each other.

"Tom, I'm terribly busy at chambers-" Wentworth starts.

"No," I interrupt, "you've just finished a case. And advocates are self-employed, so you can take time off if you want."

"Technically, but…" he starts, rolling his eyes.

Macrae leans forward and puts one hand to the side of his mouth.

"For once I agree with the goof," he says confidentially. "Not his sort of gig at all."

"Look, I know you two have your little grizzles," I say, "but we've always had fun on our adventures in the past, haven't we?"

Wentworth's eyebrows rise like a perfect pair of lemon soufflés.

"Fun?" he says.

INSERT: There then follows a lengthy series of reminiscences by Wentworth, delivered in a forthright and somewhat desultory tone. Synopsis of reminiscences:

Reminiscence 1

University field trip to Pyrenees. Easter '96. Macrae eats entire packet of laxatives in Lourdes "for a laugh". Wentworth forced to pay hospital bill.

Reminiscence 2

Wentworth's grandparents' house in Yorkshire, New Year '98.

Macrae drinks two bottles of sherry and tries to get off with Wentworth's great aunt.

Reminiscence 3

The boys win a trip to Paris in a pub quiz, July 2001.

Macrae removes his clothes during Bastille Day parade and dances naked in Trocadero fountain. Dog steals his trousers. Chaos ensues.

FITCH'S DIARY CONTINUES

"Okay, okay," I say, "but those things happened years ago. We've all matured a lot since then. No one's going to be removing their clothes-"

"Apart from the Swedish girls," interrupts Macrae.

I shoosh him with a raised palm.

"What I'm saying is that things have changed. You'd have to be blind not to see that." I take a breath. "Look at the weather. 2007 – the summer that never was. Don't you understand? This could be the start of the End. We have to get out there and find those Swedish girls now, because in a year's time, everything north of Stirling is going to be under a mile of ice."

"I don't think it's that serious-" starts Wentworth.

"But you don't know that," I say, waving my hands. "The only certainty right now is that the three of us are back together again, for the first time in years and with a little bit of time ahead of us. This might be our last ever chance to create something."

Macrae and Wentworth look at each other.

"Create what exactly?" asks Macrae.

"A book of Love," I say quietly.

Now they're staring at me. They don't see it yet. I smile and look at each of them in turn.

"Macrae's right," I say, pacing the room, "poems about Death aren't the way forward! But poems about Love, well that's very different. We'll meet the Swedish girls and celebrate their beauty by filling a book with odes to Love!"

"Dear Tom," says Wentworth, shaking his head, "it's a noble sentiment, born of your romantic heart. But my poetical efforts were produced a long time ago and even then they were rudimentary. As for Alan, and I'm sure he won't mind me saying this, there is as much chance of him writing a worthwhile poem as there is of a donkey's backside playing Rule Britannia on the clavichord."

Macrae nods.

"He's right, Fitchy," he says, "I've got fucking air for brains."

I shake my head and waggle my notebook at them.

"Forget quality for a second. As long as it's honest it has to be good. Don't you see? This is about expressing how we feel on this trip. As adventurers. As friends. As men. And that gives us total freedom. The poems will be just the start. We can keep diaries and write notes on the Way itself, draw pictures – whatever inspires us. Then, when we get back, we can publish it!"

They're still staring at me, heads cocked on opposite sides, like a pair of confused dogs.

"Look here," I say, and I scrabble around the nearest bookshelf. I pull down three old-fashioned leather-bound Moleskine notebooks. I find a pen and write a set of headings in two of the books which I then hand to the boys.

INSERT – SAMPLE NOTEBOOK PAGE

Location:

Date:

Weather:

Swedish girls met:

Wildlife seen:

Comments on accommodation (if appropriate):

Any other notes:

Creative Space:

FITCH'S DIARY CONTINUES

"Here, these headings will help you structure your thoughts," I say. "Fill the details in whenever you get a moment and do anything else you want on the Creative Space on the opposite page. The only rule is that whenever you feel inspired by Love for the Swedish girls, you capture it here."

Macrae stares at the notebook for a moment then raises his right hand.

"Can we pump them first?" he asks.

"If that's what gets your creative juices flowing," I nod, "absolutely."

"What a read that will be," mutters Wentworth.

"Shoosh," says Macrae, "he's on a roll."

I lift my head to the ceiling and spread my arms wide.

"Before the ice covers us forever," I cry, "we will build a monument to Love in the hills! And in centuries to come, when the glaciers have retreated once more, our Monument will still stand. The people then may have sprouted feelers on their heads with microchips on the end, but they'll still be people, and they'll read our words and they'll say, 'by God, those boys created something beautiful!'"

"What'll we call it?!" gasps Macrae.

I thrust a finger to the heavens.

"The Hills Are Stuffed With Swedish Girls!"

Macrae wipes a tear from his eyes. Turns to Wentworth.

"Man's a fucking genius," he splutters, pointing at me.

Wentworth sighs.

"It's all very spirited, Tom, but I wager you haven't thought about a single practicality. What, for instance, about the cat?"

"We'll take him with us," I say. "Hey, Jones!" I shout across the room, "you want to come see the Swedish pusses on the West Highland Way?"

"Mrrroww!" replies Jones, and pees on the television.

"You can't walk 95 miles through the Scottish highlands with a feline," says Wentworth.

"Fiver says he gets further than you," says Macrae, opening his wallet.

"For goodness' sake," huffs Wentworth. "This is utterly absurd."

I put my arm round Wentworth.

"You know, you're right, George. We haven't thought this through. Chances are if Macrae and I go on our own, we'll never make it. We'll be drunk in a ditch before we reach Drymen. What we really need is help – from the kind of person who understands practicalities. A man who can book accommodation, forecast the weather, identify rare wildlife. A fellow who can make sure everything goes according to plan-"

"Fuck plans-" starts Macrae.

I raise my palm to shoosh him.

Wentworth looks at me for a long moment.

"I presume," muses Wentworth, "that for this sort of venture it's very important that one has the correct kit."

"Utterly essential," I say.

Wentworth nods.

"And that one ingests enough protein."

"Absolutely," I say.

"Maps?" he asks.

"Vital," I say.

There is a long pause.

"Well, bearing in mind that you will be simply lost without me, I consent."

I smile and turn to Macrae.

"Three of your finest vodbenas, barman," I say, "and make them monsters."

FROM THE WEBSITE OF THE WEST HIGHLAND WAY

Scotland's premier long distance route

The West Highland Way is the original and most spectacular of Scotland's long distance walks. From its modest start in north Glasgow it winds its way for 95 miles through some of the most stunning scenery the country has to offer.

The West Highland Way roams over heatherclad moors and lush farmland, through deep oakwoods and all the way along the banks of romantic Loch Lomond. The path follows steep sided glens before crossing the open wilderness of Rannoch Moor and rising into the high mountains of Glencoe.

The mountains and glens abound with deer and you may also see eagles, otters, wild goats, pine martens, ospreys, kites, red squirrels and even wildcats.

There are plenty of places to stop for rest and refreshment in the early stages of the walk, and many sites of historic interest. These become rarer as the terrain gets wilder, and careful planning is required for the later stages where shelter is sparse.

Most people take around 6 days to complete the route. It finishes in the west coast town of Fort William, right at the foot of the UK's highest mountain, Ben Nevis.

Embark on this fabulous walk and you will be rewarded with an inspiring, invigorating experience that you will remember for the rest of your life.

Ben Nevis (1344m)

For many people the adventure of the Way is not complete without a final ascent of Scotland's highest mountain, Ben Nevis. Start from the Youth Hostel in Glen Nevis or the visitors centre at Achintee Farm and follow the obvious path to the top.

Despite being called the 'Tourist Route', this is a strenuous climb on a serious hill that claims the lives of expert climbers as well as novices every year. Enjoy it, but take care.

FITCH'S DIARY ENTRY – SATURDAY 22nd SEPTEMBER 2007

"Where is the fat fuck?" says Macrae, pacing up and down the concourse in front of WHSmiths, Jones at his feet.

"Don't worry," I reply, "there is absolutely zero chance that Wentworth will miss a train."

"Just like him to make a dramatic entrance, you know?" says Macrae, then mimics Wentworth in a camp falsetto: 'Don't panic, gentlemen, here I am, come to save with the day with my bulging bloody wallet'."

"He's not doing it to wind you up, Macrae, he's buying some kit and picking up food for the trip."

Macrae turns fully round to face me. His tawny face is stone-serious. I can't remember the last time I saw him like this. He says:

"I want to get something very clear before we start."

"Ah, sure–"

"You can't let fatboy get away with his usual schtick. You know – acting all high and mighty and taking the fun out of everything."

"He doesn't do that–"

"Right, 'cos you've been having a ball cooped up in that dungeon all year."

"Macrae, Wentworth has been kind to me – he just has a few eccentric ways..."

"Yeah well that's all very tragic-aristo, but I bet you a pack of king-size johnnies he'll try to suck the life out of this adventure too." He scratches the bristles on his chin and then prods me with a hard finger. "You have to stand up to him."

"Me?"

"Fucker does the opposite of what I want, but for some reason he listens to you."

"It's going to be fine," I soothe.

"Not unless you make it fine," he replies, still serious.

"Come on," I smile, "it's just a week. You managed to live with him for a whole year at uni."

"Only by staying almost permanently arseholed. You have to watch out, Fitchy, because if you don't there'll be blood in that tent."

And his eyes are drilling into me. He's really not going to let this one go.

"Okay," I say, "I'll keep an eye on things. But you have to make an effort too."

He suddenly spots something over my shoulder and breaks into a wide grin.

"Speaking of arseholes," he says, "look at the tool." Then he yells: "Oi, Mallory, where's your fucking sherpa?!"

Every head on the concourse turns to look. I spin with them to see Wentworth coming towards us.

Appearance of Wentworth: red-faced, heavily laden, dressed head to foot in ultra-modern climbing clothing.

"Told you he wouldn't be late," I say.

Wentworth puffs up and drops a pair of enormous rucksacks onto the concourse.

"All the gear and no fucking idea," says Macrae.

"There's no harm in being prepared, Alan," says Wentworth. "You can get Arctic conditions in the hills in any month of the year." He looks up at the departures board. "Now we're going from platform 14, Glasgow train, changing at Queen Street for Milngavie. I've bought your tickets, upgraded us to weekend first, and reserved seats." He points to the larger of the two rucksacks. "This bag is communal food, which I thought we could take turns carrying – Tom perhaps you'd like to go first?"

Macrae looks at me from under dark lids. I'm tempted to say something, but what's the point in that?

"Sure," I nod.

"Right," says Wentworth. "I think that's everything. Come along then, let's not dilly-dally." And he puffs off towards the barriers.

I pick up the rucksack and set off after him, Macrae's heavy stare adding to the weight on my back, and Jones trotting behind us through the gawping concourse crowd.

★

The train rattles past acres of industrial estates and office blocks. At last it crosses the city bypass and runs through fields and suddenly a delicious autumn light, as soft and warm as teenage kisses, floods the carriage. I sit back in my seat and stretch my legs out. For the first time in ages I feel like the world is full of possibilities.

"You know, Macrae," I say, "sometimes your ideas aren't entirely hopeless."

He grins. "Thank you. Shall I see if the buffet's open?"

"Why not?" I smile.

Macrae rises to his feet. Wentworth stretches a hand out into the aisle to block him.

"Wait a moment," says Wentworth. "Before you waste any money on the third-rate, additive-crammed pigswill that passes for buffet car food and drink, you must complete your menus." And he reaches into a pocket of his rucksack. "Now, I've catered for the first three days, but space dictates that after that we'll need to purchase more supplies. I went grouse shooting with Lord McLintock last year and we stopped at The Green Welly Shop in Tyndrum – it's a rather basic provisionary, but it should be offer most of the things we need to see us through to Fort William, providing-"

"Fuck you talking about?" says Macrae. "The hills are full of food! We'll catch rabbits and grouse. Salmon from the rivers and deer from the moor. Dine at nature's table. All that shit."

"Fine, Alan," says Wentworth. "You smear your face in animal droppings and boil heather for breakfast. That only leaves more goodies for us civilised people. Now Tom, please take some time now to select your menu combinations. Pick one meat option from column A, then a vegetable from row B and a desert from C for each day. Then simply record your choices in the table situated in the appendix-"

Macrae suddenly grabs the menus, shreds them violently and throws the pieces over his head. The passenger behind shouts in protest. Macrae slumps into his seat and glares at Wentworth.

George stares back.

The train clacks and rattles.

After a while Wentworth turns to me. He looks me up and down appraisingly and then peers hard at my daysack.

"Tom," he says finally, "is that all the kit you have?"

"Huh?"

He reaches over and pulls my daysack towards him. Delves a chubby hand in and pokes around.

"You don't appear to have any Goretex outer clothing. No wicking base layers, convertible walking trousers nor Nordic poles. And what, may I ask, are you intending to wear on your feet?"

I look down at my Green Flash.

"Uh, these."

Wentworth scoffs.

"You can't walk the West Highland Way in plimsolls!"

"Why not?" I say.

"Why not?" Wentworth mocks. "Tell him, Alan." And Wentworth casually turns away and reaches into the food rucksack. He takes out an oatcake and layers anchovies in neat lines on the top.

Macrae's eyebrows shoot up and freeze just below his hairline. He stares at Wentworth. Then at me. Then back to Wentworth.

"Fuck you on about?" he asks.

Wentworth chews for a second, swallows, then licks his shining lips.

"You're wearing 18-eyelet, steel-toecapped army boots, aren't you?" he asks.

"Yes–" replies Macrae.

"Not the most breathable footwear option available, but certainly a robust choice."

Macrae's brows plummet, squashing his eyes into suspicious slits.

"What he wants to walk in is up to him," he growls.

"But answer me truthfully," says Wentworth licking a finger, "you wouldn't walk in plimsolls yourself, would you?"

Huge pause.

"No."

"And why not?" asks Wentworth.

"Fuck does that matter?" snaps back Macrae.

"I'm sure Tom would like to know."

"Yes, I would," I say. "What's wrong with my bloody shoes?"

Wentworth bites into the anchovies. Chews slowly.

"Tell him, Alan."

If Macrae were a kettle, he would be coming to the boil. After a long, fizzing moment he mutters:

"No ankle support. Not waterproof. No grip."

And he glares javelins at Wentworth who turns calmly to me.

"You see, Tom? Even Tarzan agrees. You are woefully under-prepared for a trip into the wilderness. The good news is that there's a Tiso's in Glasgow. Not far from the station, in fact. We'll pop in there when we change trains and I'll treat you to a pair of Meindls." He smiles at Macrae. "The best boots money can buy."

"I'll be okay, Wentworth," I say. "These trainers have survived three Glastonburys and a Wicker Man."

He shakes his head.

"I utterly insist. Alan and I don't want you tramping into the hills with inferior ankle support, do we, old smoke?"

But Macrae says nothing. He just glares at Wentworth and strokes Jones, whose tail sways from side to side like a furry ginger cobra.

DIARY CONTINUES

I am drowning in a sea of Goretex.

Shell jackets, trousers, hats, gloves, boots, gaiters: piles of them tower around me like mid-Atlantic rollers. In front, a boss-eyed young assistant is wiping his brow. To my right, Macrae catches my eye. He is lurking by a rack of khaki shorts. His shoulders slump. His head droops.

"How are these?"

"Huh?"

I turn round to the assistant.

"Do they fit okay?" he says.

"Fine," I say, trying to work out which eye to stare at. "But you're the expert. What do you think?"

"They're our most popular boot," he replies.

"Great," I say. "We'll take them."

"Are you sure?" says Wentworth. "Berghaus might be good enough for the common man, but for those who demand superior performance in all weathers, one simply has to opt for Meindls."

The boss-eyed assistant sighs and trudges back to the stockroom.

"You sound like an advert," I say to Wentworth. "Have you got shares in the damn company or something?"

Wentworth smiles.

"Did you know that my great uncle Clarence only owned one pair of shoes in his entire adult life?"

"No. I did not."

"Brown brogues. Church's. Size eight. Was given them by his father when he came of age. Was still wearing them forty years later when he got hit by a tram. Willed them to me and now I wear them in court." He turns to me. "Quality costs, Tom. But it always, always, always repays your investment."

The boss-eyed assistant returns. Pulls out a pair of enormous walking boots from a box. Sits down on his little stool and lifts my left foot.

"You guys doing the Anapurna circuit?" asks the assistant.

"What?" says Wentworth.

"The charity trek heading out to Nepal next week. You're on that, right?"

"No," frowns Wentworth. "We're doing the West Highland Way."

The shop assistant coughs to hide a smile.

"Burma Pros are designed for extreme climbing," he says. "Not sure you need to spend that much if you're only doing the Way," says the assistant.

"My dear boy," says Wentworth. "I put no price on comfort. What do you think of the Burma Pros, Tom?"

Wentworth looks at me. The assistant looks at me. I turn and look up to Macrae.

"What do you reckon, mate?" I ask.

Macrae shrugs.

"I mean," I say, "are they going to give me enough grip?"

"Spose."

"You okay, Macrae?" I ask.

"Going to try these on," he grunts, and he plucks a pair of shorts randomly from the nearest stand and beetles off towards the changing rooms at the back of the camping section.

"Dear oh dear, what's got into him, do you think?" smiles Wentworth. He looks up at the assistant. "You know, I think these are too small. We'll try the Burma Pros in a ten, please."

★

The boots feel like I'm walking with concrete blocks on my feet. I can't help thinking that sneakers, jeans and a T-shirt is a far better outfit to walk the Way in, but I hate to disappoint Wentworth, so I let him buy me the damn things. And all the Goretex guff too.

We're at the till when Macrae comes shuffling towards us from the direction of the changing rooms.

Appearance of Macrae: red about the face; bloodshot, flickery eyes; sweaty.

"You sure you're okay?" I ask him.

Macrae coughs.

"Fine. We should go, though. Get the train."

"You going to buy those shorts?"

He shakes his head and tosses the shorts over a rack of energy bars on the counter.

"But they're nice," I say. "Perfect if the sun comes out–"

"Better hurry," says Macrae. Then he adds with a wince: "Miss it."

"I'm done," nods Wentworth, slotting his Amex back into his wallet.

We pick up our bags and I lead the boys towards the exit. As we pass through the doors to the street, the alarm barriers flash red and start beeping very loudly.

Shoppers whip their heads to look at us.

My face burns.

Suddenly a security guard is beside us, tall as a cliff.

"Can I just check your bags please, gentlemen? The girl at the till maybe missed a tag."

He shepherds us back into the shop, then reaches down and opens Wentworth's bags. He takes the items out one by one and waves them through the sensor.

"No. All clear. Try again."

Again we walk through the doorway.

Again the beeping and the flashing.

"Do you have any other items on your persons, gentlemen?"

42

"Certainly not!" huffs Wentworth.

"No," I say.

Macrae shakes his head.

"My dear fellow," says Wentworth to the cliff, "I've spent over a thousand pounds in your stores today."

"I can see that, sir, but the sensor doesn't lie. Please wait here while I call the manager."

And he reaches in his pocket for his walkie talkie.

Suddenly Macrae leans in towards me.

"We should run now," he whispers in my ear.

"Why?" I ask.

"Because I have one of their tent pegs up my bum," he replies.

Bit of a pause.

"What?"

Macrae looks down at the floor. Says softly:

"I'm sorry. I don't know why I put it up there. I just did."

Then he looks at me with those big brown eyes of his.

"Oh Macrae," I sigh. "Can you get it out?"

He shakes his head in slow sadness.

"Not right now."

"Hang on," squawks Wentworth. "You have a what up your where?!"

"I didn't realise it had a security tag, okay?" snaps Macrae in return. "Christ's sake, George, there's no need to make such a big deal out of it."

"No. Wait. You have stuffed a six-inch piece of metal up your rectum in a High Street store on a Saturday afternoon. I think that's quite a big deal don't you?"

"Not compared with getting your leg shot off."

Wentworth waves his hands. Spits in frustration:

"What are you talking about, you psychopath?!"

"Wentworth, not now," I hiss. "Now we have to run."

"What on earth do you mean... run?"

"Look. For whatever reason, the situation is that Macrae has a stolen tent peg up his arse. Now we can either stand here and wait for this security dude to get the manager and start the scene to end all scenes, or we can take our chances and leg it."

"Why should I 'leg it'? I haven't broken a law in my life and I'm not about to start now," says Wentworth.

"I know," I say, and then point at Macrae, "but he has, and he's with us now. If he gets arrested we all get into shtook."

"This is utterly absurd…"

I turn on him. Hear myself say quite loudly:

"Wentworth, this is our creative time together, do you understand? Our Monument to Love."

Wentworth looks at me for quite a while. Then he sighs.

"Can he even run like that?"

I turn to Macrae.

"Can you?"

"Run? Let me tell you, I could swim to Fort William and back with a forty pound pack, rifle and–"

I turn back to Wentworth.

"He believes so."

"Fine," says Wentworth. "But he's carrying the bags."

*

Wentworth and I sit in silence. The train jolts and sways out of Queen Street station. The window above us is jammed open. It's cloudier that it was before and chill draughts of autumn air creep drown my collar.

I shiver.

"You think the sun will come out again?" I ask.

"Hmm," says Wentworth, as the train rattles into a tunnel.

We both stare at the darkness.

"You okay?" I ask after a moment.

"Fine."

"No, you're not. Come on, what's wrong?"

"'What's wrong?' We've gone on holiday with a maniac! Honestly, Tom, if you'd just told me you wanted a break so much we could have gone to my cousin's villa in Rimini."

"The trip is his idea, Wentworth. He made it happen. And it's nice, the three of us together again-"

"'Ah've poot a tent peg up mah bluddy bum'," Wentworth mimics in a Scots-accented bass.

I can't help myself grinning.

"He's not doing it to wind you up, Wentworth. He gets confused, you know that."

Wentworth turns fully round. Jabs a quivering finger at me.

"Listen, Tom, I need to clarify something before we go any further."

"Sure-"

"I don't want that heathen doing his usual act. You know – showing off and trying to dominate proceedings with his wearying machismo." He takes a deep breath. "You must stand up to him."

"Me?"

Wentworth nods.

"The bonehead does the opposite of what I want, but for some reason he listens to you."

"Wentworth-"

"This is just a friendly request. Do this for me. Because if you don't, goodness only knows what could happen when we're out in the wilderness together."

I sigh.

"Come on," I smile, "it's just a week. You managed to live with him for a whole year at uni."

"Only by staying almost permanently intoxicated." Then he sighs and stares at me, a rosy spot in the middle of each pale cheek. "Tom, this isn't for my sake I'm saying this. He's done something today that has really only damaged himself. But that type of behaviour will escalate. That's simply how it goes with Alan. If you don't keep him in check he'll soon be damaging other things. Other people. Eventually you. And you've suffered enough."

His cool blue eyes are moist. His cheeks are now fully red. I can feel the warmth of his concern like the sun on my skin.

"Okay," I smile, "I'll keep an eye on it. But you have to try too. Come on, do it for me."

Wentworth opens his mouth to say something, then suddenly looks up over

45

my shoulder and breaks off.

I turn to see Macrae coming through the doors at the end of the carriage. He limps back towards his seat and sits gingerly down beside me.

"Hey. You okay?" I say.

Macrae nods.

"What did you do with the…?"

"Window."

"Sweet," I nod. "Well, that's that then. Now let's just try and move on, shall we? We'll say no more about it–"

"Wait," interrupts Macrae. "One more thing."

"Let me guess," says Wentworth, "you have inserted a Swiss army knife into your urethra."

Macrae lifts his eyes. They glisten in the autumn sunshine that slants in through the train window.

"I want to say I'm sorry," says Macrae. "For what happened back there."

"That's just it though, Alan," snaps Wentworth, "you always are contrite after the fact, but it never stops you going right back out and acting in an insane and antisocial manner once again."

I start to hold my hands up, expecting a massacre, but Macrae speaks softly before I have a chance to make the familiar calming gesture.

"I know," nods Macrae. "I let you guys down."

Wentworth leans back in his seat, eyebrows hoisted in surprise. Macrae goes on:

"You see, I was in the bog just now, sorting out the… problem, and it got me thinking. Fitch is right – this is our special time together. Our Love Mission. But what I did back there was thoughtless, reckless and could have fucked the whole thing up the lum. That made me feel really bad, worse even than the peg was doing, and I wanted to do something to say sorry. So I nicked these from the trolley."

And he puts three miniatures of whisky on the table.

"It's only Grouse," he says, looking at Wentworth. "But it's all I could get before the girl turned back round."

Wentworth looks at him for a moment, like he's going to hurl the whisky in his face. Then he looks at me. I stare back at him intently, my eyes pleading for peace.

The train clacks and sways.

And then Wentworth leans forward.

"Did you know," he says, picking up one of the miniatures, "that the Famous Grouse is made with Highland Park and Macallan?"

We stare at him. He unscrews the cap, lifts the bottle to his lips and downs it in one gulp.

"As blends go," he says, without a hint of a cough, "it's really rather tip-top."

He then places the empty glass container on the table between us.

Macrae and I share a smile. We reach for our bottles. Unscrew their caps. Put them away.

The little dose of warm spirit burns in my belly – briefly, but with real heat. And my heart does a flip in my chest, because it feels like something special has come into being on our draughty Scotrail train.

FROM FITCH'S CREATIVE SPACE

The Mystery of Milngavie
A Love ballad by Tom Fitch

A modern Scottish mystery!
The tourists wonder why –
a place that's spelt the way you are
is really said 'Mull-guy'.

Just like a boss-eyed monkey
or my knicker-wearing brother
you apparently look one way
but really are another.

I think perhaps the reason
we never say 'Miln-gavvy'
is so no poet ever shames you

and rhymes your name with 'lavvy'.

For that would be insulting
and you have so much that's nice
like a butcher and a baker
and a station I've been to. Twice.

You also have a Post Office
and the start of the West Highland Way
that's more than other suburbs
like bloody Bearsden can say.

So I'll always love your mystery
and your subway's spraypaint art,
yes, Milngavie don't you worry –
you'll be forever in my heart!

DAY 1

MILNGAVIE TO DRYMEN

Summary:
- *Distance: 19.5 km (12 miles)*
- *Estimated Time: 4-5 hours*
- *Height Range: 300ft (90m) ascent*
- *Terrain: The Way starts almost shyly, in a quiet lane between high street shops. It continues on footpaths, tracks and an old railway, soon leaving the town behind. You will pass across moor, through farmland and into the hills, but there are no major ascents. A deceptively easy start to the walk.*
- *Accommodation: Milngavie, Drymen*
- *Refreshments: Milngavie, Carbeth Inn, Beech Tree Inn, Drymen*
- *Places of Interest: Glengryme Distillery*

"Here we are boys, platform one at fanny central!"

"I hate to contradict, Alan, but it looks more to me like a tired Sixties shopping street with an ill-designed obelisk in the middle."

"But this is just the start of the hunt," says Macrae. "From here on out it's the wild lands and the three of us and those Swedish foxes with their fucking bazookas out."

"You really think we're going to meet lots of girls?" I say, looking around.

"Absolutely!" cries Macrae. "See, there's some already."

He points to three ladies who are readying their rucksacks by the starting point. They wear T-shirts with 'West Highland Way Sponsored Breast Cancer Walk 2007' printed on the front.

"Macrae," I say, "they have to be 60 years old."

Macrae tilts his head and re-appraises the charity ladies.

"I'd do the fat one," he muses. "But that's not the point. Point is we've seen three birds already and we haven't even started. By the time we get to Crianlarich we'll be clacker-deep in Scandinavian stunners. And the first young hotties could be just around that corner. So come on, shoulder up and let's get into those hills!"

I take a look around. It's early afternoon on a glorious late September day. The sky is a calm blue and the sun tingles the hairs on the back of my neck.

"Well," I smile, hefting my pack onto my shoulders, "why not?"

And so we start.

The path ducks away from the shops along the side of a burn. We cross a car park and then enter a tree-lined lane that runs through the northern suburbs of the town.

After a kilometre or so, the buildings beyond the trees start to fade away. We gain some height and the Way opens out onto moorland. Heather carpets the rises in purple. Small hills beckon to our left and right. Now the path turns to the north-west and runs alongside a wood. A burn chuckles at our feet, a breeze ruffles the green and golden leaves above. It's good to be here with these boys. A quiet peace settles on me.

Suddenly Macrae taps my arm.

"Look," he whispers, and nods at Jones.

My puss has drifted away from my side and is now trotting along behind Wentworth. As we watch he suddenly accelerates and leaps up the back of the big fella's rucksack. His claws hold him surely and in a couple of swift scrabbles he is perched right on top. He turns twice around, treads for a few seconds, then curls up and promptly goes to sleep.

"He has his own ways," winks Macrae.

"Phewfff!" huffs Wentworth. "We're going to have to redistribute some of this food. My pack feels like it's getting heavier with every step."

"I hear you, mate," says Macrae through a barely stifled grin. "It's funny the way your brain plays tricks on you, isn't it? Shame I didn't nick any more of that whisky. That would have pepped us up a bit."

"I may be able to help there," says Wenworth, and he reaches a hand round into a pocket of his rucksack and pulls out a hipflask. "Highland Park 18 year old," he smiles. Macrae's eyes shine.

"Oh, hang on!" I cry. "I have something too. Check this out, guys." And I delve into my rucksack, "I bought these little speakers for my iPod. Look, I can strap them to the top of my pack and we'll have tunes to get us stepping out. I've put together a new playlist specially to tune in with the vibe."

A gust blows the beech trees around us. The leaves swirl and bounce like dancers at a ceilidh. The boys smile at me.

"Come on then, Tom, play us your West Highland Way music," says Wentworth.

"You sure?"

"Yeah, come on," says Macrae. "And play it loud!"

I load up the playlist. A guitar begins to jangle as another breeze ruffles the sun-dappled trees. A few last insects hum drowsily through shafts of dusty sunlight. The Way is ours and it is glorious.

"Good fucking choice!" says Macrae.

"Yes," nods Wentworth, "rather pretty for pop music. Who is it?"

I share a quick wink with Macrae.

"A popular music combo known as the Faces. Singer's a chap called Roderick Stewart."

"Roderick Stewart...?" muses Wentworth. "I know that name..." After a moment he adds: "Did he go to Fettes?"

Macrae and I burst out laughing.

"What?" says Wentworth, blushing.

"Nevermind, George," says Macrae, putting an arm round Wentworth. "Just dig the music, brother."

PLAYLIST – 'GROOVING IN THE GLENS'

Ooh La La – Faces
Portions For Foxes – Rilo Kiley
Over The Hill – John Martyn
You Don't Know What Love Is – The White Stripes
Loving Cup – The Rolling Stones
Take The Skinheads Bowling – Camper Van Beethoven
The Boy With The Arab Strap – Belle & Sebastian
Catch My Disease – Ben Lee
Get Over It – OK Go
Sweet Jane – Lou Reed
Sick of Goodbyes – Sparklehorse
Goin' Up The Country – Canned Heat
Together – Raconteurs
All My Friends – LCD Soundsystem (Franz Ferdinand Mix)
California – Phantom Planet
Fluorescent Adolescent – Arctic Monkeys
Wish You Were Here – Pink Floyd
Mr. Jones – Counting Crows

FROM FITCH'S DIARY

If they ever turn the Monument into a film, remember to show the director the photo I took on my phone – the two of them, arm in arm, feet stepping in time, with Jones asleep on top of George's rucksack and all of us singing along to the chorus: "I wish that I knew what I know now, when I was younger" at top volume as we stepped through the sun-dappled September woods at the start of it all. A poet's moment if ever there was one. The kind you wish could last forever…

FROM WENTWORTH'S NOTEBOOK

An Observation:

Henry David Thoreau wrote: "Nature abhors a vacuum, and if I can only walk with sufficient carelessness I am sure to be filled."

While normally I detest the over-simplification of such contracted thoughts, I am forced to admit that there may indeed be 'something in' this particular little motto.

For as we proceeded thenceforth upon our path through the trees, strange notions began to spring into existence in my mind, as unexpected as they were vibrant. These were not new ideas, per se, but rather refreshed moments of mindfulness. It were as if my brain matter were a fertile bed of earth, and my keenest observations were perennial seeds planted therein and long forgotten. With every step I took, the more these kernels sprouted and the higher they grew until they began to twist and twine round one another in such profuse abandon that my rational cognition was forced into suspension.

I was filled with wonder.

And then an entirely new sensastion occured: I began to feel rather warmly disposed towards my comrade males. And if one can be permitted to employ a rather pathetic fallacy, perhaps the autumn sun did then seem to shine more richly on the golden-brown leaves of the beech wood we walked through than I ever remember it doing before.

FROM MACRAE'S NOTEBOOK

Macrae log stardate 69-69-007-fucking alpha

Mission update: Captain Jones continues to rock. Wentworth surprisingly being less of a twat than usual. Fitch is not as sad as before and getting better by the mile-

-mission going according to plan.

No fucking fanny though.

TRANSCRIPT OF A CONVERSATION FROM THE FIRST AFTERNOON

"Pass me the whisky, will you, Fitchy?"

"Sure. Hey guys, isn't it weird to think, right, that just three hundred years ago, if we'd been walking through these woods, we'd have been Jacobite soldiers? The redcoats would have control of the roads and us rebels would be hiding out in the wilderness and trying to avoid the wolves."

"Indeed, and in that era this geographical area would truly have deserved the appellation 'wilderness'. Glasgow would be nearly ten miles from here – half a day's walk. Where that bungalow is, a copse of native pines would have stood. Eagles would be nesting above that washing line, and beavers would have damned that stream."

"Beavers!? What a great fucking word. You just hear that word and you have to fucking laugh. Beavers. Fucking awesome!"

"And if we were Jacobites, right, and you came from the future somehow and said to us, in two hundred years, there'll be houses all the way from Glasgow up to here, and the woods will all be chopped down, and the wolves will be extinct, and a railway will have come and gone-"

"Even the idea of a railway would have been absurd-"

"Exactly, and you could tell them that if they looked up, they'd see giant metal canisters of people flying at a hundred times the speed of a horse off to Australia-"

"And you could get there in the same time it takes to get to fucking Wick."

"So you think of the difference between then and now, and then you think:

'Okay, so what's it going to be like three hundred years from now?'"

"A giant city like in Blade Runner, with towers and fire and lights and shit, all the way to Fort William."

"The wolves might have come back."

"No, you see, that's my point. You can't possibly imagine."

"I am imagining. There'll be aero-trams and space whisky and lasses dressed in nothing but moondust."

"No, you're missing the point. You can't possibly imagine. Okay, think of this. If you were a microbe, right, could you imagine what a human was really like?"

"Tom, microbes can't imagine anything. They don't have brains."

"Exactly! Well, that's not what I mean, but it kind of is. You see, the point I'm trying to get across is about scale. Scale and understanding. Okay, so imagine you're a microbe, and you have a brain of sorts, but not a human brain-"

"That's ridiculous. Why not just be a slug?"

"Because a slug isn't the right scale. What I'm trying to get across-"

"I could be a baby slug."

"Jesus, okay, imagine you're a baby slug-"

"Did you know that slugs can have sex with themselves? Imagine – you've got your cock here, and just there, like on the inside of your thigh... a fanny. How totally fucking awesome is that? Shit, that's the last of the whisky."

"Hold on a minute, chaps, what's that over there?"

"You're not listening-"

"Fuck me, it's only a cocking distillery!"

FROM GLENGRYME WEBSITE

Glengryme Distillery is located at Dungryme, on the south-western edge of the Scottish Highlands, close to Loch Lomond, about five miles west of Strathblane and to the north of Glasgow. The distillery has produced Highland single malt whisky for nearly 200 years.

It is reputed to be the most haunted distillery in Scotland.

Things feel wrong the second we step off the Way. The sun ducks behind a cloud and a chill breath of wind reminds us what season it really is. Ten minutes ago I would have said it was never going to rain again. Now I'm expecting cool drops on my face any second.

The boys and Jones are trotting on ahead but I'm dragging my steps. There's something about the distillery I don't like. It nestles in a dark wood at the bottom of a savage cleft in the hill. Little more than an old stone farmhouse with ramshackle outbuildings thrown at it over the centuries, it has a rotten, creepy air. You can tell it was originally built here for illicit purposes. This place was not intended to welcome visitors.

We walk through a pair of ancient black gates into a kind of courtyard. There's no one around. Even the gift shop is closed up. It feels more like a ghost ship than a working distillery.

"Come on," I say. "There's no one here. Let's get back to the Way."

"But Tom, my dear, we have run out of whisky," says Wentworth.

"We don't have to keep drinking-" I start.

"Bollocks we don't," says Macrae. "Let's see what's in here!" And he strides towards a black doorway in the stunted building to our right. "Come on, Captain Jones," he adds, "maybe there's rodents too!"

Jones's eyes go wide, his tail springs out stiffly behind him and he trots briskly after Macrae.

"George-" I start, but get no further because there's a sudden muffled 'Holy shite' from inside the building and Wentworth scurries in quickly after Macrae.

I look once more round the deserted courtyard. For a second I think I see a shadow watching me from within the dusty gift shop. No – can't be. The place is closed. But the wind is making me shiver so I follow the boys inside.

When my straining eyes finally let themselves soak up the darkness I see we're in a storehouse. Tardis-like, the inside seems far larger than the outside – stacks of black barrels disappear off into a distant gloom. But this is the oldest, dreariest Tardis ever. The crude stone walls are thick with damp. There isn't the sweet, peaty smell of a normal distillery. Here the air reeks of earth and decay. I have a sudden urge to get back into the sunshine.

"I'm not sure this is a good idea," I say. "I mean, there aren't any Swedish girls in here, are there?"

"They can wait," says Macrae, staring at the high stacks of barrels. "This is too fucking awesome."

His eyes are wide and his bottom lip hangs low like – well, I was going to say 'like a kid in a sweetshop', but 'like Macrae in a distillery' conveys the same sense of awestruck excitement and adds the necessary dash of latent evil.

"I agree, this is utterly marvellous!" says Wentworth, gripping his hands together in front of his chest. "I'm so glad we came – Alan, for once I am impressed by an idea of yours."

I suddenly realise that they aren't seeing this place as I am. Maybe they had more from the hipflask than me. The pair of them wander along, side by side, as if hypnotised. And suddenly I feel something far stronger than disgust – I sense danger.

I step over to Wentworth.

"You think this will take long, George?" I ask. "Only it's five o'clock now and it's still over six miles to Drymen. Do you think we'll have enough daylight?"

"My dear Tom, some things one simply has to make time for. Glengryme whisky, for instance, matures in these barrels for 17 years, but when it comes out… ah! it is worth it. Did you know it was voted World's Most Surprising Single Highland Malt in the competition organised by 'Whisky Magazine'?"

"No, I didn't, but-"

"I think the stills are in here!" shouts Macrae, pointing through another low doorway.

"Oh, jolly well done," says Wentworth, and before I have a chance to say anything the pair of them disappear through to the next room.

I look around for Jones, but he's gone. The shadows of a thousand barrels lurk at me. I have a horrible feeling that if I stare much longer, one of those shadows will start moving.

I follow the boys through the doorway.

★

The long, glass-fronted room looks like something out of a giant's chemistry set. Huge vessels with squat bellies and long tapering necks are connected by a labyrinth of pipes and valves. The room is warmer than the last, and a few porthole-like windows in the vessels show that they are actually in use. But their copper is tarnished and the pipes are dusty.

"Look, Tom," coos Wentworth, "the stills!" It's like he's in a trance, drunk already on the atmosphere in this place. He wanders ahead, stupefied, along a gantry.

The still next to me suddenly rumbles loudly.

"This isn't right," I say, turning to Macrae. "Place feels like it's going to explode."

But he also ignores me, and peers wonderingly in one of the portholes.

My powerlessness is overwhelming. I feel tiny and alone, dwarfed by the hideous machinery and my friends' indifference.

I grab him by the shoulder.

"Macrae," I say, shaking him hard. "This is taking too <u>long</u>!"

He stares at me dumbly for a second, then his eyes suddenly unglaze and he snaps into life.

"My God, Fitchmeister. You're right. We need to move faster."

And suddenly he slings his pack down and flips open the porthole he was looking in. Clouds of whisky vapour coil up past his face towards the ceiling. A sharp tang of alcohol kicks up my nostrils.

"Looks good," he says and pulls what appears to be a length of para cord out of his pocket. He then removes a SIGG water bottle from his rucksack and ties the cord round its neck. He tightens the knot and lifts the bottle up to the edge of the porthole opening.

Wentworth reappears at my side.

"What on earth is he doing?" he asks.

"Fitchy wanted me to get our scotch a bit quicker," Macrae says smiling, and he lowers the bottle into the porthole.

"That wasn't what I meant-" I start, frustration boiling in me like the whisky in the still.

Macrae feeds out cord.

"You do realise that you will almost certainly contaminate the whole batch?" says Wentworth.

"You don't have to have any, George," says Macrae, eyes twinkling.

"I didn't say that," smiles Wentworth. "I'll keep toot." And he walks to the edge of the walkway and takes up a lookout position.

The pair of them have gone mad. I'm just thinking how best to get them out of there when I head a strange scurrying noise. I whip my head round. I could swear I saw something duck behind those pipes. But why would someone be hiding from us?

"Oo."

The 'oo' came from behind me. As I turn back round I see Macrae peering into the still.

"What is it?" I say.

He looks up at me, eyes wide. Says:

"It's come off."

He hauls up the para cord. An empty loop hangs sadly where his SIGG bottle used to be.

"Lend me yours," he says.

"I don't have one!"

"George bought you a two litre bladder. Get it out."

"No!"

He shakes his head like I'm a small child who has said something unintentionally amusing, and then grabs me with hard paws. He spins me bodily round and I feel him delving into my pack. He finds my Camelbak, ties it onto his para cord and lowers it down the hole.

I glance back at the dark cluster of pipes.

"What if someone comes!?" I cry.

"Chuck yourself down that ladder and pretend to have an eppy."

★

Macrae peers out across the courtyard. The cobbles are damp with the thickening rain. There's still no sign of human life, but the sense of a presence here is very real. It's like the distillery itself is watching us.

"Coast is clear," he says. "Squad, let's rock."

He and Wentworth step out from the doorway.

"Wait," I cry. "Where's Jones? We can't leave without Jones!"

"Cool your jets, Fitchalicious, he's right here."

I follow his finger to see Jones crouching in the shadow of the wall. He has a large mouse in his mouth. It droops from either side of his face like a bushy grey moustache.

"See, he got a freebie too!" Macrae laughs.

The mouse wriggles in Jones's jaws, desperately trying to free itself. I know how it feels.

"Maybe we should have a look at the malting floor," muses George.

"We have to leave NOW!" I say, and start across the cobbles towards the black gates.

Suddenly I feel a fierce claw pincering my shoulder. It grates on my bones and stops me dead.

"A wee word afore ye go," creaks a voice direct from the underworld.

And the claw slowly turns me and I see a pale, withered man in a tweed shirt and leather jerkin. Was he here when they built the place? He certainly looks like he's spent more than one lifetime drinking whisky. His skin is translucent and his eyes look uncannily like pickled onions. It's not that he seems about to die, it's more like he started passing over and the other side saw what was coming and backed out of the deal half way through.

What's worse is that there's something hideously familiar about the way his half-dead eyes fasten on me. We've definitely never met before, but he's smiling like he knows me and I feel an odd closeness to him. It's deeply personal, but also shadowy and near-forgotten; like he was once in a nightmare of mine.

"Y-yes?" I say.

He juts a bristly chin at my pack.

"Ye'll need to pay for that, laddie."

"What?"

"The whisky in yer goatskin baggie."

"I'm s-sorry about that," I say, "but the shop was closed–"

"Och, there's nay harm in getting yerselves a wee dram," he sneers. "But ye always must pay."

"Fine," I say, and reach for my wallet.

"Ha! No, laddie, I dinnae want yer money."

And he leans right in close to me. It's not just his breath that smells of stale whisky, the foul spirit seeps from every pore.

"W-what do you want?" I ask. My urge to run is overwhelming. I can't bear his eyes slithering over me.

He grins.

"Your cat," he says, and he points one spidery finger towards the earth.

I look down. Jones is by my side, mouse still drooping. He looks from me to the man and back again in apparent confusion.

"Been twenty-three year since we had good mouser," the man says. "Yon moggie could have a grand life here."

And he drops to one knee with sudden, uncanny agility and extends a shrivelled claw towards Jones.

"Eh, bonny puss cat?" he creaks. "Ye fancy living out yer days hunting and sipping toddies, eh?"

Jones tilts his head on one side like he's considering the offer.

Terror lurches within me like puke. I can't bear the idea of this hideous old man even touching Jones.

In an instant I swoop down and scoop up my puss.

Normally this would result in the loss of a large amount of facial skin, but he doesn't want to drop his mouse and in my boldness I manage to get him round all four paws, so my complexion survives. A fiery glare informs me that my good fortune on this occasion should be considered unique.

"He's not for sale!" I shout. "Macrae. Wentworth. We're leaving."

And I shoo them out of the gates and don't let them stop running till we're safely back on the Way.

The man is too old and frail to chase us. But his cackling laugh scrapes down my spine with every pounding step I take.

*

"Woo hoo hoo!" whoops Macrae. "You still got it, Fitchalicious, all present and oorrect!"

The path here runs along the bed of an old railway, curving through the lush glen like a yawn. Sheep and farmhouses dot the fields. Copses of beech trees mutter like old men in the autumn breeze. We throw ourselves on the grass of the old embankment to catch our breath.

I stare dumbly at the nearest ewe.

"I don't understand why we had to run away," says Wentworth, wheezing and dropping to the ground. "He would have taken some money in the end."

"You don't get it, do you, George?" says Macrae. "Fitchy wanted to do the naughty thing." And he pulls out the whisky-filled Camelbak. "You've heard of the angels' share…" he grins, "well, this is what the bad boys get."

He grabs the tube, puts the nipple in his mouth and takes a mighty sook.

"It's the heart of the run," says Macrae. "This shit is seventy per cent."

He passes the tube to Wentworth who also takes a drink.

"Mmm," groans Wentworth, licking his lips. "Sinful and at the same time, utterly divine. Tom?" And he offers me the rubber nipple.

I take it from him mechanically and am about to take a sip, when from the corner of my eye I see Jones's mouse twitch.

I turn. The mouse's blackness reminds me of the shadows.

"Let it go, Jones," I say.

The boys are quiet. A faint patter of drizzle on beech leaves is the only sound.

The mouse wriggles some more.

"I have your sausages, puss," I say. "Please let it go."

Jones stares at me with profound cat blankness for a second.

Then the mouse squirms wildly, Jones crunches hard, the mouse gives one final spasm then flops still.

Dead.

Jones looks at me again, I swear in defiance, then starts crunching the mouse down in great gulps.

"Oh Good lord, it's eating it!" cries Wentworth, throwing a hand to his mouth as if to prevent himself being sick.

"Come on, you pansies," says Macrae, "it's his nature. And this is mine!" he adds, grabbing the bladder from Wentworth and dancing on up the track making woo-hooing noises.

Wentworth scuttles after him, complaining and fishing for the whisky.

I stare at Jones for a moment longer, and he looks back at me, frankly, as if to say, 'Yes, Macrae is right – this is how it is. This is my nature. I kill.'' Then, mouse finished, he trots after the boys.

I look at the three of them wandering off up the vanished railway, and that's when I realise: there aren't going to be any Swedish girls on this trip. Just Macrae getting drunk, Wentworth moaning and Jones killing things.

For a second I stand on my own, looking up at the sky. The sun hasn't come back out. The drizzle is turning to rain.

I shiver and a strange feeling runs through my body. It's like I can feel the approaching winter in my bones – for a shuddering second my marrow turns to snow and my muscles to ice. Then the rain splashes on my face and the feeling is gone.

With a sigh I start walking. After a minute of two I catch up with the boys and together we push on for Drymen.

Sometimes they try to make me drink. I put the nozzle to my mouth out of politeness, but I only pretend to suck. I haven't seen them having this much fun together in years, and I'd hate to rock their boat. But I'm just not in the mood for drinking. I feel like a shovel of slush has been thrown over the fire so newly lit in me.

By the time we get to the campsite it's dark and the boys are wasted. They spend twenty minutes cavorting about before eventually falling on someone else's tent. Turns out to be the OAP charity walkers we saw at the start. The poor old girls are terrified and we get thrown out of the site.

Not that the boys care. They're still giggling as I find us a spot in the nearby woods. I get my tent up and turn round to see them collapsed on top of each other, smiling and with ruddy glows on their cheeks.

I find some polythene in Macrae's pack and rig that up over them before turning in.

I'm sober but cold, and the insistent rain has soaked me to the bone.

★

DAY 2

DRYMEN TO ROWARDENNAN

Summary:
- *Distance: 24km (15 miles)*
- *Estimated Time: 5-6 hours*
- *Height Range: 1200ft (360m) ascent*
- *Terrain: Good paths or tracks most of the way. The first major climb is over Conic Hill near Balmaha. The lochside route to Rowardennan is twisty and undulating. (Please note that dogs are not allowed on Conic Hill during the lambing season, even on a lead. The season normally lasts for around three weeks at the end of April and early May. Temporary signage will be in place.)*
- *Accommodation: Balmaha and Rowardennan*
- *Refreshments: Balmaha and Rowardennan*
- *Places of Interest: Boat trips are available from Balmaha to Inchcailloch on Loch Lomond. Visitor Centre at Balmaha car park (open Easter to October). Ben Lomond.*

FROM FITCH'S DIARY

There's a 'mwuhhh' feeling I get when I wake up in a tent – horrible if I've been drinking, but still unpleasant when sober. There's also a lot of snoring going on – a giant, rasping honk from Wentworth; a machine gun rattle from Macrae; and, I can't be certain, but I think I hear a tiny purry whiffle from Jones.

Got to get out of here.

I wriggle out of my bag like a grub shedding its skin and shrug on my clothes. I unzip the flap, plant my feet in my boots and push myself out of the tent.

A little predawn light is daubing the high clouds, as clumsy and colourful as a Rolf Harris painting.

Macrae and Wentworth are lying where they fell last night, cuddled together on an unopened groundsheet under a badly put up bit of polythene.

Jones sleeps drily on Macrae's chest, but dark water has formed a puddle around the boys' legs. The rucksacks are also damp. Something tells me there will be tears when they wake.

To my left is a wood. Mist beards the trees. A gap in the trunks invites me. I run for it.

The path loops, twists and rises and falls like a ribbon on the wind. Bracken rises to my waist, a living pattern of green and brown. Moss lies deep as a duvet on fallen trunks. A few drowsy insects drone past my head. The blue-white mist rolls and coils like the exhaled breath of the forest itself.

Suddenly I step out of the wood onto a clearing.

Grassy slopes roll to a sleepy river. Just to my right, a large flat rock slants down into the water. Dew sops my trouser legs as I pace through the long grass to sit on the stone.

I've never seen clearer water. Perfect pebbles slant out into a crystal pool.

My feet feel like lumps of cooking dough in my heavy boots. My head is thick and my skin prickles.

And now my fingers are tearing at my laces. Boots and socks tumble on the grass behind me.

I lower my toes over the edge of the rock and the cool river clothes me, one delicious inch at a time.

My soul sighs.

The sensation is so exquisite that my body demands more. I unbutton my shirt and reach for my belt. It seems the most natural thing in the world: everything around me is clear and honest and true, it makes perfect sense that I should be too.

Before I fully know what I'm doing, I am sliding my naked body into the water.

Sensational.

I swim a few strokes. Laughing, gasping at the cold clarity. I whoop and splash, then I stop and just enjoy the moving water on my skin, watching the insects dance over the surface.

I pull myself from the water and lie on my rock. Dripping, smiling, clean. For the first time in ages, my brain is filled by nothing but this moment.

I lie down to dry.

Then, from the woods on the opposite side of the river, stepping calmly down towards the water, I see...

A stag.

He paces steadily across the rumpled strip of ground that separates the forest from the water.

Fifteen feet away on the opposite side of the stream, another flat rock slants down in a similar way to the one I'm sitting on. The stag paces elegantly onto this, edging forward until the bubbling waters cover his forehooves. He then bends his great neck, lowering his mouth to drink.

I see it so clearly: every hair in his rippling hide as his muscles flex, the tiny shake of his tensing legs, the wisps of breath that curl from his nostrils as he moves.

And then, at the exact second his lips touch the stream, the sun rises above the trees behind him, and his antlers splinter its fire into golden shards that pierce me where I lay.

I must have gasped, because suddenly he looks up, water dripping like molten diamonds from his whiskers, and stares dead at me, eye to eye.

But rather than bolt, he pauses. Keeps staring. As if sharing something with me. And I see that there's a light in his eyes, precious and bright. The same light that shone from Judy's eyes.

Not dropping my glance, I reach for the notebook in the pocket of my trousers. I open the pages, uncap the pen and begin to write.

The Manly Stag Of The Sparkling Waters
A Love-filled pastoral by Tom Fitch

Manly stag, are you a dream?
Noble, true and good
You drink your wine from chuckling stream
While I sit in the nude.

Proud antlers, big and velvetèd
The royallest crown of all
They look much better on your head
Than hanging on some wall.

Dewdrops shine your hairy flanks
And glisten on your lips
Little creatures line the banks
To be baptised by your drips.

You plant your hooves athwart the rock
And watch as daybreak dawns
To nature's tick, you are a tock…

No, that's not right. I scribble it out.

You plant your hooves athwart the rock
And watch as daybreak dawns
The leader of our manly flock…

Not it either. More scribbles. I look up at the stag for more inspiration and gasp with disappointment as I see him suddenly bolting for the trees. I half rise to my feet, thinking of following him when-

"Can I be sharing your rock?"

Huh?

I whip round and see…

…the most gorgeous pair of legs I have ever encountered.

Slender, tanned and beautifully toned they are standing on the bank just a few quivering feet away. They terminate at one end in a very neat pair of walking bootettes, and at the other in a pair of cut-off denim shorts.

Above the shorts is a pink t-shirt with black space invaders marching down the front. This is cropped an inch or two above the shorts' waistband, revealing a tanned and athletically flat belly. The invaders themselves are marching out as well as down, over a pair of what appear to be delightfully firm breasts.

My eyes slide up a slender neck, and on to a smiling face. At first glance, you'd say she's pretty, but look a little longer and you see that her features have an edge to them that charges her face with exotic beauty. Her brown eyes are shot through with real blackness; her mouth is a little wider and more supple than decency says it ought to be; her nose is flat, almost oriental in its provocative tilt. And, framing all this to wild perfection, a halo of rich brown hair.

Without waiting for my answer, she steps onto my rock. Those endless golden legs are just inches from my nose. But she doesn't catch my eye or say anything, she simply drops smoothly to her knees beside me, curls elegant fingers round rough stone, bends forward, plunges her beautiful mane into the pool and I lose the capacity to think.

Then she flings her head back, hair arcing like a scimitar and diamond droplets streaming into the trees like meteors.

She turns her heavenly eyes to me.

"Oh, that is better. I am always feeling so… 'mwuhhh' when I wake up in a tent. You know?"

I want to say in a very cool voice, "Absolutely, I know exactly what you mean. In fact, I was thinking much the same thing myself earlier."

"Nnnnnggg," is what I manage.

"For sure, the best thing you can do when you are feeling in such a way is come and wash yourself in the stream like a wild creature," trills the accented voice.

I don't know why, but I suddenly have a quite startling mental picture of her as a squirrel.

Her elegant fingers grasp coils of hair and squeeze streams of water free.

"Can I see it?" she asks, with a sudden nod at my crotch.

I've been so entranced by the be-denimed bend of her bottom, the bare curves of her neck, the press of her breasts against cotton and the flow of water over flesh that I have completely forgotten I am naked.

I press my notebook over my crotch.

"It's, uh, not very impressive," I say. "The water was cold and–"

"Not your penis, you crazy man," she smiles. "For sure I know what one of them is looking like. I mean your poem."

My cheeks burn.

"Oh, for sure," I mutter, and lift my notebook an inch or so. "But it isn't finished…"

She smiles and bends down to look. I feel her damp hair sweep against my cheek. It smells of summer.

She looks at the page for a long moment.

"It is a very nice composition," she says at last.

"You think so?"

The idea of her liking my work is like the first sip of cold beer on a summer day.

"Oh yes," she says. "But the subject is a little… vanilla for my taste."

"What do you mean, 'vanilla'?"

"Vanilla… how you say… it is the most basic flavour. It is straightforward. Like screwing in the missionary position, you know?"

My cheeks are now completely on fire.

"Oh. Right. But you know… it's just a poem about a stag. It's not meant to be complex. It's only meant to be beautiful."

"And yes, for sure, it is a pretty rhyme." She stares at it for another moment. "But maybe it could have something else. You know, at the end here…" And she screws her face up for a second, clearly thinking deeply. "A big finish," she goes on, "a real finger up the bottom!"

Then she puffs her proud chest out, jams her fists on her hips and recites:

"You plant your hooves athwart the rock

And watch as daybreak dawns…
And a saucy little eider duck
Nestles in your horns."

And she throws her shining leonine head back and glares down at me triumphantly.

For a long time I can say nothing. It's quite a while before I can even breathe. Then the impact of the delivery wears off and I think for a moment about the words.

"Eider duck?" I say.

"You not know her? Oh, she is a very pretty little duck. Soft feathers. So warm and fluffy."

"Right. And 'horns'?"

"Yes, you know, like his bony fingers here?"

And she wiggles her hand over her head with impossible cuteness.

"Antlers," I say.

"It is the same thing," she says.

I think about this for a second.

"But what would an eider duck be doing in a stag's horns? I mean, antlers."

"You tell me," and she smiles so widely my notebook rises an inch.

Then she stands up and looks over her shoulder.

"Well," she says, "I must go and join my friends now. See, they are waiting for me and we must walk all the way to Rowardennan today."

She points to the edge of the wood. I turn to see a pair of girls standing under a tree. They wear similar shorts and sport rucksacks.

They smile at me and wave.

I wave nervously in return.

And then without another word, she turns and walks towards them through the dewy grass.

My eyes follow her glistening calves every step of the way.

FROM FITCH'S DIARY

"Wentworth! Wentworth, wake up!" I hiss, shaking his shoulder. "Why would a stag have an eider duck nestling in its antlers?"

But I get no vocal answer, just a phlegmy bass groan followed by a loud fart.

I hop, froglike, over Wentworth's legs.

"Macrae, do you know why a stag would have an eider duck nestling in its antlers?"

"Shoot me now," moans Macrae. "Spare me the pain."

"This is important," I say, poking him. "I couldn't sleep, right, so I got up and went into the woods and I walked down to the river and I was having a swim and I was naked and then I saw this stag, see, and he made everything seem beautiful, so I wrote him a poem and that's fine right, but the really important bit is that then this girl-"

On the word 'girl' Macrae opens one eye.

"Was she Swedish?"

"Uh, I don't know, she was certainly foreign-"

He opens the other eye.

"Did she have friends?"

"Two."

He sits upright in his puddle.

"Were they hot?"

"I couldn't see, they were over by the trees–"

He grabs my hands in his. Looks up at me with his pleading brown eyes.

"With massive knockers?"

"I'm not sure if they were massive, I mean, I don't think they were small…"

Which is when Macrae goes mental.

"IT'S HA-PUR-NING!" he bellows, leaping straight to his feet and propelling the polythene sheeting towards the heavens. It hasn't even landed when he reaches down, grabs his rucksack, slings it on his back and stands there, dripping.

"Let's fucking go!"

"What happened to your hangover?" I say. "I thought you wanted me to shoot you?"

Macrae lifts his hands and uses them to hit himself in the face, alternating from side to side:

"Leftrightleftrightleftright….hoooarrgh!!!"

The hoooarrgh comes at the end of the slapping as Macrae jams his fingers down his throat and spews a horrendous brown load onto the grass beside me. He finishes puking, wipes his mouth on his sleeve and smiles.

"Let's go!"

"What about Wentworth?" I ask.

Macrae looks down at the still-sleeping bulk in the puddle at our feet.

"Leave him?" suggests Macrae.

"You know we can't do that. We're in this together."

"Then we need to rouse him. Wakey wakey, George!" Macrae bellows in Wentworth's ear.

But all this elicits is another hefty fart.

"Get up, you idle cunt!" snaps Macrae, and kicks Wentworth hard on the bottom.

This starts Wentworth into some sort of life. He raises his head.

"Will you kindly call an ambulance?" whispers Wentworth. "And the police."

"What's wrong?" I ask.

"I have been poisoned."

"Ha ha!" laughs Macrae. "It's your own fault, you fat jobby. Now get up and deal with it. We gotta hit the trail to fanny canyon."

Wentworth slowly heaves himself into a sitting position and, with a gurn of distaste, realises that he is in a puddle.

"Oh, how utterly vile."

"Come on," says Macrae, pacing in front of us, "every second you sit there feeling sorry for yourself is another second that my tassle's not getting tugged."

"I'm not going anywhere until the ambulance arrives–"

And with one brief flex of his muscles, Macrae physically lifts Wentworth clean out of the puddle and plonks him on his feet.

Wentworth stares at Macrae, astonished by this show of power.

"Now walk!" barks Macrae, and throws Wentworth his rucksack.

★

Today's route starts gently – a wide Land Rover track swinging through a pine plantation. But despite the ease of the path and the tunes from the iPod, our progress is slow. This is, unfortunately, entirely down to Wentworth.

"This is all wrong," he moans, "I can't possibly be meant to sweat this much."

"Walking is hard work, Wentworth," I say. "Plus you're hungover."

"This is far worse than a hangover. What if I have pancreatic cancer?"

"You don't have pancreatic cancer. You were fine yesterday, weren't you?"

"It presents very late, you know. And it's 95% fatal."

Macrae is raging.

"They're getting away!" he jabbers, pointing vaguely into the forest ahead. "We need to be gaining on them! Can he not walk any faster?"

"No, Alan, he cannot," says Wentworth. "And you are lucky he is walking at all in his condition. Oh God, why does my pack have to be so heavy?"

"It got wet in the night," I say. "Moisture weighs everything down more. But don't worry, it'll soon dry out."

"It can't just be that," Wentworth wails, "we must have packed some rocks up with the tent…"

Macrae looks up to the top of Wentworth's rucksack to where Jones is curled up.

"Captain Jones," he says, "there has been an unfortunate change in your transport arrangements." And he swings his own rucksack close to Wentworth's and gives a little nod of his head.

Jones stands up, stretches, steps over to the top of Macrae's rucksack, treads a couple of times and then lies down again.

Wentworth stares in horror.

"How long has that cat been up there?"

"George, shut up and accelerate."

★

After a couple of miles, the trees around us suddenly cease and the path rises onto a moor. We climb a stile and enter a sheep field which dips down to a burn crossed by a wooden bridge. We pause here for a minute, listening to its crystal music and checking our route. Our path rises up the heathery slopes of Conic Hill – a fitting name if ever there was one – hugging the northern side and climbing to a hundred feet or so below the summit.

It's not that hard a pull, but Wentworth's whining seems to make it last an age. Eventually the gradient lessens and the path curves round the side of the hill just below the summit. Macrae and I stop here, waiting for Wentworth to catch up.

Out in the distance we can see a shining slice of Loch Lomond, but the convex bulk of the hill cuts off the view of the path itself. On our left, a branch of the track zigzags up through the thinning heather to the summit.

Macrae scans the scene and points upward.

"Look! I bet we'll be able to see the fanny from up there. Come on, last one up's a poof."

And he sets off up the slope, just as Wentworth catches up with us.

"Wait, please!" whines Wentworth.

"Jesus, George," curses Macrae suddenly, "could you go any fucking slower?"

"Yes," says Wentworth. "I can stop."

And he promptly sits down.

Macrae turns to me.

"They're getting away…" he says through gritted teeth.

"Tom, will you help me?" says Wentworth. "There's something terribly wrong with my foot." And he starts taking his boot off.

I sigh.

"Okay, Macrae, we'll nip up," I say, nodding up towards the summit. "George, you stay here."

"You won't wait with me? I'm in considerable pain."

"We'll be back in five minutes," I say.

"If I haven't died by then," bleats Wentworth.

"Fuck's sake," mutters Macrae and stomps away up the track.

"Just wait here," I say to Wentworth and follow Macrae.

The path rises quickly up the slope. It feels like we're about to touch the clouds that whip by overhead. When we're out of earshot of Wentworth, Macrae turns to me and says:

"Don't see why you have to be so nice to him. It's his bloody fault he's in this state. If I was that nice to my squad we'd never get anywhere. Boy needs a fucking rocket, simple as that."

I sigh.

"It won't work, Macrae. Wentworth isn't in the marines. Shout at him and he'll simply dig his heels in more. You have to pacify him if you want to get anything done."

And suddenly Macrae's bluster drops away. He says quietly:

"It doesn't help him, you know."

I stop on the windy hillside and turn to look at my friend.

"What do you mean?" I ask.

"I mean, what's the point in sitting in a puddle all day just because someone's telling you to get out of it?"

"It's not like that-"

"The old goof's terrified of taking a risk. Making a change. Breaking routine. And he jumps on the first excuse he can to avoid facing that scare."

"He's not scared-"

"Sure it's the easy option, but if we all did that the entire human race would be sat around in fucking nappies. Which, obviously, would have its advantages every so often, but generally, you know, on a day-to-day basis, not a positive thing."

I open my mouth to say something. But nothing comes. I shut it again. Macrae goes on:

"This week is our chance to change him. Bring him out of himself. Let him see what he could be doing."

"Macrae, I don't want to change him." I reach out a hand and touch his shoulder. "Like I don't want to change you. I just want us to have a good time together as we are. Is that so hard?"

"Maybe. Maybe not. Fuck do I know. Just don't pander to him is all I'm saying. Since when do you have to do what George wants all the time?" He pokes me on the chest with a hard finger. "You be YOUR self. That's YOUR priority." He turns round. Takes a breath. Then says: "Man, look at this fucking view."

And I follow his eyes and I have to agree. The scene from the top of this hill is astonishing. Below us, Conic hill tumbles rockily down into the thick woodland. Beyond this, beyond everything, is Loch Lomond, its wide shining waters studded with autumnal islands. To our left lie the lowlands, all patchwork fields and winding rivers. To our right, the highlands – close by, the beautiful animal flanks of Ben Lomond, in the distance, the Arrochar Alps, their shoulders jagged, bristling and hunched, like approaching assassins.

For a while we share it in silence. Then suddenly:

"Look!"

"What?"

Macrae is jabbing a finger to where the main path zigzags into the wood below us.

"Is that them?" he says, his whole body poised like a hound's.

"There's certainly three of them, and they're female, but I can't see if…"

I look at Macrae. His mouth hangs open in an expectant smile.

"It could be," I say.

I expect him to leap around, but instead he lays a hand on my shoulder and says softly:

He looks me dead in the eye.

"I know you're out of practice," he says softly. "But you need to relax now. Captain Jones and I have this situation completely under control. Just kick the clutch and change down a couple of gears. We are having an adventure and you are part of it."

And his brown eyes shine and I can feel a Macrae Moment coming on. A Macrae Moment is one of those times when you are presented with a choice, and you know you should do the good thing, you're definitely going to do the good thing, but the bad thing suddenly seems like so much fun that you simply have to do that instead. It's like having a wee Macrae-shaped devil on your shoulder, grinning and whispering, "Macrae...Macrae...Macrae" and after a while, you sort of see what it's on about. It's the voice that tells you to ping that elastic band at the teacher's head rather than put it in your pencil case. It's the voice that orders another beer when you really should be going back to work. The voice that makes you want to jump off a cliff or onto a railway track, just because you can. You can't listen all the time (unless you ARE Macrae, of course), but when you do listen, the sweet release of the moment when you realise that you're actually going to along with Macrae – well, it's simply the most deliciously thrilling sensation there is.

Yes, this is going to involve being mean to Wentworth. But the naughtiness of what I'm about to do zips through me like electricity. The sun pours onto the loch and makes it shine like a lake of diamond juice. For a glorious instant I feel nineteen again.

"Do you want to do this?" he asks.

I take a breath. I smile. Nod.

"Come on then!"

And we run back to the path.

When we get back down to the junction with the main track, we find Wentworth sitting on a rock, his right boot and sock off.

"Look!" he wails, hoisting up his pudgy pale toes. "Trenchfoot!"

I peer at the sole of his foot. Under the ball of his big toe is a white bump of skin about the size of a Tic Tac.

Macrae grins.

"You know the best thing for a blister?" he says.

"No, what?" replies Wentworth.

"Piss in your boot."

"Oh, for God's sake."

Macrae winks at me.

"I'll do it if you're dry," he adds, casually unzipping his fly.

Wentworth smiles.

"You wouldn't dare," he scoffs, and looks smugly to me for support.

It hurts me, but Macrae is spot on again. I have to do this.

"I don't know, Wentworth. He's been on a few marches in his time. Perhaps he's right."

I can read the depth of my betrayal in the lines of pain on Wentworth's crumpling face. He starts to panic.

"Tom, you have to stop him!"

"He's only trying to help," I say.

Macrae delves inside his trousers and fishes out his cock.

Wentworth shrieks.

"These boots are Meindl Burma Pros!"

"This pish is Glengryme single malt." Macrae grins. "Matured in oak barrels for 17 years."

And he starts peeing.

Wentworth snatches his boot out of the way just in time. Macrae takes a step forward in pursuit.

"Eeeep!" manages Wentworth, and he jams his boot back on and takes off down the hill.

"Come back," shouts Macrae. "I'm a qualified first aider!"

Macrae gives me a double thumbs-up, and we set off after galloping George.

★

Balmaha nestles at the bottom of the hill in a little cove surrounded by deep woods. The village is no more than a handful of buildings dotting a bend in the single-track road. There's a pub and a shop and a little harbour where a few white boats bob and lurch drunkenly, their masts clanking on the boisterous wind.

Further out on the loch, steep tree-covered islands rise from the choppy water. Their clustering canopies of golden russet, dark green and ochre brown leaves make them look like vast florets of half-submerged and slightly stale broccoli. (Fitch note to self: does this sort of detail make a good simile or a bad one? Check this out and consider 'like giant autumnal afros' as possible alternative.)

Our path pops us out onto the road and starts again on the other side, curving away alongside a small pebbly beach. A few Sunday driver families are mooching around the waterfront, pushing prams and keeping dashing kids off the road. Opposite us is a stone pub with a garden and ancient waterwheel. To our left is a low whitewashed village shop. Beside that, set back a bit from the road, a wooden bench offers a place to enjoy the perfectly pretty scene.

As we reach the bench, Macrae jumps up onto a bollard and eagerly scans the road up and down.

"There!" he cries, pointing to an old-fashioned cart that stands in the beer garden of the pub. Neatly lined up against the wooden spokes of the cart's wheel are three pink and light-blue rucksacks.

"They must be in the boozer! Fucking fantastic, let's get in there. See, George, wasn't that worth it?"

He doesn't wait for an answer before skipping across the road to the pub and going in.

Wentworth wheezes to a halt beside me.

"Do you think this will shut him up?" he asks, and slumps down onto the bench.

My friend is rasping heavily. Sweat has plastered his hair to his face. His cheeks are bright red and smeared with dirt. It suddenly occurs to me that he isn't having a good time.

"Listen, George," I say, "I'm sorry about the piss in the boot thing–"

He somehow manages a refined smile and lays a delicate hand on my arm.

"Tom, you never have to apologise to me. I know you always have the best intentions. Perhaps now Alan has found his wenches he will stop causing us such mischief."

And again his lips curl elegantly upwards and his eyes crinkle nobly.

Does he really think that about me? Or is he forcing himself to be forgiving? Either way, his decency makes me feel twice as dreadful about what I did.

There must be some way I can be nice to both of them at the same time…

But I don't have time to finish that thought because suddenly the pub door flies open again and three blurry shapes in baggy T-shirts come rocketing out. They zoom through the beer garden and grab up the pink and light-blue rucksacks, throw a final panicked glance behind themselves, then shoot off along the loch.

The OAP charity women whose tent the boys fell on last night.

A second or two passes, then Macrae trudges out of the still-swinging pub door. He walks dolefully across the road and drops onto the bench beside us.

"Knickers," he says.

I take my rucksack off and put an arm round each of my friends.

"Never mind boys," I say, "we gave it a good shot. And look, it's still a beautiful day."

I look around at the scene in front of me and try to feel inspired. But my heart isn't wholly in it. Pretty though the boats and the buildings are, there's something primitive about this landscape. If a pterodactyl wheeled out of the forest, swept down and hooked an infant in its cavernous black beak I wouldn't be at all surprised.

TING!!

The bell from the shop chimes beside us, and the second it does, the sun finally breaks free from the scudding clouds, flooding the village with golden light and vaporising my daydream.

Something is different about the world.

The boys sense it too. And without a word we turn as one and see, stepping in sun-drenched slow-motion from the whitewashed cottage that holds the village stores, with rucksacks on their backs and Fab ice lollies in their hands –

Three deliciously attractive girls.

They climb the few low steps from the shop door and cross the road in front of us. As they pass, the glorious sunlight shines from their legs, their hair and the ice crystals on the lollies. On our iPod Lou Reed sings about Sweet Jane and the whole world sparkles.

The girl in front is the one I was talking to earlier. She looks even lovelier in the sunshine, her deep dark hair and tanned skin outrageously exotic in the Scottish autumn scene.

Her two friends follow behind. The first of these is rather tall and broad, with brown hair in a strict bob. Her face is striking – almost masculine in its handsomeness, but the features are fine and her complexion as white as marble. She'd make a great model for a statue of an ancient queen. There's also something profoundly regal about the way she holds herself – very upright and together, like she's afraid of what would happen to her muscles if she let them relax.

The other girl is short, with long blonde hair, huge blue eyes and pouting lips as red and moist as fresh blood. Like her friends she wears rather short shorts revealing a slender pair of legs. Above, she wears a low-cut yellow vest-top that shows off her equally shapely arms and her noticeably large breasts.

"Is that…?" whispers Macrae.

"Yes."

"We have hit the fucking mother lode," says Macrae, breathing like a bull.

A few metres ahead of the girls the path dives into the woods. It will be difficult to approach them in there. In a moment they will be gone from this little patch of sunshine.

"Go!" says Macrae and shoves me into the road.

I jerk to a stop and turn round. I feel like I'm in a school disco.

"Why me?"

"You fucking know them!"

"I spoke to one of them for about a minute."

"When you were bollock naked. If that's not an 'in' I don't know what the fuck is."

And he steps forward and pushes me again.

"Alright, Jesus, I'll go," I say, "just don't shove me."

I look back across at the girls. They're nearly at the gap. Another few seconds and they'll be gone. I sling my pack nonchalantly on my back. Unfortunately it snags in an overhanging tree branch and the effect is less effortlessly manly than intended. Then I jog over the road to intercept the girls.

"Hello again!" I say and stop trotting as casually as I can.

The lead girl looks up, and as she does she tosses her mane of hair, so proudly, so wildly, my breath sets in my lungs like glue. She takes her Fab lolly from her mouth with an audible 'pop'.

"Oh, it is Mr Crazy Poet."

I grin and bob my head like an idiot. An insanse urge to get on my knees and lick her legs floods my system. Got to stay focused.

"J-j-just wanted to say thank you," I manage.

"What for?"

"Inspiring me."

She half smiles then sees that the other two girls are grinning at her, mischief glistening in their eyes, and she stops, as if catching herself.

"Pff, it was nothing," she says, and pops her lolly back in her mouth. But she doesn't walk away.

Macrae jams a spiky elbow in my ribs.

"Oof! So, uh, are you ladies from Sweden?" I ask.

"Yes, Malmo," says Tess. "How did you guess?"

"Well, Macrae-"

"That's me," says Macrae, diving forward and pumping the blonde girl's hand. "Bloody pleased to meet you. He's Tom. The goofball is George. And you girls are…?"

"I am Nina," replies the blonde girl. "She is Gertrud (the tall girl) and that is Tess (the girl I was talking to)."

"What bloody lovely names," says Macrae, staring hard at the blonde girl's chest.

The waters of the loch lap gently at a little beach on our left.

"So what are you doing in Scotland?" Macrae asks Nina's breasts.

"Well," starts Nina, "Tess just split up from her boyfriend and we heard about the kilts and-"

Tess whips round and glares at her friend. Her soft rosy skin has hardened, like nougat left in the freezer. And she holds herself rigid like that, as if afraid she might shatter into a thousand sweet shards.

Nina stutters and changes tack:

"Uh, that is, I mean, we are in a… erm… nature club together. We hear Scotland is good for that, so we decide to visit, and…"

"So it was very nice to meet you," starts Tess, her voice quavering ever-so-slightly, "but we have many kilometres to walk today." And she starts towards the entry to the forest. Nina and Gertrud start to follow.

Macrae glares at me, jaw clenched hard.

I know I have to act, but for a moment I can't move. It's the first time she's displayed anything other than total confidence and I'm entranced. I swear the way she half drops her head in embarrassment makes the sun shine brighter. I can't let that glorious light slip away.

"That's amazing," I say, stepping forward, "because that's why we're doing the Way too. To study… nature. In fact, we are writing a book about it."

Tess pauses. Nina and Gertrud look at her. Gertrud turns to George and raises an eyebrow.

"All of you?" she asks.

"Well," says Wentworth, "Tom here is the real creative genius, but I am also helping, and Alan is trying his best. Most of the time."

"Look," says Macrae, pulling out his notebook. "I got a jotter and everything!"

Nina smiles at Tess who pauses for a second. She's caught. She wants to be part of the group, but something in her is yelling 'bolt'. I don't know how I'm so in tune with her, but I know she can't let this go without a fight.

She turns to me. Her skin is still tight but a tiny smile is toying with the stiff line of her lips. The masts of the boats in the bay chime like bells in the breeze. The sunlight gleams on her hair.

"So here we are, all of us interested in nature," she says, her proud eyes shining.

"Seems like it," I smile.

"But you look more like city boys to me." And she tilts her head back a little, lifting her chin royally into the air.

It's a challenge. I know that much. The boys know it too. I can feel their eyes on me, begging me to say something. But what?

And then it comes to me.

"We live in the city, Tess," I nod, "that is true. But we have been roaming these hills since we were boys. Alan knows all the plants and good things to eat. George has the whole area mapped in his head. As for me, well, I know about the wild creatures." I tilt my own head back, mirroring Tess. "In fact, there's a place near here, really rather close, where I can show you a true Scottish wildcat. If you wanted to see…?"

Now the girls are edging in close, pretty eyes wide.

"Oh yes!" says Nina.

"Please!" adds Gertrud.

Tess just nods.

I say nothing for a second, then I look around, as if searching for a scent. I pretend to catch it, then follow my nose, moving in widening circles before suddenly I dart back into the middle of the group.

"There!" I whisper, and point to the top of Wentworth's rucksack.

The girls see Jones and instantly melt.

"Oh, what a cute puss cat!" cries Nina.

"Isn't he lovely!" says Gertrud.

"He's up there again?!" squawks Wentworth.

Unbelievably, Jones lets the girls stroke him. He even purrs a little.

Tess turns to me and I see she's smiling and happiness surges in me because it feels like an old friend has just come into the room.

"Taking your cat walking," says Tess, shaking her head. "You are such funny boys." And she's staring right at me.

I feel like a long-forgotten power is once more flowing through my muscles.

"Let's walk together," I say. "And we'll show you a place to pick wild blackberries."

"Sure."

"Okay."

"That sounds much fun."

And the girls start on up the lochside path.

Macrae grabs me.

"So. Fucking. Smooth," he hisses in my ear, then slams a mighty paw round my shoulders. "My boy is back." And he thumps me so hard between the shoulder blades I can't breathe for two minutes. Which is actually fine, because it takes me that long to stop grinning.

FITCH RECOUNTS MACRAE'S FIRST CONVERSATION WITH NINA

It's ace to see Macrae in action again. He certainly doesn't hang about. He just peels away with Nina and starts gabbing. He turns his whole body to face her, even when walking, like she's the centre of his universe and he's stuck in her orbit.

I want to start talking to Tess, but I guess I'm a little shy. It's been so long since… I don't know, it just feels weird. So I keep one ear open to what Macrae is saying to Nina, keen to pick up a few tips. Their conversation runs something like this:

"So you girls're in a nature club."

"That's right."

"What is that, volleyball in the scuddy, that kind of thing?"

Nina smiles.

"No," she replies, "watching wildlife. Birds and beetles and little mouses. Do you like nature?"

"Like it? Sweetheart, I fucking love it. You see that sparrow? I love it. That tree? Love it. That sheep? I fucking love it."

"You are a man who loves sheep?" she asks with a shine in her eyes.

Macrae's eyebrows crumple in confusion. I smile to myself. I can't remember the last time I saw a girl check him like this.

"I don't want to shag it or anything. Who would? Well, I know some guys have, but you've got to be in one fuck of a drought before that seems like a good idea, know what I mean?" He smiles. "Course, if you were a sheep, I might reconsider."

"What?"

"I mean, if I was a sheep too. I'm not saying if you were a sheep and I was me I'd pump you. I mean, I might, I couldn't honestly say right now- anyway, shit, forget this."

"Yes."

"I'm sorry, I didn't mean it in a bad way," he says, then cracks a massive grin at her. "Do you get it?"

"What?"

"Baa-d way! Baa, like a sheep."

"I may be a Swedish person, but I know that is not a good joke."

"Right. Piss poor." He scratches his backside. "So what do you do?"

"I'm a physicist."

"Magic. Got any brufen? My head is fucking banging."

"Not a pharmacist. A physicist."

"I know that. I was joking. I've got a degree you know. No, that's a lie. I never graduated. Thick as a pie."

"What is... pie?"

"Shit, I'm not making much sense here, am I? But you know, Nina, there's a reason for that. You see..."

And he grabs her arm and turns her towards him and, with his big brown animal eyes looking right at her with absolute seriousness, says:

"I've been dreaming about a girl like you for a long, long time."

"How long?"

"A million years. Maybe more."

I swear, the girl visibly melts.

WENTWORTH RECOUNTS FITCH'S CONVERSATION WITH TESS

I accept that our species must procreate. But what I do not understand is this obsession so many males have with pursuing women. I have observed it often throughout my life, but in Alan Macrae this particular compulsion has surely reached its zenith. I truly believe that not a minute goes by when he does not think about that most basic of all human actions, the procedure of coitus. How dull and repetitive it must be to live in his world.

Nor am I against women per se. I have had many pleasurable conversations with females on topics covering the spectrum of human intellectual achievement, from literature and music to the sciences and philosophies. Indeed, the tallest of the three Scandinavian ladies whom we met today at once demonstrated that she is a woman of both immense sympathy and considerable intelligence. I have to say, I was rather charmed by her.

But this all-consuming and interminable pursuit, this incessant desire for unnecessary intimacy... these are things I simply cannot countenance.

Personally, of course, I do not have to countenance them. I can simply side-step the issue and employ my time more usefully. Tom, however, is less objective when it comes to such matters. Although not cut from the same cloth as Alan, he is nevertheless a man who is swayed by fashion.

And Alan has designs upon him.

He is desperate for his complicity. Such is Tom's charisma that a mere smile from him is enough to calm the hottest fires of Alan. His approval mitigates the excesses of Alan's behaviour and halves the burden of his insanity – as proven by the rather crude incident with my Meindl Burma Pros on that infernal hill.

Most of Alan's childishness is, of course, harmless. And I could allow it to continue with nothing more than a few checks and restraints were it not for an additional and far more worrying consequence that it has created.

I refer to the three Swedish females with whom Alan has conspired to ally us. One is, as I mentioned before, intelligent enough, and makes for better than average company; the second is a harmless trollop – but the third is something more dangerous.

A lioness.

She has a certain athleticism about her, a carefree, creative spirit and a pretty face that are as beguiling as the velvety paws of the great cat. But in her heart... ah, there, my friends, she is a hunter of primal ruthlessness.

Read the following transcript of the conversation between them which I overheard and see if it is not plain that I must be on watch for my friend Tom, and must, when this vigilance produces the opportunity, put into action such plans as may save his soul and his sanity from the extreme danger in which Alan has placed them:

"So what do you do when you're not enjoying wildlife?" Tom asks Tess.

"I am... dancer!" she exclaims, throwing her arms in the air and twirling on the spot in a somewhat ostentatious manner. Tom watches her for a moment and, true to his considerate nature, actually manages to feign interest in this display of idiocy.

"Wow, really? What, like ballet?"

"Poof! That is so fucking formal. Who wants to see some skinny flicka in a custard costume rubbing herself against a gay man's trouser package?"

"Um, not me."

"Absoluut!"

"So, ah... what sort of stuff do you do?"

"I have my own solo show."

"Wow. Cool. What's it about?"

"Well, it is not completed yet. That is why I am on this trip, for inspiration. But I know what the theme will be."

"Tell me!"

She then speaks as if reading from a theatre review:

"It is the epic show of an eagle's life quest. The journey of a beautiful, noble and ruthless bird as she strives through her harsh mountain environment from fledgling to hunter to mate and mother."

"Gosh, sounds dramatic. What's it called?"

"'Fly Eagle, Sing Eagle, Fuck Eagle.'"

"Right. Aha. Pretty um... memorable."

She shrugs.

"It is crazy I know. But there is no time in this life for, how you say – pissing around the place. One minute we are here, walking beside the pretty water, the next minute – PAF!!" She slams her fist into her opposite palm, "an asteroid lands on your head, turns your brain to lava and poof!! – you are dead as shit. So I decide I want to call my show ' Fly Eagle, Sing Eagle, Fuck Eagle' – and I think, yeah, why fucking not?"

He looks away out at the loch for a second. I assume that like me he is trying hard not to laugh at this cretinous creature, but after a while he turns back round to her and says"Tess, have you always been a dancer?"

"Since I was three."

"Wow."

He kicks a stone. For a moment they walk along in silence. He looks like he is thinking of a way to politely tell her to push off, but after a while he surprises me (and her) by saying:

"Tess, about my poem. The one I showed you earlier."

"Mr Manly Stag?"

He nods.

"Well, I was thinking just now about what you said about the eider duck, and I suddenly realised that that's a great idea for an ending because if the duck was a female and she built a nest in a stag's antlers it would represent, you know, the gentle balance between male and female. The fragility of it all. Maybe."

She turns towards him.

"Is that what you really believe?"

He stares at her for a long time in conversational terms. I estimate ninety seconds. He finally says:

"No."

Her eyebrows arch like a pair of black cats stretching.

He goes on, a little sadly:

"For a moment there I had a notion it's what you believe. And that made me want to believe it too. But the fact is…"

"Continue."

He throws his hands into the air in a rather dramatic gesture.

"I don't know what I believe! And that's my problem, you know? I want to write poems that are all deep and philosophical, so I look at things and try to see the meaning there, but whenever I put the words down it never seems to come out very deep at all. And then I meet someone like you, a truly creative person, a real artist, and I just think… maybe that's because I'm just not a very deep person, you know?"

"Hey," she says. "I am thirty-two years old. You know how many people came to my last show?"

"No-"

"Seven."

"Oh. Per night?"

"In total."

She takes his hand and says:

"It's not about getting to the meaning. It's about enjoying the journey."

And they walk on together. But I can tell they're simply humouring each other. There's no real spark there.

FROM MACRAE'S NOTEBOOK

So the good news is that we've got to this place on the loch and I've just about not fucking chinned Wentworth and we've caught up with the three birds and for once things are looking rosy.

One's a big old unit not a pig but a bit smug looking. Perfect for George. Second one's nice enough bit of a dopey pus but good pins and that dreamy artist look about her. Fitchy is going to go for her I can tell. And she'll do him good. She's not the marrying kind but she's into him and she'll suck his bobby clean off if he doesn't blow it. But the third one. Fuck. Me. Blonde and horny as hell and I swear you would not fucking believe the tits on this girl.

I'm not kidding at times like this I wish I was creative like Fitch cos then I could think of some cool way of describing these tits to you. Poetry I mean. But they are just so fucking astonishing it's like they've melted my eyes right out and gone in through the holes and somehow replaced my brain and now they're just bouncing around in there and ringing a bell – dingalingadingadingding – as what's left of me dances around with a stiffy doing a mad Jimmy Saville impression waving my hands and going 'Eeeuurghh-eeee-urrghh-eeee-urrrghhh!'

As you can imagine this has royally fucked my noodle so there won't be any poetry I'm afraid.

Now like I say this is all the good news. But the bad news is that I've started talking to this bird and I'm giving her my grade-A chat and she starts laughing at me. Turns out she's a fucking psychologist or something and is a superbrain as well as a superbod and she's finding things funny that I simply don't understand (probably due to that tool Saville).

At first this pisses me off. Then I figure ah what the hell. Least the girl's laughing.

So I just mong out and keep chatting away being myself and making crap jokes and she keeps on laughing hysterically at fuck knows what and after a while we kind of reach this sort of balance which is a bit of a turn up for the books because it lets me keep an ear on George.

This is important because we are in a delicate situation here and the silly cunt could fuck this whole thing right up.

He needs watching.

Not cos he's nasty cos he isn't. He may not like me very much but he thinks the sun rises out of Fitchy's hoop and he wouldn't do anything to upset him. But there's something not right there. Something maybe he doesn't know about. Something he just can't help. Fat fucker's just so hung up. Listen to this conversation which I was wigging on right and you'll see what I mean:

The big bird looks sideways at George who is limping like a saddo.

"Are you okay?" she asks.

"I'm sorry, what?"

"You appear to be in pain," she says, pointing to his foot.

"Oh, I have sustained a blister."

The ostrich extends her neck like a raccoon stole her egg.

"What!?" she squawks. "Alert your friends, we must stop!"

George flaps his hands at her.

"Calm down, my dear, please. I've already told them. Their response was far from sympathetic and their proposed treatment decidedly unscientific, I can tell you."

"Let me have a look at it."

George goes stiff. His white face is like a wet flannel thrown against a wall.

"W-w-what?"

"I am a doctor."

"You are?"

"Yes. A dermatological surgeon to be precise."

"Oh, goodness me, ha ha, no, it's not that serious."

Which is a twat thing to say. This chick is plainly hot for you George. Ten minutes in and she's asking to touch your body. The correct strategy is of course – stop and let the girl remove your boot and wait till everyone else is out of sight then take your trousers off and tell her there's something wrong with your balls as well.

"Okay," says the ostrich, "I was only offering to help."

There's a pause then George says clearly realising he's fucked up:

"But perhaps you could advise me of any method or technique that may prevent it from getting any worse?"

Big bird nods.

"One key to blister prevention is to keep your skin as dry as possible. When significant forces are applied to dry skin, they tend to quickly tear off the very outer layer, called the stratum corneum. Although that sounds bad, the displaced cells actually form a sort of protective barrier over the remaining skin."

I know what you're thinking – fucking yawnsville. But the point is that she may be being boring but she's being boring about shit she's into. Really into. Which is a fucking result this early on. It's a signal clear as day and George can see it. The problem is that he isn't letting on that he sees it.

"I say, this is most fascinating," is all he says.

"On the other hand, wet skin is the true blister culprit, because surface tension created by the thin coating of water holds skin cells together, impedes their movement, and thereby hikes the frictional effect-"

And so it goes on for mile after mile and not a word of it getting him anywhere.

Because the man is completely fucking uptight.

FROM FITCH'S DIARY

Suddenly the six of us spill into Milarrochy Bay, a crescent moon of pebbly sand backed by trees. To our right, beneath the patchwork canopy of autumn leaves, thick bushes beard the path.

It's a lovely spot, and we break from our pairs here, each of us spinning in their own circle, entranced by the never-ending landscape of trees, loch, islands and hazy mountains beyond.

I walk over to the bushes. Nestling under the leaves are little clusters of fruit, shining like treasure.

"Over here, ladies," I cry. "Look, wild blackberries."

The girls step forward to the bushes.

"I've never seen berries so big," says Nina.

"The one good thing about a wet summer," grins Macrae. "Makes them juicy."

I dig my Frisbee out of my rucksack.

"We'll put them in here," I say.

And so we start scurrying round the bushes, harvesting the ripe fruit and piling them in my Frisbee. After twenty minutes of laughing and throwing we have a glorious pyramid of gleaming berries. We sit on the grassy bank in a line, looking out at the loch and passing the heavy Frisbee from hand to hand.

For a moment we all just sit there, eating together in silence as our fingers stain ever darker with sweet crimson blood.

"Isn't it mad," I say eventually, "that all this used to be under a mile of ice. Great glaciers freezing and crushing everything in their path."

Everyone munches for another moment.

"And yet, if that had not happened," says Tess, "this beauty we see now would not exist."

Her hair flicks and floats on the breeze as she stares out at the water. She pops another blackberry into her mouth and at that very second a hot light surges within me. Pure creativity is flooding my veins. Ideas for poems dart and shine inside me like a shoal of fish in the sun.

I look out to the islands.

"You know, I hadn't thought of that," I say after a moment. "They are beautiful. And each in its own way. With its own unique character."

Tess smiles at me as she chews.

Wentworth leans forward and says:

"The islands are indeed different in many respects, Tom. Geologically speaking, the south-eastern section of the loch is in the lowlands and the rest in the highlands. We are actually sitting on the cusp of an enormous fracture in the surface of the world."

The girls nod and look out at the water. Macrae yawns loudly. Wentworth ignores him and continues:

"They also vary in their flora and fauna. In fact, one of them – Inchconnachan – is one of the very few places outside Australia which has a viable population of wallabies."

"Wallabies?" asks Gertrud.

"Pish!" cries Macrae, and pings a berry right off Wentworth's nose.

"It's true," continues George. "The landowner, Lady Arran Colquhoun introduced them in 1975, intending to start a wildlife park, but the plan never came to fruition. The wallabies roamed wild and actually settled into their new habitat. Now there is a stable population of around 28."

"How fucking high was that bitch?" snorts Macrae.

"Occasionally," continues Wentworth, "the loch freezes over and one crosses the ice onto the mainland. Where it usually gets hit by a truck on the A82, to the enormous surprise of the driver."

"Hah!" scoffs Macrae, but his bluster drops after that and I notice his eyes drift out over the water.

Again, the light in me burns.

"What I find amazing though," I say, "is that creatures so far from home could live here, thrive, and find peace in the hills of Scotland."

"That is such a poetic thought," says Tess. And she holds me with eyes that are themselves heavy berries, ripe and dark and full of life. I swear, if she'd looked like that one millisecond longer I'd have kissed her then and there.

But suddenly Gertrud says:

"Oh dear. We have eaten all of them."

And she holds up the now-empty Frisbee.

"I did not realise how hungry I was," says Nina, licking a suntanned finger.

"Let's pick more," growls Macrae.

"Better than that," says Wentworth, pulling a map from his pocket. "Look, we're nearly finished for the day – Rowardennan is just up ahead. I believe they have a rather splendid bar there which overlooks the water. Its seafood is reputed to be particularly exquisite."

"George," says Macrae, "sometimes you could almost pass for a human being."

"From your lips, a most incredible honour," smiles George.

And as one we jump to our feet and happily reach for our rucksacks.

*

After an hour or so, the track rises a little over a hillock and at the crest Macrae suddenly extends his arms and stops us, letting the girls walk on a little.

"Oh boys!" says Macrae licking his lips. "Tell me this isn't heaven and I'll tell you you're a pair of lying cunts."

I smile. The scene below is almost impossibly attractive.

The wood around us opens out into a wide, grassy clearing. This rolls down to the loch, giving us a clear view of the mountains on the opposite side. A large white building perches on a rise at the edge of the water like a nervous swimmer. On the wall facing us is written "Rowardennan Hotel". To the right of the building is a curving beach with a pier at its far end. At the rear of the hotel, a wide terrace has been built out towards the water and a bar opens out from the hotel through French windows. This terrace is rich with happy drinkers, their pints shining in the sun like jewels. The evening air is still and genuinely warm – it feels more like high summer than autumn, and the clink-ting of glasses and high music of female laughter that drift through it across the soft lawn are utterly intoxicating.

Wentworth and I are about to set off down the hill when again Macrae holds us back.

"If this turns into an orgy," he says, heavy seriousness weighing down his round brown eyes, "I don't mind you boys having a shot on Nina as long as I get first go. That girl's special to me, okay?"

"How nice to see, Alan," says Wentworth, "that chivalry still thrives in our modern age."

"Right," nods Macrae, "just so long as we're clear." And then he grabs our hands and presses something into them. I look down. A pair of condoms nestles in my palm.

"That's me down to my last twenty," he says, "so if you boys need any more you'll have to go to the machine in the bogs." He smiles. "Good luck, lads," he adds, then throws an arm briefly around each of us before stepping forward and leading the way down the grassy slope to the bar.

★

The six of us go in through the front of the hotel, snake our way through reception and enter the bar. The room is a curious blend of old-fashioned hunting lodge and modern gastropub. Stags' heads hang on the walls alongside chalkboards with the day's specials; the bar is ancient mahogany, but it's backed by angled mirrors and glitzy glass optics. The best thing though, are the huge French windows which take up the whole back wall and open out onto the terrace and its stunning view of the loch.

We pick our way through the clientele – a mixture of Way walkers, ramblers and mountain bikers who also use this area – and step up to the bar.

A suntanned barman with corkscrew hair, freckles and a broad, chipped-tooth grin bobs towards us.

"Afternoon, guys," he says in a friendly Australian accent, "I'm Brian. What can I get you today?"

"Well, Brian, that's an incredibly complex question," says Macrae. "I see you have Colonsay lager there – a very fine brew. So we'll start with a dozen of them to take the thirst off. Then some double vodka tonics to revive the spirits and better bring five or six bottles of red to help us get our chill on."

"You guys going to be eating?" asks Brian.

"Fucking right we are, mate," says Macrae. "I'm so hungry I could eat a scabby camel's cock."

"Nice one!" chirps Brian. "Here's some menus, I'll pop out in just a second and get your orders."

"You, mate," says Macrae, "are a prince among men." And he scoops an armful of Colonsay lager bottles and leads the way out into the sunshine.

"Can you believe," smiles Macrae, holding his three beers in his paws and expanding his arms to encompass the happy scene before us, "that we have a whole week of this?!"

Which is when a voice, as deep and cold and echoing as a cracking glacier, booms from the far side of the terrace:

"Hello again, Tess!"

Tess whips round.

We follow her gaze to see three guys in tracksuits sitting at a trestle table. They rise to their feet and as they do I actually hear myself gasp – I have simply never seen such prodigious specimens of masculinity.

Their shoulders are as broad as Siberia and the veins on their necks as thick as the Volga. They wear identical white tracksuits with red piping down their scarily triangular shoulders. A badge on the left breasts of their absurdly bulging chests bears a logo: two clenched fists raised in triumph above the words written in red capitals: "Moscow Gymnastic Team". In front of each of them is a barely touched slim-jim of orange juice.

We stop where we are, halfway across the decking. Disappointment clings to me like somebody else's sweaty gym kit.

The first of the three Russian colossi steps away from the table and moves like a panther towards Tess.

"Nice surprise to see us, yes?" he says, cracking a huge blonde grin, and kissing her lingeringly on both cheeks.

Tess totters back in surprise.

"B-b-but you had gone back to Russia!" she says.

The guy's cliff-face cracks into a smile.

"Our trainer he was so pleased with our victories that he give us some relaxing time. So we thought, why not go to Scotland and surprise our nice Swedish girls?"

"Are you not pleased to see us?" says the second Russian, stepping forward and facing Nina.

"Woah dragon," says Macrae, inserting himself between them. Then he asks Nina: "Who're these tubes?"

And the Russians turn and look at us for the first time. They size us up with one glance and their top lips instantly contort into Billy Idol sneers.

"Please, Tess," says the first Russian, "will you not be introducing us to these gentlemen?"

Nina and Gertrud flash nervous glances at Tess. She fires a similarly pained one back.

Then she looks round at me and smiles in what is clearly meant to be a reassuring way. But then there's something odd behind that smile, something that doesn't fit – a doomed air of self-preservation. Like the autumn trees trying to hold on to their summer leaves.

I have an urge to step forward and stroke her cheek.

She steps in between our ranks and makes the introductions.

"Boys, this is Uzeyir, Wassily and Zinaida. Some Russian… friends of ours. This is Tom, George and Alan." Then she glances at me and adds: "They are proud Scotsmen."

The way she flicked her eyes at me when she said that makes the breath seize in my lungs. Was that a plea for help? It looked like it, but surely Tess wouldn't need my help…

But I don't have time to think about that because suddenly my hand is shaken by a JCB.

"I have pleasure to meet you."

And I'm staring up into the monolith of Uzeyir's face. He passes my crunched hand on to Wassily and Zinaida as we all shake in turn.

"Hi."

"Hi."

"Hey."

"Hey."

"How jolly nice to meet you all," says Wentworth.

"Gaaaaar!" Zinaida roars back at him.

"Goodness, is he ill?" asks Wentworth, cowering in alarm.

"Please excuse Zinaida," says Uzeyir, "he is not so good with words."

"That's okay," I smile as we dump our packs and take up position on the long bench table, "I don't expect him to speak our language. After all, we can't speak yours."

"It is not English that is the problem for him," replies Uzeyir with a calm smile. "It is Russian."

"Goooorrr!" booms Zinaida suddenly pointing at Jones.

"But he likes your funny fat cat," grins Wassily, his eyes narrowing to slits. "I think he wants to make friends with it."

Zinaida is reaching a huge meat hand towards Jones. My puss is in a corner between the wall and our rucksacks and for a second it looks like the Russian is simply going to grab him.

Macrae snaps his fingers in front of Zinaida's face, stopping his lunge.

"First," says Macrae, "that's muscle, not fat. Second, he's not an 'it' he's Jones. Third, Boris here is going to keep his paws off, capiche?"

Zinaida stares down at Macrae. Macrae stares right back up.

I have this horrible feeling like I've walked out into the middle of a rope bridge and only just noticed that the ropes are actually lengths of licquorice and at any second the whole thing will crash into the chasm.

"Geerrr," growls Zinaida at last and withdraws his hand.

"We understand each other just fine," says Macrae.

Jones, fur standing high on his back, withdraws haughtily from the corner and reclaims his dignity by lifting his tail and spraying on Wentworth's rucksack.

For now, my bridge holds firm.

"Please," says Uzeyir. "Join us." And he nods to Zinaida who picks up the nearest bench with one hand and plonks it down next to their table.

The Russians make sure the girls sit in between them, while we line up opposite. Although they seemed like the identical triplets of Zeus at first, now we're closer I notice a few differences between them. Uzeyir's blonde hair flops over his eyes and his chin has an imperious upward tilt. His eyes are wide and crystal blue and seem constantly amused. Wassily has the same thick fair hair, but he wears it slicked back in a razor parting. His eyes are thin, his nose sharp, and his lips so narrow and bloodless as to be almost translucent. The third Russian, Zinaida, is taller and broader than his colleagues, making him a full foot higher than Macrae when they shake hands. Every inch of him – even his face – is covered with muscles that strain and squirm beneath his skin like snakes in a sack. His blonde hair is shaved close to his enormous muscled head.

Out of the corner of my eye I sense the girls looking at each other. There's a strange quietness hanging over them, faint but definitely there, like a cloud of midges.

"So, um, how did you guys all, er, meet?" I ask in what I hope is a cheery manner.

Uzeyir grins.

"We stay in Malmo for two months, training for the European athletic championships. We meet these girls one day and they become like our… good luck charms! With them as inspirations we easily win our events. It was such a shame when we had to part. And so when we get our time off we come looking for our lucky little girls."

And he slides an arm round Tess's waist.

"How do you know them?" he asks me.

Before I can answer, Tess coolly removes Uzeyir's arm from her hips and leans forward.

"The boys are walking the West Highland Way like us," she says.

Uzeyir nods, steepling granite hands to sandstone lips.

"Yes, we heard about this. A gentle – how you say? – stroll through your little hills."

"Stroll?" I say. "These hills can be pretty tough, you know." And I point to the Arrochar Alps across the loch which, despite the glory of the evening, carry darkness around their shoulders.

"Zey are nothing compared wiz ze mountains in Russia," says Uzeyir. "How big is your Ben Nevis, a thousand metres?"

"1344," says Wentworth.

Uzeyir leans forward.

"Last year we climbed Mount Elbrus, the highest peak in Europe. It is 5,642 metres." He leans back, grinning.

'That is almost four times bigger than your weeny little Nevis," laughs Wassily, pinching his fingers together in a 'tiny' mime.

"Guuur," adds Zinaida.

"Well," says Tess, "we are not here because they're big, we're here because they're beautiful. And," she adds, nodding at me, "because of the wildlife."

She smiles at me and again the pleading in her eyes tears at my soul.

Uzeyir leans forward. His mouth splits over his teeth like a wound.

"Is that so?" he says. "When we were training for the Siberian Championships, we lived in a cabin in the Irkutsk forest for six months. At night the wolves would howl us to sleep."

"And when we go to wash in the river in morning," adds Wassily, "the bears are catching fishes for their breakfast."

Uzeyir nods.

"One time when on the top of the snowy cliffs, we even see a Siberian tiger!"

"Garr!" roars Zinaida.

"Yeah, alright, we get the idea," mutters Macrae, "mountains, wildlife, you cunts sat on a rock having a wank, we're with you."

Nina's mouth drops open in thrilled shock and she slides a smile at Gertrud. It only lasts a heartbeat, but I swear I see danger there.

Uzeyir cocks his head at Macrae.

"So what animals have you seen?" asks Uzeyir.

My licquorice rope bridge is getting rained on.

"Uh… well, we haven't been going that long," I start, "but this morning a stag–"

"A deer?" asks Wassily in apparent innocence. "Like Bambi?"

And now the wind is starting to blow.

Tess leans forward.

"Yes," she says, "but Tom wrote a poem to him and transformed his humble animal body into high art."

And she smiles at me and for a second the world steadies. Then I clock Uzeyir's sneer and everything lurches hideously.

"Is that so?" he muses, leaing forward in apparent fascination. "I would very much like to hear that. Could you speak it out to us?"

I think of my Manly Stag poem and it just seems so small, so silly, so... weak compared with the gathered armies of their muscles.

"It's not quite finished-"

"Yes it is," says Tess.

"I mean, I don't want to show it to anyone yet-"

Tess frowns.

"You let me see it earlier," she says.

"That was different," I say.

She sinks back in herself, like a puppy with a wounded paw.

"How?" she croaks.

"We were... I was... there weren't any... other people there," I manage.

"What kind of artist cares about what other people think?" she blurts out.

A bloody hurricane just hit my bridge.

I look at Macrae. He's biting his lip in frustration. Wentworth looks like a firework just went off in his face. As for Tess, her dark eyes shine with hope. I know I have to say something important. But my brain is literally empty. I have nothing to give. I'm falling...

"I'm not sure you could call me much of an artist-" I start.

"Oh," says Tess – a curious, almost involuntary syllable. She drops her eyes and scans the ground for a moment, as if reading the terms of my treason there. Then she stands, drawing her elegant frame up to its full proud height.

"I... am going to bed," she announces, and she spins away from the table.

"See you in the morning!" calls Uzeyir after her. Then he turns to Nina and Gertrud and says: "We are thinking we will walk this Way with you. It sounds like so much fun."

But they don't reply, and after a moment they rise and follow their friend, eyes lost in the far distance.

Now there's just the Russians smirking at us as amid the clank and chatter of the pub.

Suddenly the cheerful Aussie barman bounces up.

"Here's the rest of your drinks, guys," he says, laying down a huge tray of clanking glasses and bottles. "Now, you decided on your food yet?"

"Three steaks," grins Uzeyir. "Very bloody."

"Nice one," says Brian. He looks at me. "And how about you fellas?"

"You can ram your food, Brian," says Macrae, and he slings an arm around me. "Come on, mate," he soothes, "let's find a spot to camp."

I'm too stunned to take much in as Macrae leads the way off the terrace and along the shore. But I do remember we have to go a long way from the pub before the lapping of the loch drowns out the Russians' laughter.

★

Some time later I'm sitting in my tent, rain pattering on the flysheet, Wentworth curled on his sleeping bag in his tent, the pair of us forlornly watching Macrae attempt to coax a fire into life.

"Smokers!" curses Macrae suddenly as his tinder sizzles and dies for the tenth time. He springs to his feet and boots his carefully structured triangle of sticks into oblivion. "Fucking Russian cocksmokers!" And he stalks away from our rude little campsite, the sparks of his shattered fire zinging around him like fireflies in the darkening forest.

"I believe," says Wentworth, "that is my cue to retire."

He pulls his Audrey Hepburn book from his rucksack and unzips his sleeping bag.

"You turning in too, Tom?" he yawns.

"Might just have one word with him," I say.

"You sure? You look simply exhausted."

"Won't be long," I smile. "You get your head down."

And I leave him in the warm sanctuary of the tent and pad into the rain after Macrae.

Fifty feet away, in the velvet heart of the twilight wood, I find him. He sits with his back against a huge shaggy oak, slugging hard on a bottle of Colonsay lager.

I sit down with my back to the same oak, both of us facing the loch. Jones crouches above us on a low branch, looking in the same direction, his dangling tail slowly whipping back and forth.

Macrae hands me his beer. Without a word, I accept it and take a slug. It is still cool and utterly delicious. I move to hand it back. He stops me with his left hand while lifting a new bottle with his right. He puts the bottle in his mouth and pops the cap with his teeth.

For a second we just sit there and drink. It doesn't seem so cold here in the woods.

"What happened?" I say.

"I think that's obvious, Fitchy. Boris, Morris and Horace fucked us," sighs Macrae. "We got our work cut out now if we're going to get that ride."

"You sure? Didn't Nina say earlier that they came on this trip because Tess split up with her boyfriend? She didn't look that keen on him if you ask me. Maybe they are just going to be friends now."

He cocks his head and stares at me from the side of his eyes.

"For such a clever boy you can be surprisingly thick when it comes to women. Didn't you see those guys back there? Hear their boasting? And how many blokes you know would fly from fucking Russia to Scotland to be friends with a bird?" He snorts. "Fitch, this is a war where the winner takes all and both sides know it. The girls do too. Hot little bitches love the idea of guys battling it out for the honour of ramming them. Makes them feel prized. And that makes them wet. I tell you, when this thing is finally decided, whoever comes out on top is going to get his jockeys ripped off in a cocking nanosecond."

I stare at the mossy ground.

He takes a slug of his beer.

"You tried your best in there with your poetry manoeuvre, but unfortunately our enemy's counter attack was impressive. If we're going to defeat them we need a plan that is powerful, devious and final." He looms at me out of the gloaming. "A mega-strategy."

"Do you have any suggestions?"

Macrae rubs his hand thoughtfully over his stubbly chin. He says:

"Yes."

"What?"

"Wallaby."

He looks out across the loch. Sips his beer.

"Macrae – what are you talking about?"

"Look, the girls love wildlife, right? They're here in Scotland to see nature. They practically creamed their cut-offs when Wentworth told them about wallaby island. Imagine how impressed they'd be if we could show them a real live one!"

"I don't understand it and already I know this is a dreadful idea."

"That's just because you're not on board yet. When you see it from the bridge of the good ship Macrae, you'll know it makes perfect sense."

"Like putting a tent peg up your arse did."

He shakes his head and waves his hands.

"I was confused then. But my thoughts are clear now. My piss in the boot idea got Wentworth going, didn't it?"

"I suppose-"

"Right then."

"Right then what? Macrae, even if I admit that it might be an okay idea in principle, how do you suggest we go about putting it into action?"

"Simple. We wait till it's completely dark then just swim over to the island, put wallaby in a rucksack and swim back."

"You're a lunatic."

"Just think how buzzed those chicks are going to be when we parade it at breakfast!"

"Macrae, we can't start swimming around Loch Lomond in the middle of the night!"

"When we were on exercise on Indonesia I swam two miles across shark-infested waters to the beach bar in Bali and back every night."

"Comparing this terrible idea with another terrible idea does not make it less terrible. It'll be freezing cold and dark and dangerous and I'm simply not going in. Besides, why would you even think of swimming when there are all those boats behind the pier?"

His eyes flare wide. He lobs his beer bottle into the bushes, throws an arm around me and says:

"Now that is mega-strategic thinking. Let's fucking go!"

"Crap."

★

We wait until the pub has long closed and all the drinkers have settled in for the evening. The only sounds now are the lap of the water on the shore and the soft night twitterings of the forest creatures. When the last light has been turned off and the stars are ruling the sky, Macrae gets to his feet and dusts himself down.

"Operation Wallaby is a go," he whispers.

As I pointed out, there are a few boats at the back of the pier, but they are all tightly secured and battened down. A little way further we find a small dinghy which is open, but it has an enormous engine that would surely wake everyone from here to Balloch even if we could jump it. Those are the only boats in this bay, so we head back into the trees and climb over the headland into the next one. It's hard going, but after a while we notice that the moon has risen. Nearly full, her soft light gives the woods a surreal glow. And when we get back down to the water's edge, the reflection of her flying high over the night-cloaked mountains stops me dead in my tracks.

I'm still staring at the beauty of it all, trying to find some breath, when I hear Macrae.

"I found her!" he hisses. "Come here!"

I pick my way over to where he's standing, a little way back from the shoreline with a leaf-covered tarpaulin at his feet.

"The Good Ship Macrae," he beams. "Isn't she beautiful?"

I'm staring at an ancient rowing boat with flaking paint and about six inches of moss in the bottom.

"Is this going to float?" I ask.

"Course it is!" says Macrae. "Would Jones and I take you out in an unseaworthy vessel?"

"You will forgive me if I require something a little more buoyant than the blind optimism of a madman and a ginger cat."

"Sh! Do you want to give the game away? Now see if you can find a dry spot for these beers."

★

With the playful slap-slapping of the water on the hull and the drip-splash of the oars as I lift them in and out of the water, I'm seriously beginning to need a pee.

Macrae sits facing me in the stern, still drinking Colonsay lager. The last time I looked Jones was behind me, paws on the prow, scanning the moonlit horizon.

Sweat drips into my eyes despite the cool of the autumn night. We've been out on the water for over an hour and I'm getting a little tired of it.

"Why do I-?" I start.

Macrae leans forward.

"Sh!" he hisses.

I take a calming breath and whisper:

"Why do I have to do all the rowing?"

"Are you trained in night-time animal tracking?" whispers Macrae in reply.

"No."

"Well I am, and Captain Jones was born with that particular skillset, so get your hands on those oars and pull until we say otherwise."

"Can you at least," I say, hauling the boat forward, "tell me which island we're going for?"

"The one with the wallabies on it."

"Obviously, but which one is that?"

"Fatboy said was called 'inch' something."

I hold the oars above the water, dripping.

"Macrae, there are twenty-three islands in Loch Lomond and they don't have bloody signposts on. Tell me you've brought the map."

"Let's try this one. This looks good. I think this is it."

"Macrae, it's about forty feet across. How could a colony of twenty-eight wallabies live on that?"

He looks at me like I'm mad.

"In their burrows."

"Wallabies don't live in burrows."

"Right, right, well let's find an island with trees on it, then."

"No, they don't live up trees either. Macrae, out of interest, do you actually know what a wallaby is?"

"That's it! That one there. Come on, row faster."

Six islands later and I'm close to complete exhaustion. We've gone ashore on all of them, hauling the boat up on the pebbles before disappearing into the undergrowth for a fruitless wallaby hunt. My arms are aching from the rowing, my legs are jammed with thorns and my face is thick with stinging sweat and grime.

"That's enough," I say, as I pull us away from the shore once more, "I need bed more than I need any damned wallaby."

"Wait!" says Macrae, leaning forward. "Look there!" And he points over my shoulder.

I turn round to see Jones twitching his nose at yet another fabulously beautiful moon-shrouded island.

"This has to be it!" he says.

"No, Macrae," I say, "it doesn't."

★

Ten minutes later we're hauling the boat up onto pebbles again. A silver-plated beach curves away on either side and in front of us is a thicket of the densest undergrowth yet. Macrae points forward and smiles.

"Right then, here we go!" he whispers. "Remember, nice and quiet." And he paces deftly towards the bushes, Jones at his side.

How can he possibly have so much energy? It's taking every ounce of my will just to keep myself from collapsing where I stand like a puppet with its strings cut.

I step forward after him and kick my shin straight into a log. I tumble to the deck, cursing and crunching into the pebbles.

"I told you to be quiet," he says, looming over me.

"Jesus, that's it!" I snap. "Listen, Macrae, it's got to be four in the morning. It's starting to rain. I'm shattered. Let's just go."

"Sh!" he hisses.

"What?"

"Look at Jones!"

Jones has slowed to a panther crawl. Suddenly he stops dead, eyes blazing in the gloom. His tail shoots upright and 'poofs' to the volume of a feather duster.

"There!" says Macrae.

Through the trees at the edge of the water, a shape is moving.

"I'm not sure that's a wallaby," I say. "It's got a fish in its mouth."

"I don't care if it's got the Declaration of Arbroath up its arsehole. Bag the bastard."

★

The journey back is more dream than reality. Am I really lying on damp moss in a rotting boat, a twitching sack beside me, or am I in a silken berth in in a luxury yacht, Captain Macrae whistling at the wheel?

Is that the first grey light of dawn over the eastern hills or just the lights of St Tropez harbour as we ease home? And the softness caressing my face, that cannot be rain, it must surely be the gentle breath of Tess herself.

I sigh, and sip at a little sweet sleep. Delicious. If only I were a little warmer, I could drink my fill...

And then Jones, my little puss-man, pads gently onto my chest, treads once, and lies himself down, a purring bundle of warmth...

...and I am gone.

★

The unmistakeable sound of rain on a tent.

The unmistakeable smell of camp-cooked food.

The unmistakeable sight of Macrae, peering in my tent flap, drizzle sparkling on his wiry hair.

"Rise and shine!" he beams. "I've made you boys breakfast."

And he thrusts something towards me.

I wriggle up onto one elbow and try to focus on what he's holding out. Close inspection reveals it to be a plastic bowl filled with an odd-smelling, lumpy grey broth.

"What is it?" I ask.

"Stew!" cries Macrae, prodding a spoon towards the heavens.

"What kind of stew?" I sniff.

"Stew McGoo."

"Aha. And what is in 'Stew McGoo'?"

"Nutrients!" beams Macrae, jabbing the spoon skywards again before forcing it on me. "Now eat it while it's hot and then get up. We have something amazing to show the girls!"

★

Fifteen minutes later I struggle out of the tent into the grey light of a dull morning. There's only a light mist of rain falling now, but the way the clouds are rolling fatly down the hills, it could well get heavier.

Wentworth appears at the mouth of his tent.

"My word!" he says, slapping his arms around himself. "I never thought one could sleep so well without silk sheets. I have to say I feel jolly marvellous. Thousand times better than yesterday. How are you this morning, Tom?"

"Still a little tired," I say. "And I'm not sure I thought much of breakfast, did you?" I add, an odd-tasting belch escaping my lips.

"Actually, I thought it was rather nice – salmony and creamy but with a little bite to it in places. Reminded me somewhat of great aunt Claudia's kedgeree."

Suddenly Macrae appears from his bivouac, clutching an oddly bulging rucksack.

"Right," he says, "here's the plan. The birds're up there having some scran," he says, nodding at the hotel, "and those Russian pricks aren't up yet. So we have to strike now."

Wentworth gently swivels his head to look at me.

"What is he talking about?" Wentworth.

Macrae slings the bulging pack on his back and stares at me expectantly.

"Well…" I start, then pause. "Probably best just to see for yourself," I add. "Come on." And we set off across the clearing.

★

On the terrace, awnings have been hoisted over the bench tables. The girls sit under them, sipping steaming mugs of coffee, munching on toast and looking out from their haven at the rain on the loch.

They break into smiles as soon as they see us. We smile back. But as we approach, memories of how we parted crack at everyone's confidence and our conversation is chilly.

"Morning."

"Hey."

"Hi."

"You sleep well?"

"How you say, like a tree. You?"

I smile. Nod.

"Like a tree also."

"You would like to have breakfast?"

Macrae nudges me.

"Uh, no, we've already eaten. But we would like a moment to, uh… show you something."

"A very very special thing," adds Macrae. And he takes off his rucksack and plumps it, upside down, on the table in front of them.

Something about the way it sags there gives me a very weird feeling. Stew McGoo rises in my throat, forcing me to swallow unpleasantly.

The girls stare first at the rucksack, then at us. Wentworth looks equally perplexed. I turn to Macrae who is parading up and down like an impatient peacock. Suddenly he leans towards me.

"Say something," he hisses.

"Say what?"

"I don't know! Something. Poetry. Build me up." And he glares at me.

I look at the girls. They are also staring at me. I clear my throat.

"Uh, well. As you ladies know, being such, um, fans of nature, there are very many beautiful animals in Scotland." I smile. They nod. I go on: "And from the noble stag standing silhouetted on the heather-clad mountainside to the mighty sea eagle, soaring high over river and glen, all of them are beautiful in their own way."

The girls look excited. I continue:

"But perhaps none, not one of them is quite so beautiful in its…" I look around at them again. Now they are waiting on my next word with bottom lips hanging low. "…unexpectedness as the creature you are about to see."

They edge forward on their bench, thighs jiggling with anticipation.

"Ladies of Sweden," I continue, rising in excitement, "I give you, the rarity of rarities, the beast of beasts, the treasure of the highlands, here he is… the Last Lost Wallaby of Loch Lomond!"

"You fucking dancer," winks Macrae, and whips up the rucksack.

fuck

me

But I've barely had time to take in the awfulness of what is now displayed when I hear the sound of bolking. I spin to see Gertrud and Nina clamping their hands to their mouths and bolting for the loos.

"Come back," says Macrae sadly. "He wants to talk to you – look, he's smiling."

"I told you, Tom," says Wentworth, also throwing his hand to his mouth, "he's nothing but a savage!" And he's gone after the girls.

I turn to look at Tess.

She turns from the table to face me. Her wide brown eyes are bubbling with angry tears.

"I thought," she says through gritted teeth, "you were man with warm heart. But this… this is the most… coldest thing I have ever seen."

Then she too is gone.

Leaving just me, Macrae and the… creature on the table.

I stare.

I stare and stare and stare.

For a brief moment a wave of anger rises within me. I have a hideous urge to hurt Macrae, physically damage him so he cries out in pain. Then I look at his face, the features I know so well – swarthy and boyish, smiling and scared, and I think – what's the fucking point?

I take my old friend to one side. Say to him quietly:

"Macrae, what's this?"

111

"Wallaby."

I sigh.

"Really?"

"Yes."

Pause.

"Where's its pouch?"

Macrae pulls out his enormous survival knife.

"You want it to have a pouch?"

Another sigh.

"I want it to be a wallaby."

"It is." He points with the knife. "Wallaby."

"No, Macrae, it's a dead otter. Into which you have sewn my Frisbee."

Long pause. He drops his big brown eyes to the ground. Says softly:

"Is it that obvious?"

FROM MACRAE'S NOTEBOOK

DAY 3

ROWARDENNAN TO CRIANLARICH

Summary:
- *Distance: 22.5 km (20 miles)*
- *Estimated Time: 6-8 hours*
- *Height Range: 800ft (240m) ascent*
- *Terrain: This is by far the roughest section of the Way, particularly north of Inversnaid where the path makes a tortuous route along the side of Loch Lomond with many ups and downs. A full, hard day's walk but the scenery is superb.*
- *Accommodation: Inversnaid, Inverarnan, Beinglas Farm*
- *Refreshments: Inversnaid, Inverarnan*
- *Places of Interest: Rob Roy's Prison and Rob Roy's Cave*

FROM FITCH'S DIARY

I stare at the dead otter.

A gentle misty rain permeates the air between us. It glistens on the creature's fur and makes its nose appear moist, despite the lack of life within.

Its eyes seem accusing, even in death. "Why?" they seem to say. "Why did you have to do this to me?"

The wind presses cool droplets onto my cheeks. They gather there and call to the moisture in my eyes to join them.

I look out across the water. Heavy grey mist is rolling down the sharp hills, blunting their ridges and covering huge forests with unspeakable ease. How easy it is for the clouds to obliterate them.

How much easier still for those clouds to obliterate me.

FROM WENTWORTH'S CREATIVE SPACE

I don't particularly care for otters. In fact, I find them rather unpleasant creatures, what with their slippery skins and soulless, beady eyes.

But I do care that the death of one has upset Tom. As I predicted, Alan's lunacy is slowly destroying any chance we have of civilised conversation on this misadventure.

Look at Tom now! Still sitting on that rock at the edge of the loch, cradling the dead otter in his arms. If I didn't know better, I'd say that -

"We're in danger."

I turn round. Alan is standing beside me. But he doesn't engage my eyes, instead he stares straight past at Tom. His face is tight, his eyes narrow and animal-like.

"I beg your pardon?" I say.

"Look," Alan hisses into my ear. "He's gone into one of his states. Thinking about bloody Death again."

"And whose fault is that?" I say, taking care to spell each syllable out slowly and clearly. "You're the one who butchered the helpless animal."

"It was mostly dead anyway. Wasn't much air in that bag."

"That's hardly the point-" I start.

"Alright, Jesus, so I made a mistake! I didn't mean to fuck things up. It all

made sense at the time. I can see now there were a couple of minor oversights in the mega-strategy-"

"Minor?!"

"-but the point is that now the girls have left. And those Russian tools have gone with them. And he's about to write a bloody poem to that thing."

"So what if he does?"

Macrae sighs and turns to face me.

"You really don't see the danger?" he asks me, his animal face surprisingly gentle.

"Oh, I think there's a definite risk to the local wildlife," I say.

"Sit down a second, George," says Macrae in a quiet voice, and points to a mossy log. Grudgingly I obey, and he sits beside me.

"Listen, mate, I know you think I'm a total tosser. And that's fair enough, in many ways I am. But I'm not asking for you to do this for me. I want you to do it for him."

Typical Macrae. Masking his true feelings with a sheen of self-awareness and consideration. But I'm not going to fall for it.

"Asking what exactly?' I say.

"I know that you looked after him back in Edinburgh," he starts, "and that was kind of you. But you have to admit that getting out of that place has done him a fucking power of good. He's been having fun. He likes that Swedish bird and she likes him."

Why yes, Alan, Tom does indeed seem to have been enjoying himself on the walk. Just as I myself have encountered the odd pleasant sensation. But this is nothing to do with your stupid carnal monkey plans. It's because, like me, Tom's sensitive heart responds to nature. And no matter how often you try to turn him against me, like you did on that infernal hill, you are simply fated to fail. When, Alan, will you realise, that he simply doesn't want what you have to offer?

He shuffles even nearer to me.

"But now we have an enemy on the battlefield," he says. "And if we're going to defeat it and get Fitchy laid and generally save his brain, we have to pull together here."

This from the man who yesterday was trying to urinate in my boot. He really must think I'm an idiot.

"If we let those birds get away, and he starts back down that Death poetry route, he's going to freeze up again and this whole trip will have been wasted."

Because you won't have had your filthy way with those women.

"So when he comes over here," Alan continues, "I need you to help me get him back on the trail of the fanny. As soon as possible. It's what's best for him. You do see that, don't you?"

And he stares at me, clearly expecting me to agree. But all I see is yet another self-seeking Macrae ploy. Admittedly more complex than he normally manages, but still selfish in the extreme.

"Look, here he comes," hisses Alan. "For Fitchy, now, remember!"

And suddenly Tom is standing in front of us.

"Hey Fitchalicious!" says Macrae with a rigid smile. "How's tricks?"

"Can you both join me by the shore, please?" asks Tom.

Macrae looks at me, then back at Tom.

"What for, mate?" he says.

"I've written an elegy to the otter-"

Alan shoots a 'told you so' glance at me.

"Nononono noooo," he gushes, laying an arm around Tom's shoulder, "none of that dreary poetry pish."

"-and we have to bury it."

"Don't be soft," laughs Macrae. "Drop-kick it into the loch and let's get grooving. Before you know it we'll be at Crianlarich. I've heard there's a bunkhouse there, owned by this crazy Swiss dude who's put open-air hot-tubs out behind the chalets. Imagine that, us and the Swedish birds all soaping each other off and looking up at the stars. That's the way forward now, right George?"

Tom looks round at me. His mouth is smiling calmly, but his eyes swirl with confusion.

"George," says Alan. "I'm right about this, aren't I?"

In the corner of my vision I can see Macrae waggling his thick black eyebrows at me.

And suddenly, like a door opening in the forest, my path is there in front of me, clear and wide. To borrow one of Alan's beloved military metaphors, I now have a strategy. I must take any little chances that come my way, building my strength, entrenching my position. Then, when my final opportunity comes... I can rout the field and take the prize.

And perhaps at last Tom and I can spend some civilised time together.

I take a deep breath and stand beside Tom.

"No, Alan," I say, "you're not. An elegy for the poor little creature sounds like just the thing."

FROM FITCH'S DIARY

We're standing on the edge of the grass at the little bay just past the hotel.

Macrae is on his knees in front of me, stabbing at the turf with his knife. He thrusts the blade hard into the ground and violently twists it, for some reason staring all the time at Wentworth.

I don't mind why he's doing it, I'm simply glad the boys came round to my idea. It makes it so much more meaningful now we're going it together.

When he has a hole dug, I approach and lay the otter in it. Then I step back and we all stand round the grave, just staring for a moment. It seems absurd, I know, but the sight of that little creature brings tears to my eyes. I swallow, and look out at the mist coming over the loch.

I shiver – it definitely feels like the weather is on the turn.

"Gentlemen," I say, "we must make our peace with nature. George," I cough, "would you like to say something?"

"What-? Oh, of course."

He steps forward to the very edge of the grave, smiles at me and clears his throat. Then he says:

"We would like to thank the spirits of the forest, the loch and the high-topped hill for the life of this otter. May its little soul rest peacefully in fish-filled paradise."

I nod at him in thanks. He steps back.

"Macrae?"

He steps forward to the grave. I think I hear him mutter "twat" as he passes Wentworth.

"Yeah, listen, Mr God or whoever," he starts, "I'm sorry we killed your otter. Really I am. But you know, maybe if you hadn't made it look so much like a damn wallaby this whole thing could have been avoided."

"Very nice," I say, wiping away another tear. "Now it's my turn."

FROM FITCH'S CREATIVE SPACE

The Grey Mist of Sadness
An elegy by Thomas J. Fitch

Mist covers all in its grey sadness
Rolling down the hills profound
Hiding the pain and the madness
And an otter buried, in the ground.

Your lowly cloak unmans the highest
Shrouding proud and craggy peaks
That is wet, which once was driest;
Even my Goretex jacket leaks.

Otter! Oh otter! That swam so fast
The grey mist caught you dozing
Your time for swimming now is past
The pool of life is closing.

What a lesson here is shown
By lifeless paw and dullèd nose
The truth that every man must own:
One day my feet will decompose.

Epilogue:

Mist do not cease; pray, never stop
Flood the world and drown my pain
And leave me just a falling drop
In your everlasting rain.

Tears stream down my cheeks.

I close my notebook and look up.

The boys are staring at me, mouths wide.

"You can cover him now," I whisper.

Macrae drops to his knees and starts scooping the pile of earth over the otter. After a couple of handfuls he suddenly sits bolt upright.

"Hey," he says, looking up at me with bright eyes, "you want your Frisbee back?" He pulls out his knife. "Won't take a jiffy."

My lip begins to quiver.

I manage to shake my head.

Alan ignores me and reaches for the otter.

"Seems a shame to waste quality sporting equipment–"

"Alan!" hisses Wentworth.

"Alright, Jesus! Only trying to help."

And he scoops the spoil of earth back over the otter, thankfully covering it from sight.

I'm glad we did that, but something is still weirding me out. The feeling I had at the distillery has come back – only stronger. Now I have the sense that the mist is here to chill me, seeping icily through my bones, nerves and flesh.

Making me numb.

FROM WENTWORTH'S NOTEBOOK

We still have to pack up camp. This takes a while – but I don't mind. Every minute we waste is another minute we aren't doing things Alan's way. And we waste quite a few, particularly when I keep dropping tent pegs and forgetting sleeping bags…

Alan's glaring eyes tell me this is a dangerous game, but pooh! – it's worth it just to see him squirm.

Finally we head back to the path. The Way idles out of Rowardennan, its wide grassed track winding sleepily through the woods. For a mile or so it silently rises and falls and we walk it wordlessly.

Tom stares at the track just in front of his feet, strangely preoccupied. Alan stomps on ahead, trying to encourage us to walk faster. I smile along at the back, relishing the tension.

After a while we reach a fork. I check OS sheet 56. One branch goes more-or-less straight; the other takes a detour before rejoining the main track later on.

"This one," I say, and lead us down the longer way.

*

After a couple of hours of rollercoaster walking, the Land Rover track narrows to a path and the going gets harder.

It twists and rises, forcing us to scramble over roots and rocks. It's rather as if the forest resents the Way's incursion and permits a traverse only grudgingly. One sympathises.

On top of that, the mist has thickened further, greasing every branch and stone. We are all soon scrambling on all fours rather than walking.

But for once the hardship hurts me not: we are running seriously behind time. The girls will be far, far ahead of us. If I keep this up there is no way we'll catch them today.

With a surge of pleasure I see that Alan, too, has realised this. Rock and root now irritate him intensely and his curses echo into the foggy wood.

Tom is shivering and his face is a little pale, but the main thing is that Alan is on the back foot.

*

Several long hours later we come out of the woods. The path has risen a little on the hillside and in front of us now it drops away, revealing the next section of the walk. The loch is behind us and the glen has narrowed, a river flowing along its floor. Just ahead, we can see a rude farmhouse with a boggy sheepfield in front of it. To the left of this, a little bridge carries the path over the river towards some lights in the trees.

We pause on a rise in the path, perspiring as we peer into the lowering gloom. Tom is really rather wan now, and starting to wheeze a little. Pefect.

"Is this Crianlarich?" asks Alan.

"I suppose it must be," I reply.

"Thank shite for that," says Alan. "Come on, Fitchy, let's get down there and make it up with the birds."

"Oh no, wait," I say, consulting my map. "My mistake, this is Inverarnan. Crianlarich is another seven miles further ahead."

Alan's eyes bore into me. His mouth is a steel wire.

"Then we'll have to double our speed," he says.

"I don't know," I say, "Tom looks a little peaky. And it has turned rather chilly. Now, I seem to remember there's a very fine pub in Inverarnan with a real fire. Let's pop in there for a sec and get warmed up."

"But the girls are in Crianlarich!"

"I don't care if Noam Chomsky is in Crianlarich," I reply. "We aren't walking seven more miles without a rest."

"If we just walked a bit bloody faster he'd be fine!" says Macrae. "Come on, Fitchy, you're up for a couple more miles, right?"

Tom pauses. His eyes seem focused on something very far off. Shudders wrack his body and he has his hands clasped in his armpits.

"You hear that?" he asks, cocking his head on one side and looking round the bar like a nervous bird.

"What, mate?" says Macrae.

"The voice!" Tom whispers. "It said, 'Enough of thish running shit'. Came from over near Jones…"

"Fuck's sake, George," hisses Alan in my ear, "that cunt Connery is messing with his brain again. We need to hit the road now."

"You can carry on ahead and we'll catch you up later if you like," I say. "But I really think he needs a break, old bean."

Whereupon Tom sneezes, right on cue. Bless him.

Alan exhales and utters one simple curse. He shoots me a ferocious glance, then stomps off towards the lights in the distance.

I smile to myself and walk Tom slowly across the river.

MACRAE'S SAMPLE NOTEBOOK PAGE

Location: Fucking Inverarnan
Date: Monday the 10th of Fuck
Weather: Fucking pish
Swedish girls met: The fanny fucked off
Wildlife seen: 1 otter. And the cunt died.
Comments on accommodation (if appropriate): Fucking pish
Any other notes: Fuck off
Creative space: Wentworth is a twat

FROM THE WEBSITE OF THE REIVERS INN

For more than 300 years the Reivers inn has been welcoming weary Highland travellers. Originally it was the hangout of cattle thieves ('Reivers') who used the inn and its lands as a base to seize animals being driven to market in the south.

Its rooms are notoriously haunted with the spirits of drinkers past, including old George, the cattleman whose ashes sit in an urn beside his favourite seat, and the ghost of a young girl who drowned in the river behind the bar in 1837.

The reception hall and bar also play home to a remarkable collection of stuffed wildlife, including a full-grown grizzly bear! Indeed, the interior of the inn has barely changed from the days when the bandits drank their illicit whisky by candlelight.

Visit us, and you are guaranteed a trip back in time to a bygone age, with equally old-fashioned prices!

FROM MACRAE'S NOTEBOOK

I said that George would try to fuck stuff up and here he is trying to delay things and get us off the Way. But being right is no help to me now because

Fitchy really does look in a shit state all shivering and clammy and the way he's staring into space is freaking me out a bit so we really are going to have to stop.

Oh Georgy boy is a tricky prick and no mistake.

He's even found the perfect pub to plug his evil plans into. I used to think that boozers are like blowjobs because even the bad ones are basically good but when we walked in the Reivers I remembered this lass called Valerie. Bags of enthusuiasm bless her but she also had these goofy big teeth that kept snagging on my banjo string and then she started blowing into my boy like he was some kind of damned trumpet. I swear every second she was down there was terrifying.

Well the Reivers is to pubs what Valerie is to blowjobs.

You're only just in the door and there's a stuffed bloody bear in front of you with its head all wrong and one paw gone manky. Then you turn left into the bar and the black old ceiling's sagging over your head like you're walking in under a fucking dragon. Where the walls aren't covered in soot, they're dotted with portraits of drunken old tools too faded to recognise.

As for the bar itself well it slouches like all the beer and whisky spilled over the centuries has seeped into its fibres making it totally pished. The huge fire looks like it might have steps at the back leading down to hell. Stuffed wildlife crowds every shelf and nook and behind the bar is a grey-haired dude so decrepit he looks like one of the portraits from the wall come to life.

A place like this might tip Fitchy over the edge. We need to make this as short a stop as possible.

Georgy you got a battle on your hands.

FROM WENTWORTH'S NOTEBOOK

I know I'm doing well because, to my increasing delight, Alan is getting himself worked up. The pub, normally such a happy place for him, is now a source of irritation. Well, my little chicken, let us tread this path a little further together and see where it leads us.

"Oh," I say as I lead the way into the shabby saloon, "how quaint!"

"Quaint?" snorts Alan. "Place is like a fucking crypt. What's with all the dead

animals? And bloody Skeletor behind the bar."

He speaks very loudly, but the ancient barman just stares into space, deaf to any insult.

"Hush, Alan!" I say. "There is no need to offend the locals. Not everyone is as cosmopolitan as you." And I turn to the barman. "A sweet sherry please. Tom, what would you like?"

"He'll have a treble whisky," barks Alan. "And one for me as well. You chin this, Fitchy," he adds, "get a quick toasting by the fire and we'll soon have you back on the trail."

But Tom doesn't answer him. He drifts right past him to where that infernal cat lies on the floor on the hearth. He gets down, rolls on his back and cocks his hands and feet in the air like paws.

"Do you exshpect me to tokk?" he says.

Alan's eyebrows rear like stallions.

"Make that two sweet sherries," I say to the barman.

FROM MACRAE'S NOTEBOOK

I've seen Fitchy do a pile of crazy shite like the Saturday he took his kit off and tied a bunch of balloons to his balls and danced through Covent Garden. But that was funny crazy and this is sad crazy. He's lying on the fucking sooty flagstones talking to Jones. I haul him to his feet and sit him down beside me and stick a drink in his hands.

"This has all gone to pish," I hiss at George, slugging my whisky.

"I really don't know what you're complaining about," sneers George, "this whole thing was your idea."

I jab my finger at him.

"Rattling Swedish birds was my idea," I say, "not sitting around mooning at each other in this teuchter's toilet. Look at the state of him!"

"Distraction, that's all he needs." He leans forward. "Tom, I believe you brought your travel Scrabble?"

"Board games!?" I say.

"We could play noughts and crosses if you'd prefer, Alan," he says.

I give him a Macrae mad stare. He thinks I'm a moron. And maybe I am. But I'm a moron who cares.

"Fine, George," I say, "get your fucking Scrabble out."

FROM WENTWORTH'S NOTEBOOK

I reach into Tom's rucksack and pull out the travel Scrabble. Alan moves the drinks aside and we set up the board. I offer round the bag of letters.

"Shall we draw?" I ask.

As we take our letters, the fire in Alan's eyes tells me that we're playing for more than a high score here. Fine by me, old bean.

We all draw seven tiles and lay them on our racks.

"And now to see who goes first," I add, and hold the bag out.

Alan draws Q, I get a T. By wiggling the bag I make sure Tom gets an A.

"Well done, Tom!" I smile. "You start us off. And here's to a jolly game!"

And I lift my sherry glass.

Tom looks at me a little vacantly. Alan mutters something unintelligible and looks down at his letters.

The fire crackles as we consider our racks.

But I've barely assessed my letters when Tom simply picks up his first two tiles and lays them down as they are, starting on the centre square:

O   W

I look down at the board.

"O-W" I read. "Ow?"

"Ow!" he mumbles. "As in pain."

"Tom, I'm, ah, not sure... is that really the best you can do?"

"I got a whole load of Xs and things," he mutters.

"But you must be able to do better than ow," I say. "You can prefix that with practically any consonant and make a better word – Bow, Cow, How, Low, Now, Mow..."

"He's not an idiot, George," snaps Alan, somewhat childishly.

"It's alright, Macrae," says Tom, calming him down with a gentle hand. "I see what he means. I was being a bit slow." He looks back down at his letters. "I can do

125

something else." And he reaches down and adds two more tiles to his word:

L Y

I peer at the board.

"Uh, Tom," I say, "should that be an 'N'? Surely you mean 'only'?"

"No," he replies. "I mean 'owly' – being like an owl."

Alan grins at me. The sight of his teeth is really quite annoying.

"Love it!" he says.

"I'm not sure that's a word either, Tom," I say.

"You get 'ducky', don't you?" says Tom.

"That's a different part of speech-" I start.

"And 'titty'," Alan adds.

I sigh. Tom is clearly enfeebled. There is no point dilly-dallying here. Besides, I have an excellent word to place.

"Alright," I say. "You can have 'owly'. But please try a little harder next time. That's one and four and four and one makes ten and a double word, twenty. Now, my turn."

I lay down my letters, descending the board and using the 'O' of OWLY.

B

I

J

O

U

"Bijou?!" squawks Alan. "That's not English. That's frog or something."

"How very perspicacious of you, Alan. It has indeed come to us from French. However, unlike that language, which is administered strictly by the Académie Française, English has no official governing body. A word can come from anywhere, and once it passes into popular parlance, it is accepted and when the next edition of the Oxford English dictionary is updated, it is included. This flux – or rather, the acceptance of this flux – is a major factor in the continued dominance of English as a world language."

"Aye, very good, but you're still not fucking having it."

"I am. Aren't I, Tom?"

Tom is staring half in fascination, half in fear at the cat. I tap him on the shoulder.

"'Bijou' is a word, yes Tom?"

"Think so," he mutters. "Means small."

"You're just saying that because he let you have 'owly'," snaps Alan.

Execllent – I don't think his primeval temper will be able to cope with this much longer. I smile and methodically start to tally.

"Three and one…" I count, "…and eight for the J and one and one makes… fourteen points."

"Pish," Alan snorts. "A waste of a good J."

"Well, of course, I was slightly hamstrung by the fact that Tom placed his 'O' on the centre square. If he had positioned it one square to the left, I would have had-"

"Yeah, but he didn't," interrupts Alan, "and you got fuck all and now it's my go." He smiles and leans forward. "And I got to tell you now… it's a fucking beauty." He lays down his letters, running across from the B of bijou.

A W B A G

"Makes it fourteen and on a double word, that's twenty eight."

I lean over the board.

"B-A-W-B-A-G" I read. "What's that? That's not a word."

"Fuck you talking about?" Alan says, and he grabs his crotch and gives it a shake. "Bawbag."

I smirk at his idiocy.

"If by 'bawbag' you mean 'ball-bag' then you are, of course, wrong on two counts. Firstly it's a compound noun requiring a hyphen. Secondly, you are rendering it in the lowland Scots idiomatic slang pronunciation which certainly isn't permissible."

"Look," says Alan, waggling a forefinger at me, "you said yourself the English language is about people talking, right? So. How many times have you heard people say 'bijou' recently? Fuck all. But how many times do you hear 'bawbag' on the streets of Edinburgh? 'Hey, bawbag, geez a light.' 'This kilt isn't half scratching mah hairy bawbag'. 'Youse guys are a bunch of bawbags.' So you tell me, Mrs Vorderman, which is the proper word?"

And he stares at Tom expectantly.

I also turn to Tom. He pauses for a long time, looking between the two of us. I can't believe he's even considering this…

"You did give me owly," he says suddenly.

This isn't how this was meant to go.

127

"That's different!" I splutter. "Owly wasn't worth very much."

"It was worth more than fucking bijou," Alan laughs.

"ALRIGHT! You can have your bloody bawbag!"

"Thank you, George," says Alan, and he grabs my piece of paper. "So, the scores at the end of round one: I'm in the lead with twenty-eight, Fitchy-baby's in second with twenty and bringing up the rear, on a whopping fourteen, the man who threw his J away... George Wentworth!"

Now he's really starting to annoy me. He should have retired gracefully from the field by now.

"Can we just move on to the next round, please?" I say.

"-yeah, fine, happy to-" Alan fires back.

"-excellent-"

"-no problemo-"

"-good-"

"-cos I got another belter lined up already."

And Alan leans towards Tom and says to him in a mock whisper:

"How many zeds are there in 'jizz'?"

And a burning anger rises up inside me like a tsunami, drowning all my senses and towering over my reason. I grab hold of the Scrabble board, and Alan grins hugely and I'm just about to throw the board at him and he's daring me to do it with his eyes and I know that doing it is exactly what he wants and Fitch is looking sadly at the two of us but I'm just about to do it anyway to shut his stupid animal face up when-

BRRRIIINNNGG

-the phone behind the bar rings.

We all turn.

And something strange happens.

FROM FITCH'S DIARY

"Reivers," creaks the ancient barman, picking up the phone.

And that one word is like a magic password. A stone door rolls away from in front of my eyes and light floods in on me.

There's a pause as the caller speaks.

"Och, hello, Donald," smiles the barman in recognition. "How are you?"

The light intensifies into heat, and I don't know how, but I can sense that this call is in some way for me.

Another pause. "Is that so. Och, what a shame. I'll see. Bye bye."

He puts the phone down and calls out to us:

"Are you laddies staying at Bridge of Orchy tomorrow night?"

The warmth floods my veins like a shot of amphetamine.

"That's the next stop, right Wentworth?" I ask.

Wentworth nods slowly.

The ancient barman continues:

"Have ye seen any Swedish lassies on yer travels?"

I sit bolt upright on my stool like a meerkat.

"Of course," I say, nodding rapidly. "What's the problem?"

"That was Donald from the Bridge of Orchy Hotel on the telephone," replies the barman, "seems they've had a wee fire in the kitchen. Yer Swedish friends have booked some rooms in the bunkhouse which are still okay, but the ovens and the back of the bar are in an awfy state, so they won't be able to get any food or drinks."

Now I leap to my feet.

"But the Bridge of Orchy Hotel is the only place to eat for about ten miles in any direction!" I shout at the barman.

"Aye, laddie, that is true, but it cannae be helped. I suppose all ye can do is let the lassies know and take it from there."

I look down at my two good friends. The memory of today – my sadness, their bickering – is cast off me now like a cloak. Jones twists on his back in front of the little fire and meows his toasted pleasure.

"Boys," I say, "I have a plan."

★

"Right," I say, leading the way out of the pub and back into the trees. "It's too late to press on tonight, but there's a campsite just over the river. We fling up our tents, grab a quick bite and get an early night. Tomorrow we get up just before dawn, break camp fast and hit the road. The girls have a seven mile head start on us and we'll need to get that under our belts sharpish if we're to warn them in time."

Macrae strides along beside me, nodding furiously. Wentworth scurries to keep up.

"I also want to say sorry," I continue as I lead us back over the river to the field by the farmhouse. "I lost the plot a bit back there. I was wallowing in... well, I don't exactly know what, but I was wallowing all right. I forgot all about The Hills Are Stuffed With Swedish Girls and that was totally selfish of me. We're on this adventure together and I should never have forgotten that."

Macrae stops me.

"It's okay, mate," he replies, "you're firing with all guns again and that's all that matters." And he slaps me heartily on the back. "Isn't that right, George?" he grins.

Wentworth smiles, a little lopsidedly.

"Of course," he says.

And I sling an arm round each of them and the three of us walk together to our campsite, a still-glowing Jones trotting along behind.

FROM MACRAE'S NOTEBOOK

Fuck you, George, you lost!

FROM WENTWORTH'S NOTEBOOK

I'll bet you consider this a victory, don't you? Well, my fine fellow, you may have won that round, but the fight is far from over. And the gloves are now off. In this contest no quarter will be asked or given.

You have my word on that.

DAY 4

INVERARNAN TO BRIDGE OF ORCHY

Summary:
- *Distance: 32km (21 miles)*
- *Estimated Time: 6-8 hours*
- *Height Range: 1700ft (510m) ascent*
- *Terrain: The path and tacks are mainly well-surfaced, much of the way consists of an old military road. Moderate ascents and descents. The way bypasses Crianlarich to the west, but a spur path leads into the village, the halfway point on the route. A long but straightforward day of glen and low pass walking amid stunning mountain scenery.*
- *Accommodation: Crianlarich, Tyndrum, Bridge of Orchy*
- *Refreshments: Crianlarich, Tyndrum, Bridge of Orchy*
- *Places of Interest: Grey mares tail (waterfall), The Falls of Falloch, Cononish Gold Mine, St Fillans Chapel, (remains) – It was raised to a Priory by Robert the Bruce in 1318 and thereafter enjoyed some measure of privilege and protection from the kings of Scotland.*

Crisp air.

Sharp sunlight.

A snapping fresh autumn day, as cool and clear on my soul as the dew on my bare feet. The sun hasn't yet climbed above the towering hillsides, but already the last snakes of chill mist are evaporating above the river. It's going to be a beauty.

And what a night's sleep! Not a twitch, a turn or wisp of a dream. I feel ten feet tall and bulletproof as Macrae and I take down the tents and Wentworth cooks up a truly delicious breakfast.

"Right," I say, peering at the map as we munch on sizzling bacon and slurp coffee. "The girls are seven miles further on than us. They've got six miles to go till Tyndrum, which is the last chance of a shop. After that it's six more miles through the hills to Bridge of Orchy and starvation. We need to get them in this level stretch here between Crianlarich and Tyndrum so we can warn them and they can stock up at the Green Welly." I slug the last of my coffee.

"That's a long day," murmurs Wentworth.

"Aha," I nod, "and we're going to have to shift it if we want to catch them in time. So get that coffee down you."

Ten minutes later, with the sun just tousling our sleeping-bag hair, we're back on the Way and starting the pull up Glen Falloch. The path is wide and easy going, rising and dipping like a wave as it climbs up into the heart of the glen. Watching the boys it seems like the ripples in yesterday's stream have calmed. Our mercy mission has united us, and we soon settle into a good pace which even Wentworth keeps up.

The river Falloch chatters rowdily through the rocks to our left. The odd car zips along the A82 on the other side. Above that rolls the single track of the West Highland Railway, which has joined the glen from a notch in the hills. As we mount a rise in the path and stop for a second to slug some water from a stream, the morning train to Oban curves over a viaduct opposite us, its windows shining in the early rays of the sun. The driver toots his horn and we wave, the childish fun of it all spurring our steps even more.

Path, road, river and railway wind closer as they rise up the glen, twisting over and under each other like a clutch of ribbons. After an hour or so we cross the river, duck through a sheep creep under the railway, then a tunnel beneath the A82, and suddenly we're rising along an old military road, wondering how many thousands of boots have walked this way before us. How those ancient solders must have hated the path that took them nearer nothing but bloody death in the mud of an unnamed glen. How much more we have to look forward to.

To the east, the mountains rise closer than they have done yet: the long ridges of Beinn Chabhair; the sharp top of An Caisteal; muscular Beinn a' Chroin and Cruach Ardrain; with the classic mountain cones of Ben More and Stob Binnein framing the scene.

Macrae is in his element; it's all I can do to stop him galloping off up the track with Jones on top of his pack. Wentworth is suffering with the quick walking, but fair play to him, he is digging in with a determination that is joyous to see. He obviously really cares about the girls, too.

After a couple of hours, we reach a dense wood where the path divides. As we stop to check out the sign that stands at the junction, Wentworth slumps to the ground, face shining with sweat.

The Way continues left to Tyndrum, a spur drops to the right to Crianlarich, The girls will have walked that way last night into the village and will have had to come back up the spur to rejoin the Way.

"Fine," says Macrae, "left it is." And he turns towards Tyndrum.

"Wait a second," I say. "It's only just gone ten. What if they haven't left yet? We'll be ahead of them."

"So we get to Tyndrum and wait."

"But they might be ahead of us. And if we wait we'll miss them. We need to know for certain."

"But it's almost a mile down into the village. We go down to have a look and we risk being even more off the pace."

"You also risk being struck forever from my roll of pleasant persons," puffs Wentworth.

I sit down to think. I'm ten seconds into formulating a plan when the sudden noise of an engine makes me look up. Rising through a forestry break just ahead is a Land Rover. Its tyres spit grass and its engine whines as it accelerates towards us.

To my considerable surprise, Macrae steps right out into the path of the vehicle and waves it down. The driver stands hard on the brake and brings the Land Rover skidding to a mud-spattered halt.

Hunched over the wheel is a tweed-hatted, green-jacketed ghillie with astonishing blue eyes and the bushiest ginger beard I have ever seen. His eyes scan us rapidly as he stops beside us. A shotgun stands propped up on the passenger seat.

He rolls down his window.

"Git oot the bloody way, ya crazy bugger!" he yells, then sucks a chunk of his beard into his mouth and chews on it aggressively.

"Sorry to bother you," says Macrae, "but have you seen three fit birds and three twats in track suits?"

"No, ah bloody haven't. Now get out mah road. Jesus Christ!"

And he jams the Land Rover into gear.

"Mackay Brown," says Macrae.

"Whit?" cries the ghillie, spinning back round to face Macrae and chomping on more beard.

"Unique round action," says Macrae, nodding at the shotgun, "with bow-type mainsprings. Very reliable."

The ghillie puts the Land Rover into neutral. Chews slower.

"Hunting man?" he barks at Macrae after a moment.

"No," admits Macrae, shaking his head. "But I know beauty when I see it. Like those girls up ahead of us..."

The ghillie sucks another huge tuft of beard into his mouth and grinds on it. Macrae goes on:

"The twats with them are Russians." Macrae leans towards him and whispers confidentially: "You know that Russians poach deer with AK-47s?"

The ghillie's eyes go wide.

"No!" he jabbers.

Macrae nods.

"Mow them down they do." He sniffs. "By the dozen. While they laugh. And most of the animals, well, they just lie there and rot. Sometimes they use tanks. Whole herds at a time – vaporised. Ah well, nice chatting to you." And he starts to move away.

The ghillie indulges in one last bug-eyed moment of chewing that is so vigorous I fear he might actually tear his whole beard out by the roots. Suddenly he jerks a thumb over his shoulder and blurts out:

"Saw them aboot two mile back in the forest there. If ye get a leg on, ye'll catch them just before Tyndrum!"

"Thanks," smiles Macrae.

"Nae bother, boys." His eyes sparkle. "Gie them both barrels."

The ghillie gives his beard a final vicious chew, sticks his Land Rover into gear and revs away up the track.

Macrae turns to us and cocks his head on one side expectantly.

"Come on, Wentworth," I say, "just a little bit further."

He sighs and gets to his feet as we turn west and follow the sign to Tyndrum.

★

The path turns west and rises high into the forest. Leaves and pine needles carpet the track. We trot down some contours, dip under the railway again, then cross road and river to the glen floor.

We're on a good metalled surface now and we fairly fly past farms and a ruined church before swaying back across the road into a dense wood. The sun batters down through the trees, incredibly warm for autumn. Yesterday's moisture rises from the mossy ground, turning the forest into jungle. My thermal is sticking to me and I'm just considering taking a layer off when-

"There they are!" cires Macrae, stopping dead and pointing.

I follow his quivering finger to see the three girls and the Russians standing by a junction in the path. Ahead of them, the Way continues straight on through the forest. To the right, a small road turns right into the village of Tyndrum.

"Come on," hisses Macrae, and leads us sneaking through the trees. We get to within a few yards of them, then tuck in behind a shrubby rowan tree.

The girls have taken off their rucksacks and are sitting on the low wall of a bridge over the river. They look hot and tired. Nina has her boots off and is rubbing her feet. The Russians stand a little away from them, cocky and impatient. They are removing their tracksuit tops and tucking them onto the back of their packs. Their absurd chests now bulge in immaculate white t-shirts.

We crouch, sweating in the bracken, their conversation filtering to us through the trees:

"Phew, it is so hot…" complains Tess. "Do we have to go so fast?"

Wassily finishes tucking away his top. His muscles shine in the golden sunlight.

"Why don't you take off your shirts?" he suggests, with a dirty sneer and a wink at Uzeyir.

The girls ignore him.

"We wish you had not made us walk on so far yesterday," says Gertrud. "We are so tired today."

"Yes, can we stop for a rest in that village?" says Nina, pointing towards Tyndrum.

"Pffff!" scoffs Uzeyir. "A rest? When we have set off only so recently? How stupid!"

"Yah," agrees Wassily, "we must press on to the Bridge of the Orchy. There we will rest and eat."

"…but my feet are so full of pain…" says Nina.

"Pain is in the mind, not in the feets! Have some vodka!"

"But I do not like vodka…"

Macrae turns to me, a big grin on his face.

"Sweet!" he whispers Macrae. "They're fucking it up worse than we did!"

"The poor, weary things," says Wentworth. "We must get down there and tell them about the hotel this instant!"

"Exactly," agrees Macrae, "this is our chance."

And he steps out from the edge of the forest. I'm about to set off after him, when I thrust out a hand and grab his rucksack.

"Wait," I hiss, pulling him back into the trees. "I have a better idea. They're dragging the girls all the way to Bridge of Orchy right? And we know that when they get there they're going to go hungry."

"Yes…"

"So we don't tell them."

The boys stare at me, mouths handing open. I go on:

"We wait here till they're out of sight, then we nip into Tyndrum. We head to the Green Welly and pick up some barbecues and a stack of supplies. We then

136

jump the afternoon train to Bridge of Orchy, get there before they do and set up a feast down by the river. The girls arrive, get upset because of the state of the hotel, then we pop out of the trees, barbecues bursting with delicious hot food, wine on hand and… generally save the day."

"Fantastic fucking idea, mate!" says Macrae, slinging an arm round me. "Man, I wish I could come out with shit like that." He bangs the side of his own head percussively with his fist. "If. I. could. just. think. fucking. straight…"

"Wentworth?" I ask, turning to face my weary pal.

"Anything that involves less walking and more eating is fine by me," he smiles.

"Great," I say, let's wait until they get out of sight and–"

"OHOHOHOHOH!" rattles Macrae suddenly, his face reddening as if he's about to give birth. "Permission to amend plan slightly, sir!"

"Go on," I say.

"I'm thinking that maybe while you guys rock into Tyndrum for the barbecues and salad and beers and stuff, me and Captain Jones can bomb up into the hills and hunt down some fresh meat."

"I suppose so," I murmur. "But be care–"

"Awesome!" cries Macrae. "Don't start things till I get there. And now there's just one more thing I have to do."

And without a further word, he sprints stealthily up the track towards the departing Russians, Jones speeding behind him.

"What on earth is he doing?" asks Wentworth.

"I'm not sure…" I reply.

And I can only watch in astonishment as Macrae sneaks right up to the Russians, reaches out and grabs Zinaida's tracksuit top from the back of his rucksack, and then bolts into the forest.

A split second later, Zinaida turns round, looking suspiciously at the track behind him. He scans the forest, black eyes burning, then turns back round and walks on.

"I'll tell you," says Wentworth. "He has finally gone…"

And then, as suddenly as he disappeared, Macrae appears from the trees. He is wearing the white tracksuit top, its hood pulled right up. He smiles broadly and waves at us then is gone again.

"…completely feral."

"He's happy," I say. Then I hear myself take a deep breath and let it out with a sigh. "Come on, let's get to that shop."

★

The Green Welly is the garage that got ambition.

I remember when it was nothing more than a few petrol pumps and a manky toilet. Macrae and I used to hitch from here when heading up to Glencoe. But that was more than ten years ago. Now it's a minimarket with tearoom and gift shop attached. Stuffed with coach loads of tourists and OAP day trippers, normally I avoid it.

But today, it's perfect.

Cheese and bread, salad and fruit, dips and crisps, snacks and veggies, a couple of boxes of wine and some beers – all tumble happily into our trolley.

"Not exactly gourmet," sniffs Wentworth, "but it will have to do."

And then we cart our swag back down the main road and head up the zigzag road to Tyndrum Upper station.

We sit on the platform, looking out at the majestic corries and ridges of Ben Lui and eating a pork pie. Then the train comes.

Sweetly on time.

FROM THETRAINLINE.COM

Trains from Tyndrum to Bridge of Orchy
Outward journey: Tuesday 25 September 2007
Depart 14:51
Arrive 15:04
Changes 0
Duration 0:13

FROM FITCH'S DIARY

From Tyndrum the train skirts the hill, climbing to the head of the glen. The Way winds up below the track and we haven't gone far before we spot the girls and the Russians, slogging up the path.

"Look, there they are!"

As we pass, the girls look up at the train.

"Duck!"

"Did they see us?"

"Don't think so."

And then we're rattling over the pass and dropping down into a new glen towards Bridge of Orchy.

"Did you see them?" I say excitedly. "They don't look at all happy with the Russians! They were walking ten yards behind them." I smile. "You know what? I think this is actually going to work."

Now the country is really opening out. Ahead, the flank of Beinn Dorain rises in one elegant curve from glen floor to its 3,000 foot summit. The railway curves round its base, over two spectacular viaducts.

"Glorious, isn't it?" I say, leaning back in my seat and chewing on an extra hot Pepperami.

Wentworth nods but says nothing.

"We should come back here one time and do that steam train ride," I add, waggling my snack for emphasis. "Harry Potter and all that."

Wentworth takes a breath.

"This train goes to Fort William, doesn't it?" he asks.

"Eventually," I say. "Why?"

He looks at me, his eyes level.

"We don't have to get off at Bridge of Orchy," he says, leaning forward with a sudden passion in his eyes. "We could stay on to Fort William, get a taxi to Inverness and pick up a flight. This time tomorrow we could be in Rimini, spending some civilised time together."

I stare at him for a long second. Then I burst out laughing.

"Oh George, you are funny. Come on now, grab the bags, we're nearly there."

FROM MACRAE'S NOTEBOOK

Macrae log stardate 36-24-36-banjo

This is more fucking like it. Fitchy-Baby's back to his best and now Captain Jones and I are deep in enemy territory crawling over burn and brae hunting nature's bounty.

The Captain is proving himself to be the most remarkable attack cat and we have intuitively worked out a very efficient hunting technique:

Stage 1 – Jones locates the prey with his superior sensory equipment.

Stage 2 – We stalk said beast together utilising a simple yet elegant pincer manoeuvre.

Stage 3 – Jones approaches stealthily from the front before suddenly exposing his position thus alarming the creature and causing it to bolt in the opposite direction.

Stage 4 – I spring from the heather and chop its head off.

The only problem is how we are going to transport all this meat from the mountain. Oh hang on a minute will you look at that beautiful bastard...

FITCH'S DIARY CONTINUES

There's not much to Bridge of Orchy except the hotel, the bridge and a few scattered houses. A big sign by the side of the road reads – "HOTEL CLOSED, SORRY" and as we walk past we can see that the rear of the building is a little blackened.

We cross the ancient humpback of stone that bridges the boisterous river Orchy. The Way heads on to our right, out of the village towards the real wilderness of Rannoch. Between this track and the water the riverbank is flat and grassy. It's the perfect spot to camp. Wentworth and I drop our bags, set up our tents, lay out the barbecues and kick back on the grass to wait for the girls.

It's a gorgeous afternoon. The sky is sheet blue above green and gold mountains. The chattering river and birdsong soothe our ears. The air smells of heather and pine woods.

So why am I nervous?

"You fancy a beer?" I ask Wentworth.

"Suppose."

"You don't have to."

He nods at me. Why's he nervous too?

"How long do you think they'll be?" I ask.

"Couple of hours. Three maybe."

We sip our Arran Blondes.

"God I'm getting hungry," I say. "Hey, what meat do think Macrae will bring?"

"Hah! If he ever shows."

"What do you mean by that?"

"By now he's probably smeared his face in badger dung and gone to live in a cave."

A long pause. Another slug.

"He'll be here."

★

Three hours and five beers later, and Macrae still isn't here.

"Shit, where is he?"

"I don't know. But I do know who has arrived," says Wentworth, pointing up to the opposite hillside.

I follow his finger to see the girls and the Russians stepping down the hill towards the village.

"Shit no."

"Excrement yes."

"Where is he? He said not to start without him."

"Told you."

"It's okay, they're not at the hotel yet…"

"They've seen the sign," says Wentworth.

141

It's true. Tess reads the sign and her face darkens. She throws her hands high in the air, and turns questioningly to the Russians. From where we sit we can hear their shouted conversation.

"What is going on?!" she exclaims.

Wassily and Uzeyir shrug. Zinaida looks blank.

"I will find out," says Tess, then curses under her breath and stomps up the entrance steps into the hotel.

The Russians just stare after her and giggle inanely at each other.

"Where is he…?" I mutter, scanning the road for Macrae.

"You should learn never to rely on him," sniffs Wentworth.

"This isn't helping, Wentworth…"

At the hotel, Tess storms back out, even angrier.

"It is true!" she cries. "They cannot cook for us!"

Gertrud and Nina groan.

Tess glares at the Russians.

"What do you suggest we do now?!" she demands.

"We have some chocolate bars…" starts Uzeyir.

"Pah! You are hopeless! A bunch of stupid egos, not men!"

"Oh man, this is our perfect moment. Come on Macrae…"

"You might as well count on the wind to come when you call," says Wentworth.

"Here comes a bus," says Nina, looking up the main road. "We could take it back to that last town."

"Good idea!" cries Tess, and they cross the main road to the bus stop. The yellow and blue block of a Citylink bus is rolling and bouncing down the road.

"They're leaving."

"For fuck's sake Macrae, why can you never-" And then I hear it.

CLOP CLOP CLOP behind me.

I turn and my mouth drops open to say something, but the words evaporate on my tongue – I am facing a truly astonishing sight:

A highland cow, with thick ginger fringe and wide horns is walking down a forestry break on the hillside. By the cow's side, steering it by one of its horns, is Macrae. Sitting regally on top of the cow's withers, his whiskers hoisted high and proud, is Jones. Lined up along the cow's back are four haunches of venison, six grouse, two pheasants and several large salmon.

Macrae grins and waves as he leads the shaggy beast across the road and up towards us.

All we can do is stare, open mouthed.

"Hold these," he says, slinging about half the fish, meat and fowl on the ground beside me, "and hide under the bridge." He then leads the cow over the hump towards the Russians, who are standing by the side of the hotel, trying to work out what to do.

"Hey guys," he calls to them, "what's going down?"

"This stupid hotel has shut the kitchen," replies Wassily, "and now our Swedish girls are leaving on the bus."

"Aw shit, what a bummer. But hey, we got some barbecues and beer and stuff and look, all this fresh meat too. Way enough to share. You think the girls'd like some?"

"Yah, of course, but–"

"Well, why don't you show them our hairy friend here and see if they'll stay for a bite, and I'll go and get the barbecues fired up."

The Russians can't believe their luck.

"Yah, sure."

"Cool," smiles Macrae, and turns away. He takes a step then quickly spins back.

"Oh, one more thing. I found this blowing about on the hillside. Thought maybe one of you guys had lost it."

And he hands Zinaida back his white tracksuit top.

"Thanking you much," grin the Russians.

"No problemo, fellas," smiles Macrae, and then casually turns and walks back towards us.

The Russians stare after him for a moment, snorting and sniggering in their own language before starting towards the road.

Macrae is still sauntering, but as soon as he's over the crest of the bridge he breaks into a run. Suddenly he's on top of us, Jones at his heels.

"I told you, get under!" he hisses.

"What the hell have you just done?" I ask.

"Don't argue, just go!" And he bundles us round the side of the bridge and under the stone arch.

"Any second now. Watch."

From where we are we can just peer up and see the Russians approaching the girls at the bus stop.

"All I see is them about to do the heroic thing with our girls," I say. "You completely threw away our advantage-"

"Patience," he says. "Just another second…"

And then, from somewhere above us, I hear a rumble. It grows in volume and violence until the whole bridge shakes and a vehicle zooms over our heads. We stretch ourselves a little higher to get a glimpse of the road and watch, fascinated, as a muddy Land Rover screeches up right in front of the Russians.

They all stagger back in astonishment as the bearded face of the ghillie we met earlier leers out at them.

"Savages!" he screams.

The girls now step back from the road, letting the bus pass clean by them. They stand quietly, keenly observing the ensuing drama.

The ghillie is almost bursting, spitting tufts of his chewed beard at the Russians. He leaps out of his Land Rover and starts waving his shotgun in the air.

"Thieving savages!"

Suddenly there's another roaring vibration and another vehicle passes over us. We look up to see a police car screeching to a halt beside the Land Rover. A young policeman jumps out, jamming his hat on his head. The ghillie yells at him:

"Here they are, Tam!"

"Dougie, for Christ's sake put that gun away and let me handle this," hisses the policeman. Then he turns to the Russians. "Boys, you're going to have to come with us."

"What for?"

"You're accused of poaching."

"What is 'poaching'?"

"This, ye thieving bugger!" cries Dougie the ghillie, grabbing a grouse from the cow's back and waving it in Wassily's face. He turns to the policeman. "Look! They've stolen Hamish an' all!" he cries, pointing to the highland cow. "Poor confused beastie."

"But it was not us who was taking these animals," wails Wassily, "it was those men over there!"

"Over where?"

We duck down as they look round.

"They must be hiding-" starts Uzeyir.

"Lying hound!" barks the ghillie, "I saw ye masel' in yon white tracksuit, and ye've got the evidence in your hands!"

"But-"

The policeman sighs.

"Come on, no arguments now," he says to the Russians. "Just get in the car and we'll discuss this in the station at Kinlochleven."

And he shepherds the Russians into the back of his police car.

"You wait there, Hamish," says the ghillie to the highland cow. "I'll get you later." Then he gets in his Land Rover and drives off after the police car.

The river babbles behind us.

I turn at Macrae.

"Genius," I say. "Genuine genius."

Macrae shrugs and modestly stares at his feet.

"Afraid I can't take all the credit," he says, kicking a stone into the river. "It was mostly Captain Jones' idea. He is steadily proving himself to be one of the great strategic thinkers. In fact," he beams, "he deserves a promotion!" Macrae looks down. "From now on," he says, "you will be General Jones."

And he salutes my cat.

"Go on, like I showed you!" he whispers. And to my astonishment, Jones slowly raises his right paw to his ear.

"A privilege, sah!" whoops Macrae, saluting triumphantly in return.

"Oh Jones," I say, "where's your dignity?"

"Ram your dignity," smiles Macrae. "And go and get the ladies. Come on General, let's get ourselves outside this fish."

And he picks up one of the salmon and walks over to the barbecue, his superior officer twisting through his legs.

PLAYLIST FOR A PICNIC BY THE CHUCKLING RIVER ORCHY

Itchycoo Park – Small Faces
Lay Back In The Sun – Spiritualized
Go Your Own Way – Fleetwood Mac
Happy – The Rolling Stones
Not So Manic Now – Dubstar
Roll Away The Stone – Mott The Hoople
Waterfall – Stone Roses
Sunny Afternoon – The Kinks
Do You Realise? – The Flaming Lips
The Bucket – Kings Of Leon
Together – Raconteurs

SELECTED MEMORIES OF THE PICNIC BY THE RIVER AT THE BRIDGE OF ORCHY HOTEL

Fitch remembers…

Tess, walking slowly down from the hotel, her girls flanking her. She stops in front of me, plants her golden legs a little apart, and puts her fists on her hips.

"I think that you are being naughty boys," she says. Her face is strangely stern, and for a second I think she's angry. Then her sensual mouth smiles broadly and her eyes shine like the golden sun itself. "We thank you for your badness."

I glance at Macrae. His grin is from ear to ear.

"Our pleasure," I say. And I step forward and hold out my arm. "Now," I continue, "the barbecues are lit, the meat is marinading, the cheese is cut and the beers are cooling in the river – I don't suppose you ladies are hungry?"

"Starving," she says, and takes my arm.

And now the hills recline above us like hungover giants. Hamish the highland cow stands dreamily to one side. The river rolls in front, the golden rays of the sun fingering its froth. (Fitch note to self – think of something better. Sounds a bit rude.) The Stone Roses have never sounded so beautiful.

The six of us are sitting back in a moment of happy silence, the detritus of a delicious meal scattered around. Jones is flat out on his back in feline ecstasy, his fish-filled ginger belly curving towards the sun. The wine is flowing. I have a beer on the go as well. I look at Tess's wide brown eyes and can't remember a time I felt so chilled.

"Man, look at his 'do," says Macrae, pointing at Hamish. "He's like a rock star of the bovine world."

"He is pretty cool," I say. "He's just hanging there, soaking in the vibe."

"He looks to me like he wants to party," says Macrae. "Hey, do you think Highland cows like beer?"

And he leaps to his feet and steps over to Hamish.

"Alan, a cow cannot possibly digest complex carbohydrates," says Wentworth.

"Don't be such a fucking cube, George," says Macrae and holds up his bottle of Arran Blonde towards the beast. Hamish immediately flops his lips round the bottle and slurps the beer down.

"Man, he's totally chinning it!" cries Macrae.

Nina laughs at him. Macrae smiles back at her.

"That is completely irresponsible—" starts Wentworth.

"It is very warm I think," says Nina suddenly. "Time now to cool my feet in the river," and she stands up and steps away towards the water. Macrae looks around at us, then takes the beer bottle from Hamish and puts it down.

"Better check she doesn't fall in," he says, and walks after her.

There's a very brief pause. The river chuckles some more.

"And I think I would like to try some digestive stretches," says Tess, smiling and cocking her head at me. "That patch of grass over there looks perfect."

Then she too is up and walking away to a spot a few yards away.

I turn to Wentworth.

"Better help her... um, digest," I say, and I am also on my feet. I follow Tess, leaving George alone with Gertrud and the heavily purring Jones.

Hamish, meanwhile, has found another Arran Blonde and is sucking hard at it beneath his rockstar fringe.

Macrae remembers…

Man will you look at her. Lying back on the bank with her bare feet splashing in the water and her soft voice singing along to the music god she's so fucking hot I'm surprised the water isn't steaming.

The urge to just run up and grab her fanny almost gets control of me. Luckily I wrestle it back inside in time.

"Hey, Nina!" I say, and sit down beside her on a rock that juts out into the river.

I look into her eyes and smile then squint as if recognising something, and say:

"You know," I say, "you remind me of a famous Scottish engineer."

"Who?"

"No, Thomas Telford."

"Shit, I got that wrong. You're meant to say, 'What?' You get it? – 'Watt'. Steam engine dude."

She stares at me like I just farted in her beer.

"Fuck it," I say, "I can't do this shit. Look, Nina, I'm going to be straight with you here. I'm not the fastest brain around. In fact, I got a head full of mince. So I can't sit here and talk to you about physics and that pish. But what I can tell you, and this is provable by immediate observation, is that your tits are causing an equal and opposite reaction in my trousers."

For a second I think she's going to bolt. She holds herself tense and upright. Then she suddenly melts and eases closer.

"You know," she says, "most men, when they hear of my profession, they are either scared of me, or they pretend to be able to converse with me about things that they do not understand. But you do neither. You make silly jokes and talk to me about sex."

"Hey, sorry, I'm calling it as it is-"

"No, do not apologise," she smiles. "It is a great turn-on."

I shuffle a little closer. The warm autumn air catches in my throat and makes me swallow with a weird gulping noise.

"Yes, I am a brainy woman," she goes on, "but that is not all I am. Sometimes I want to be a… sexual woman too. And then I do not want sophistication. I want..."

"A bit of rough? Well, sweetheart, that is pretty much my defining characteristic. I mean, Christ, I killed a deer today with my bare hands."

"You did?!"

And I swear she gasps and clasps her hands to her chest and tilts her head back like some dopey bird in a black and white movie. I smile to myself. There's blood in the water.

"Yeah. And then I stood naked in a freezing waterfall catching wild salmon like a bear."

"Mmmm! More!"

She shuffles closer to me and I see her eyes are glistening.

"I haven't worn underpants in eleven years."

"Oh, you stinky old goat, that is so bad!"

"I don't see you running away."

"No. But if I did, how long would it take you to catch me?"

"One frightened, frantic heartbeat."

"Oh God!"

Fitch remembers...

"Are you boys brothers?" Tess asks me. She holds a plastic cup of red wine in one hand, an oatcake with cheese on it in the other as she stretches back on the grass.

"No, no," I reply. "Just old uni friends."

"You seem so close." She sips again.

"You think?"

"Oh yes. They care very much for you. It is obvious."

"God, I don't know about that," I say, reaching for my own wine. "Sometimes I feel like I spend my whole time trying to stop a fight erupting. And then the next moment I'll look at them and out of the blue I'll get this surge of affection for the crazy old buggers, so strong inside it's like sickness." I pull my knees up to my chest and rock back a little. "I guess you could say in that way they're like the brothers I never had. I'm an only child, you see."

"You are? Me also."

"Shit, really?"

I let my knees go and lean forward.

She looks down at the ground for a second.

"Well, I had a younger sister, but she died."

Suddenly I shiver.

"Is that so?" I choke.

"Yes, she was only six years old. She got some horrible disease. Poor little Inga."

She sips her wine once more and I feel like a tiny wind is starting to blow inside me, whipping itself into existence, hard and cold.

"Something like that," I start, the words freezing in my throat, "must be hard to get over."

She cocks her head. A memory drifts like a cloud over her face.

"We used to dance together, Inga and I," she says. "But she was so much better than me even though she was younger. She was like a little- how you say, big white bird?"

"Swan."

"Swan, yes. And when she died, it seemed so unfair, that this beautiful, talented little swan was taken and me, this great big lumpy thing was not. So that is when I thought of my destiny. I swore an oath. I said, 'my dear dead sister, I will dedicate my life to your memory. I will become the dancer you never could be!' And here I am, twenty-six years later, still dancing my little shows to seven people." She looks down at her cup of wine. "I sometimes wonder if that oath was a good idea." And she drains her plastic cup.

I lean forward.

"Of course it was!" I say.

She lifts her eyes. Their lustre is somehow fragile, like porcelain.

"You have not seen me dance," she says.

"I don't need to," I reply. "I know you're sensational!"

"You are a very sweet man."

And she lays her hand on mine and lightning hits me from a cloudless sky.

My body jolts, my brain zaps and in a single flash of understanding I feel free for the first time in years. I realise, as clear as the mountain waters before me… I have never wanted anything in my life as much as I want this girl in this moment with me.

I love her.

She turns and stares out at the hills. The sun is starting to go down and the sky over the hills is a dozen shades of awesome.

"Oh it is so beautiful here," she says, "my heart could sing!"

My heart is already singing. More than that, my fucking soul is on fire. It's all I can do to say:

"Let me write you a poem."

She whips round, head cocked on one side.

"You would do this for me?!" she asks, luscious eyebrows arching.

I bend closer, my face now just inches from hers.

"I will immortalise you – if you'll let me."

"Of course!"

Macrae remembers…

I lead Nina away from the group and under the bridge just so we can get a bit of privacy you understand. And I'm standing there with her and the river's burbling away and the old stones are above us and I look down at her lovely blonde smile and her smashing creamy tits and I suddenly feel as horny as a troll which if you're not exactly sure how horny that is well I can tell you it's very fucking horny indeed.

But I pause for a second cos I always think that this moment just before the kill is the best. You know you're going to kiss her. She knows she's going to let you. You know she's going to let you. She knows you know that too. There's like this unspoken moment of sweet surrender that is totally intoxicating and I want to drink it all in for as long as I can and get right pished on it.

So that goes on for about two seconds then I think enough fucking philosophy and I grab her and pull her towards me.

"My goodness," she gasps, "what is that in your pocket?"

"That, professor, is my particle accelerator," I reply. "Would you like to see it?"

"Is it dangerous?"

"Very."

"Oh, yes please!"

Wentworth remembers…

This is utterly the last straw. Look at the pair of them. Exposing themselves to the mercy of those girls. Alan is a lost cause, of course: a rutting man-puppet, completely controlled by his sinister animalistic hormones. But Tom is an innocent: there is hope for him and he should be rescued from the grasping claws of that harpy-woman.

I must act now.

But it is simply impossible to think: the previously intelligent Gertrud has suddenly become intensely tiresome.

"Tomorrow's route looks most interesting, don't you think, Mr Wentworth?" she coos, poring dumbly over the map and moving uncomfortably close to me. "We must cross the largest moor in Britain passing all these beautiful mountains here-"

She pushes the map in front of me causing her arm to press against mine. I don't know whether it's the surfeit of barbecued venison in my belly or the gross bloom of her perfume, but something is making me feel awfully queasy.

"It is certain to be most fascinating," she continues, "but also jolly long and hard-going, wouldn't you say, Mr Wentworth?"

Oh, how sordid. Alan and his mate have disappeared under the bridge. To rut there in the filthy shadows like a pair of goats, no doubt. And look at that… thing beside Tom! She's practically writhing on that grass as he writes his poem. They're going to start kissing in a minute, and then I really will be ill.

"I suppose the possibility of viewing wildlife in the wilderness will take our minds from the effort," continues this interminable female beside me. "There are still so many of your wonderful beasts that we want to see. Tess in particular, she wishes more than anything to see an eagle – it is her dream. Do you think we might possibly see one of those on the moor of Rannoch?"

I wonder, if I gave her a hearty shove, would the current catch her before she could scream?

"I said, Mr Wentworth, do you think we might see an eagle tomorrow?"

And I'm on the verge of attempting a physical proof of that conjecture when suddenly it comes to me. My final opportunity. My strategy. Simple, complete, decisive.

I turn on Gertrud.

"She dreams of eagles, you say?" I muse. "Doesn't seem much of a dream to me. There's a spot not far from here where I could show you a dozen of them."

"What?!"

"Oh yes," I add casually, and then flick my finger at the map. "You see the name of that hill – Tom Dubh-Mor. It's Gaelic for 'Crag of the Plentiful Eagles'."

"Are you sure?" she replies. "I thought the Gaelic for eagle was iolair?"

"No no no," I smile, "that's the modern Gaelic. This is all ancient Gaelic. Really, it's practically nothing but eagles there. Soaring and swooping and filling the sky with their awesome majesty."

Her eyes shine. She leans forward and places her hand on my knee.

"Could we go there?"

"Oh no."

"But you said it is not far!"

"It's only a few kilometres off the Way, but as you yourself remarked, we have a very long stage tomorrow, and we don't want to be delaying ourselves just for a few birds, do we?"

"But Tess is crazy about eagles!"

"Really?"

"Yes! She will want to see them very much – I must tell her most immediately."

"If you think so."

"Of course!"

And she skips down to the water's edge, leaving me in peace, blessed peace.

I believe I deserve another piece of venison.

Fitch remembers…

"It hasn't worked," I mutter. "I'm going to have to start again." And I move to tear my poem up.

153

"No!" she cries, and leaps off the grass towards me. "Let me see."

"I don't know," I say, putting the notebook behind my back. "The metaphors have gone all weird."

"I bet they are fine!" she cries, and dives forward, throwing her arms around me to seize the pages.

The world slows.

Her hair presses soft against my cheek. I can see the perfect curve of her neck arcing away below my lips. My nose is a plain bare inch from her ear, drinking in the intimacy of her warm scent. The light of the setting sun blinds me.

And then she's gone, away from me again, my words in her hands.

She stares at the notebook for a long time as I shake on the riverbank.

"What do you think?" I say.

She swallows. Then looks up at me, her wide eyes slung with tears.

"It is the most beautiful poem I have ever read."

"You don't think the rhythm's a bit wonky?"

"You have captured my spirit. I find it thrilling."

And she steps back towards me and puts her hand on my thigh.

Instantly there's a strange, sudden movement in my trousers. Like the twitch of a dead frog, laid out in the lab and electrocuted.

I put my hand on hers.

She lets out a little gasp.

I move my face towards her and–

–Gertrud looms up in front of me.

"Tess! Tess! We can see eagles tomorrow!"

Tess jerks away, brown eyes wide, her hand flying from my leg.

"No!"

"Dozens of them!"

Tess looks like she's about to explode.

"Where?!" she steams.

"We must make a small diversion from the Way, but Mr Wentworth says it will be worth it – we are certain to see them flying all so beautiful above a cliff!"

"Then we must go to bed now so we can get up early! Tell Nina."

And the two of them start to move away.

"Hang on a moment," I say, "Seems a shame to go to bed now. Just when we were having such a… lovely conversation about your, um, sister…"

She leans forward.

"Don't worry," she says. "You have given me wings in your poetry and that is wonderful. But seeing an eagle is just about the sexiest thing I can think of. And if I saw a dozen… ooh la la!"

And she pats my thigh again, higher this time, pressing the heel of her hand into my tense flesh and holding it there, just a little longer than she ought to.

"Right, everyone!" I say. "Bed time!"

Macrae remembers…

This girl's got greased silk fingers and a gob like a soapy hoover. She may have a doctorate in physics but she's also got a PhD in playing with my balls and I'm sitting back enjoying the lesson when-

-suddenly Gertrud appears under the bridge and starts rabbitting on about eagles and next thing I know Nina's pulled her hand out of my shorts and the girls are heading off to bed.

I stomp off to see the boys.

"What the fuck's going on here?" I demand.

"The girls want to get up early and see some eagles," says George, sliding his eyes sideways and picking at a piece of melted cheese.

"What?!" I shout.

"It'll be okay," smiles Fitch dreamily, "eagles make her feel sexy."

"For your information, I was already feeling sexy. In fact, Nina was very kindly wanking me off. Then you cunts go and mention the eagles and she stops. Now, are either of you going to finish the job she'd started? No. Course not. I'm going to have to go into those trees and bloody do it myself."

Which tells them how it is and makes me feel a bit better. But I still have to go into the forest and pull my wire which is a bit disappointing all things being considered.

On The Terror Of Beauty
A sonnet by Tom Fitch

A symphony of birdness deftly played
O'ertopping highest mountain, glen and hill
In the school of birds you make the eagle grade
And carve the air beneath you to your will.
But little creatures, mouse and bat and vole
Espy you and all thoughts of beauty flee
Their frantic eyes look only for a hole
Or gap perhaps in rotten stump of tree.
And what if wings from back of mine doth sprout?
And lift me high – what would you think of me?
A fellow eagle to soar with all about?
Or a sparrow snack to set you on for tea?
I do not care. I risk my neck, O Tess
And bare my heart to your feathered sexiness.

DAY 5

BRIDGE OF ORCHY TO KINLOCHLEVEN

Summary:
- *Distance: 32 km (21 miles)*
- *Estimated Time: 7-9 hours*
- *Height Range: 2900ft (870m) ascent*
- *Terrain: You are now about to cross over Britain's largest and wildest moor. When conditions are calm this is a deceptively easy walk, but remember that the Way is extremely exposed with no shelter and in bad weather Rannoch Moor has to be taken seriously. Do NOT stray from the path as there are places you can sink into a peat bog. In adverse weather Ba Bridge marks the halfway point; turn back if in doubt about your safety.*
- *Accommodation: Bridge of Orchy, Inveroran, King's House, Kinlochleven.*
- *Refreshments: Bridge of Orchy (hotel), Inveroran (hotel), Glen Coe Ski Centre, Kingshouse (hotel).*
- *Places of Interest: Glen Coe Ski Centre. The Devil's Staircase: at 1850ft this is the highest point along the Way.*

Fwap.

Patter.

Fwap fwap.

Patter patter.

Huh? What's going on? Why's it so cold in here?

Fwap fwap fwap.

Patter patter patter.

And what's flapping so hard? Is there a bird in the tent?

I dig a knuckle into my sleep-clogged eyes and wriggle my sleeping bag over so I'm lying on my belly.

What the hell-?

The outer door of my tent is wide open. Persuasive gusts of wind are tugging the triangle of material towards some imaginary dance floor. A gentle but insistent fall of rain has soaked the inner cotton door. Through this glistening window I can see my kit in the doorway area, now exposed to the elements.

Shit!

I rip the zip round, thrust out a hand and grab one of my boots. The inner lining is sopping. I tip the boot. Water plashes out onto the grass.

Damp condenses on my spine. I shiver. I'm absolutely positive that I shut that flap when I came to bed. This isn't right. There's something intrusive about the way the rain has come into my tent. Another shiver.

"Wakey wakey rise and shine, breakfast's here, time to dine!"

Wentworth's cheery schoolboy face bobs into the mouth of the tent like a cartoon sun. In his pudgy right hand he holds a bubbling pan of what appears to be omelette.

"Wentworth," I ask slowly, "did you get that pan from my rucksack?"

"Mushrooms and peppers and a healthy dose of cheese!" he beams, nodding at the pan.

"Because you didn't close the tent flap. Look at my boots."

I pour the other boot out, right in front of him.

He wafts my irritation away with a flick of his hand.

"What's a little damp when you're got eagles for afters?!" he says, lofting his chin to the grey heavens.

I'm about to have a go and then I see the happy sheen in his eyes. And reflected in that dewy joy, I see Tess, holding her arms wide and circling around me, her brown eyes wide with gratitude…

My anger dissolves like rain in the river.

"Sure," I say, "what are a couple of damp feet between friends?"

"Good chap," he grins, "now eat up your nummy nummy brekko and let's get a-rambling!"

I shrug myself from my cocoon, pull on my waterproof and exit the tent.

Just to my right the river crashes against the rocks. It has risen a full two feet in the night – a foot more and it would have washed our tents away.

I look up.

The hills that swept up above us so majestically yesterday have vanished, replaced by a blank grey wall reaching right up to heaven. Ribbons of silver mist drape the lower forest like huge garlands of out-of-focus tinsel. (Fitch note to self: reconsider this simile for 2nd draft – 'huge grey draught excluders'?)

"This isn't right."

I look down to my left. Macrae is sitting cross-legged outside his tarpaulin staring at a bowl of omelette, his eyebrows piled up on top of each other like crashed cars. He looks up at me, still perplexed.

"Cunt made me breakfast," he says, cocking his head at Wentworth.

"I know," I say, sitting down beside him with my omelette. "It seems odd. But we can't moan at him when he's whinging and when he's happy. This eagle adventure has really fired his imagination. He's finally getting into the trip and we should be glad."

"I don't know," replies Macrae. "Look at him. Eyes all glassy and grinning like a Scientologist – I don't like it." He sniffs at the omelette. "I don't like it at all." And he flings his food into the pounding river just as Wentworth appears with two plastic mugs of steaming coffee.

★

I finish my thoroughly delicious breakfast and we decamp. Then we walk back over the bridge to the bunkhouse.

There's a small porch outside the door and we shelter under it as we try to work the security lock. Suddenly the door swings open from the inside and the girls come out. They are completely kitted up in their bulky waterproofs. For a second we are all huddled together in the doorway. It's a moment of unexpected closeness. I smile at Tess, but there's a strange chill about her face and she doesn't smile back. She just looks at me, her brown eyes glowing in the deep cave of her hood.

I sense the closeness turning to awkwardness. The intimate languor of last night seems to have been washed away by the downpour. The waterproofs have formed a barrier to us as well as the weather. Instinctively we know that the girls want more space, and we step back out into the rain. It patters noisily on our Goretex.

We try to regain a little friendliness with some greetings, but they sound oddly formal.

"Good morning."

"Hey."

"How you doing?"

"Great."

"Good to see you."

"You too."

I catch Tess's eyes again, searching for a little warmth.

"So," I say, "you looking forward to seeing the eagles?"

She looks directly at me, and her eyes are suddenly the lights of a runaway train, roaring down a tunnel, out of control.

"Of course," she says. "Why wouldn't I be?"

"We did not sleep so well," says Gertrud. "The roof leaked."

"And it is still raining now," says Nina. "It will be hard to see the eagles."

They speak almost an explanation of Tess's shortness. But it's entirely unnecessary. It was a stupid question.

"Well, as long as we all give it a try," I say.

"I don't know, Fitchy, it's getting worse," says Macrae, looking up at the slanting rain.

"Just a little shower," trills Wentworth. "Soon pass."

"Bullshite," says Macrae. "This is a front. Check out the shape of the clouds

160

above the Black Mount. It's in for the day. At least."

Then suddenly his eyes go wide.

"Hey, look – here's an idea!" he cries, and jabs his finger at a sign pinned on the inside of the open bunkhouse door:

Autumn Ceilidh
Kinlochleven Village Hall
Wednesday 26th September 2007
All Welcome

"That's tonight!" Macrae continues, turning round to face us with wide, excited eyes. He whips back round. "You girls fancy a bit of Scottish dancing? We could hop on a bus and get there early. See if we can rustle up some kilts!"

"Oh, absolutely yes!" smiles Nina, clapping her hands and bobbing up and down on the spot.

Tess glares at her.

"Now, Nina," she says solemnly, "you know how much I like dancing. But surely you have not forgotten the importance of the task we have to do first?" And Tess swivels a heavy-lidded gaze at me. For a second the sensual promise I saw last night shines in her eyes. It's the light at the end of the tunnel, and for that I'll do anything. "Isn't that right, Tom?" she adds.

"Absolutely," I say, delighted that she has spoken my name. "Eagles now. Dancing later."

Macrae stares at me.

"Fair enough," he shrugs, "but in precisely one hour you guys are going to have ice-cold drips running down crevices you didn't even know you had and you'll be wishing to fuck you'd listened to old Alan."

"Miaow!" whines Jones suddenly.

We all look down. He crouches awkwardly below us, drips from the porch roof wetting his fur.

"Yes sir, General," says Macrae and slips off his rucksack. He fishes out his tarpaulin and loops it over the top of his pack. This creates a little gap, a backward-facing hole. Jones climbs into this den and curls up as tight as he can.

Macrae hoists his rucksack onto his shoulders and without another word we set off. It's eleven thirty.

And it's odd, because I don't turn my head, I just stare straight at the path to avoid the rain – but I'm sure I can sense Wentworth smiling to my right and Macrae chewing his lip to my left.

FROM MACRAE'S NOTEBOOK

Macrae's log stardate 666-24/7-bumhole

Pish.
Pish.
And double fucking pish.
First he disrupts a very beautiful handjob and now he's taken shitting on my chips to a whole new level – he's playing with those girls and messing with Fitchy's mind. Which is just not fair because girls love to be played with and Fitchy's mind is already pretty messed up.

He's just not helping things you know what I mean?

Wouldn't surprise me if he'd got his uncle bloody Windermere to bring the rain on.

There's trouble in those clouds, I fucking know it.

FROM WENTWORTH'S NOTEBOOK

Ah, the refreshing bead of dew on one's brow! Caressing the poet's skin and cooling his mind.

I am pleased to report that the walk is finally enjoyable. A little damp, yes; but for once there is neither inane chatter nor sordid innuendo. Just the cleansing silence of man in the wilderness.

And the sweet anticipation of a pleasure planned and won.

FROM FITCH'S DIARY

Everyone has their hood up. We plod silently along the muddy path like blinkered horses. Only Wentworth has anything approaching a spring in his step.

The rain comes steadily down as the path loops round a long loch, passes through dripping woods, then starts to rise.

Suddenly the trees have gone. Scrubby heather extends away on all sides until swallowed by the rain in the middle distance. I feel strangely exposed in the bubble of my hood. Like there's some huge cliff or skulking creature out there in the mist, always just out of my restricted view.

I suddenly feel very alone. I have an urge to talk to someone.

I step to my left and twist my head round to look at Tess.

"I was thinking about Inga-" I start, talking to the side of her waterproof hood.

"What?" yells Tess, turning her head towards me. The rising wind presses rain onto her face.

"I said, 'You made me think-'"

"You want a drink?!" she squawks.

"No. I'm talking about your sister."

"You have a blister!?!" she yells back.

"Forget it," I say, shaking my heading and turning back to the puddles on the path.

And then I feel it – a stone-cold sliver of water sliding down my neck and round into my armpit. Unbelievably ticklish and shiver-inducing. I try to rub the chill away, but the drip escapes and slides like a razor down my ribs.

I look up to see Macrae raising one bushy eyebrow at me.

*

We trudge on into the rain for a couple of hours that seem like days. My back, inner thighs and armpits are streaming with icy water. I'm trying to find the source of the leaks when I bump into Wentworth.

He has stopped on a flat wooden bridge that carries the Way over a bustling river. He reaches a gloved hand deep into a pocket of his waterproof and pulls out a map. He consults it for about half a second then jams it back inside.

"Well, here we are, Bridge of Ba, tra la la. That cottage up there is where we realign." And he looks out across the moor.

"Realign?" asks Macrae. "What are you talking about?"

"Eagle Crag is over that way," Wentworth replies, wafting a hand out to the wall of rain that constitutes the east.

"Er, what?" says Macrae.

"Where the eagles are," says Tess, eyes smouldering inside her hood.

Macrae stares at her for a second. Then he turns. Looks at me like he can't quite believe what he's hearing.

"Fitchy. We're not walking out onto that moor," he says. "This weather is serious. We're going on a few klicks to the Kingshouse and then we're getting the bus to Kinlochleven, where we will go to the dance in the warm village hall and drink beer."

Wentworth reaches up and pulls his hood down. Rain instantly beads on his pale skin. He grins. For some reason, the sight of his teeth makes me feel a little dizzy.

"Is that all you can think about," he says slowly, "drinking?"

Macrae freezes.

He looks Wentworth up and down very closely, as if searching for a stain on his clothing.

"The beer, George, is incidental. It's the getting out of the freezing fucking downpour that's my main motivation."

"Oh, I see," says Wentworth, his pudgy head nodding. "You're wimping out."

I've never seen Macrae so still. Drops of water hang motionless on the edge of his hood. The only noise is the background rustle of rain on heather.

His animal eyes are full of fire, and for a second I think he's going to pounce on Wentworth. But as he stares, the fire seems to cool.

Then, slowly, gently, he backs away from Wentworth, like he's seen something dangerous in him.

And when he speaks, the words are full of the usual confidence. But there's a quiet shake in his voice that I've never heard before. Like the first faint rattle before your exhaust falls off.

"George, you maniac, be quiet for a second. Fitch. Mate. I know you've got on lot on your mind right now, but you have to listen to me when I tell you this

– you don't fuck with Rannoch Moor. The marines, they've trained me in some places – Sutherland, the Grey Corries, Knoydart, Cape Wrath. Snow-blown, wind-torn shitholes every one. But you know where they don't train?" He jabs a brawny finger into the mist. "Out. There."

"You know what I think?" says Wentworth in a loud, bold voice. "I think he's just jealous because I'm the one who had the idea of going to Eagle Crag."

Macrae coughs. For a second I think he's choking. Then the cough turns into a spluttering, disbelieving laugh.

"Oh George," he gasps at last, "you really have no clue. Listen. A hundred years ago, when they built the Blackwater reservoir – which is just over those enormous cunting hills over there – the Irish navvies that made up the workforce used to schlep over to the Kingshouse inn on a Friday night after a week of work – a week of work, incidentally, like you and I have never known – to get pished. And then, pished, they'd schlep back. All summer, autumn and winter this would go on. And in then, in the spring, when the snow melted, they'd send a cart over to pick up the piles of bodies they'd find. Dead. Fucking. Drunk. And fuck knows how many they didn't find." He throws his arm out. "Christ, look at it! Six hundred million square feet of peat moor. No paths, no roads, no deer tracks. The railway runs over the best of the ground and even that is fucking floating. You think I'm joking? Look it up when we get back. That railway line has no foundations. It floats on a drenched bed of dead Irishmen. There is no way you're getting me out there in conditions like this to look at a fucking bird's nest."

Wind.

Rain.

Both of them smacking Goretex.

"Then don't come," says Tess.

Another rain-blown pause.

"What's that, sweetheart?'"

"You don't like getting wet – poof! Don't come."

Macrae cocks his head and looks at me, eyebrows arched.

Where the hell has this come from? Everything was going so well. Now I feel like the path is dropping away beneath me. As sudden and terrifying as a landslide.

I step into the middle of the group.

"Guys guys guys," I soothe, "there's no need to be like this. Why don't we just walk out there a little bit, see if it's still raining, and decide then?" I smile.

"No, Fitch," says Macrae, squaring his shoulders. "This is the Way." And he points to the tarmac path below our feet. "That is suicide," he adds, pointing out to the moor. "You decide now."

I can feel Tess staring at me. Her thoughts are written on her face like graffiti: 'Yes,' she's thinking, 'you decide now.'

"But you take risks all the time," I say to Macrae with a high laugh.

"Yeah, I do." He glances at the girls. "But I don't make others take them."

"What about that time you made me snort gunpowder?"

"That was different," he mutters. "There was no one else, just us-" then he smiles and lays a hand on my shoulder, "-and you're just as much an idiot as I am."

My eyes flick towards Tess and her reaction to that gesture of Macrae's terrifies me. Her upper lip wrinkles in a sneer. Her eyes shine with scorn. And again I don't need words to understand things perfectly. Because I know that this is it. I have to go out there. Right now. Or she'll be lost to me forever.

I suck in a breath.

"Maybe I'm not."

Macrae takes a step away from me.

"What are you talking about, mate?" His voice hangs deathly in the shroud of mist around us.

"Look," I say, "the girls really want to go and see the eagles-"

"I don't," shrugs Nina. Tess glares at her. She drops her eyes.

"-maybe we should give it a shot," I continue. "It's only September. How bad can it get? And you know, we have maps and phones and stuff. Even if it does turn nasty, we'll be okay."

"You guys have to realise-" starts Macrae.

"No, what you have to realise-" says Wentworth, stepping forward, and he suddenly looks every inch of his six-foot frame, "-is that we're tired of listening to your self-serving macho bullshit nonsense. The only reason you want to avoid this little détour is so you can get to Kinlochleven quicker and have sex!"

"What?" squawks Tess.

166

Nina shrugs – is that so bad?

"Oh, he wants you to get there too, Tess," roars Wentworth. "So you and Tom can do the same! That's all it's about for him-" and he jabs his finger at Macrae, "sex."

"George, you prick-" starts Macrae.

To my incredible surprise, Wentworth presses forward, squaring his chest against Macrae's.

"Deny you said those words!" Wentworth spits. "Deny you said, 'It's all about getting him laid'!" And he points at me.

I look at Macrae. He drops his eyes. I look at Tess. She is aghast. I want to feel angry, I want to feel outraged, I want to say something. But all I can do is stare.

Macrae still glares at his feet. He says:

"I don't want to get into some fucking legal argument, George, because that's not what I meant-"

"But is that what you said?!" bellows Wentworth.

And then, slowly, Macrae lifts his eyes from the wet road and even in ten years of his heaviest hangovers, I've never seen them look so dead. He says:

"Yes. It is."

There's a long pause. Then Macrae turns to me. Says ever so softly:

"Fitch. Look at the General. The toughest bastard I ever met. And even he's advising against it."

It's too late now. I'm in with both feet.

"Yes, Alan," I say, "but he's just a cat."

And the very last bit of sunshine fades from Macrae's face.

Then there's some sort of gap in reality. A shrug between what was meant to be and what really is.

And the next thing I know, we're buttoning up our Goretexes and heading out off the path onto Rannoch Moor.

And I'm looking back at the even track of the Way and it's surreal, because my last sight of civilisation is Macrae trudging into the gale towards the Kingshouse inn, with Jones peering back at us from his cubby hole, a faint glimmer of worry in his pocket-tiger eyes.

Then the rain thickens even more and the two of them are gone.

★

I don't remember ever seeing Wentworth so jolly. He practically skips along the scrawny path like the fat fisherman on the old Skegness posters.

"Come on, you lazy bones!" he cries over his shoulder. "The eagle-weagles are waiting!"

Tess, too, is full of energy. She flies along between banks of heather, her legs graceful despite her thick waterproofs.

Gertrud's face is flat as a slab of rock. She seems resigned, like she has somehow been here before.

While poor blonde Nina just seems sad. She keeps looking back over her shoulder, like she's hoping to see someone there.

But there's nothing behind us. Just haggard clumps of heather and then, after a few hundred feet, a closed wall of mist.

As for me, I'm strung out at the back trying to work out what the hell just happened. I feel like I walked into a cinema, sat down with my popcorn, there was a big dramatic ending then everyone left.

I can't believe Macrae sometimes, really I can't. I mean, maybe 'self-serving macho bullshit nonsense' was a bit over the top, but he certainly can be stubborn. He talked himself into a corner there when he knew he was in the wrong – why else would he have backed down from Wentworth like that?

And why did he admit to that stuff about getting me laid? Jesus, I'm embarrassed now to look at Tess. But I have to say something. Can't walk along feeling like this.

I jog on up to the front of the group and fall in step with her.

"Hi," I say. "Listen. I must apologise for what my friend-"

"Why?" she interrupts. "You did not say it."

"I know, but-"

"Pfaff! Don't worry. What someone else thinks is not important to you-" and she peers sideways at me out of her hood, "-is it?"

"No no no of course not-"

"Good. That is the best way to be. Don't give a fucking fuck about any of them." Then she smiles and says softly: "Besides. We all have needs."

And she winks at me and my breakfast flips in my belly.

The path trickles on for an hour or so then reaches a derelict hut.

"This way, team!" trills Wentworth. But as we follow him round the corner of the tumbledown building we all stutter to a halt.

I've done my fair share of hillwalking, and normally I love the wilderness- But this is different.

It's simply one of the bleakest places I have ever seen.

There are no trees. Scrubby heather is studded with jagged rocks. Peat hags, gnarled like gargoyles, add a little variety. Dead ahead of us lies a ragged, inky loch. It sulks malignantly beneath bulging rainclouds. Mounds of peat and stone protrude from its black surface like half-drowned whales. I know you couldn't ever get whales up here, and it's pretty difficult to drown one, but damn me that's what these islets look like.

"We're going out there?" chokes Nina.

"Of course!" replies Wentworth. "This is where the moor really begins."

And he starts briskly forward onto the pathless acres.

Tess follows him then, after a moment, Gertrud. Nina hangs back for a second longer, biting her lip and looking over her shoulder. And I have to admit, a splash of her nervousness spills over me.

There's an inhuman emptiness here. A void surrounds us and I have the lurching feeling that we simply aren't meant to be in this place.

I shiver.

For a second I feel like a spaceman, hanging by a thread a million miles from home. I look up at the receding figure of Tess, and let her gravity pull me deeper into the blackness.

★

We pick our way along the snaggly shore of the loch for an hour or so, then leave the water and continue across open heather.

For some bizarre reason, Wentworth has taken his hood down and is providing a commentary to our walk:

"From a distance, and on a map, much of Rannoch moor looks flat. But this is merely an average, fooling your eye and the coarseness of cartographic scale. Close up, it's a labyrinth of ditches, mounds, muddy streams, lochans and peat bogs…"

His relentlessly cheery tone is completely at odds with his subject matter and the wilds around us. And I don't know whether it's that or just the exertions of traveling here, but something seems to be sapping the energy from Nina's legs. She is starting to lag behind.

"This landscape is geology in action," continues Wentworth. "Ten thousand years ago, a vast plateau of ice stretched above our heads. I know that seems like too long a timescale to imagine, but it's really rather recent-"

Nina stops to take a breath. Her face is red. Her eyes cast around helplessly.

"Imagine Scotland is a man," Wentworth booms. "Thirty years old. For the first twenty-nine and a half years of his life he lived in the tropics, amid vast lizards and ferns the size of oak trees. Three months ago, he moved to the arctic. The cold was vicious – it crushed the tropical jungle to death and buried it under rivers of ice 3,000 feet deep. A mere three hours ago, things warmed up and the ice departed, carving out the glens like cheese and forming the land on which we walk. Twenty minutes ago, men started farming here. The sun of our civilisation has shone for a little over eight minutes. On a scale like that, our endeavours seem rather trivial, no?"

Nina stumbles off a peat hag. She pitches forward, puts out a foot to steady herself and skids. For a second I think she's going to faceplant into the mud, but she gets her hands out and uses them to break her fall.

Her gloves and sleeves are coated in thick peat slime.

She curses in Swedish and flaps her arms against the heather to clean them.

"What then is your life to Scotland?" Wentworth goes on. "Nothing but the song of a lark. The ripples of a stone falling in a loch. A single breath of a stag, sucked in and blown out into the timeless mist-"

If that's true, I start to wonder, then for how many microseconds have I known Tess? I can't begin to make the calculation, but the whole relationship thing seems suddenly laughable. Its supreme futility climbs on top of me like a glacier, grinding me into the landscape as it flows slowly into the west…

"I'm hungry!"

Huh?

I turn round.

It's Nina. She has stopped on a peat hag, arms folded across her chest.

"It's not far now," says Wentworth.

"I don't care," says Nina.

"Don't be so idiotisk," says Tess. "We will eat when we get to Eagle rock."

"Idiotisk yourself!" snaps Nina. "I have hunger now!"

The girls are glaring at each other.

Wentworth steps slowly in between them.

"You know, Tess," he says, "those eagles have been there for thousands upon thousands of years. I'm sure they can hold on another twenty minutes. Don't you think, Tom?"

"Uh, yes," I nod. "Of course."

But I haven't really thought my answer through.

★

We can't find any meaningful form of shelter so we have to stop for lunch half standing up, half crouched against a peat hag. The rain clatters against our Goretex jackets as we take off our rucksacks and close in together.

"Now," says Wentworth, "you will be pleased to hear that I have saved a large portion of leftovers from our feast yesterday."

And the girls' faces brighten up – even Nina's – as he reaches into his rucksack.

But instead of the delicious collection of breads, meats and salads that we are all expecting him to remove, all he pulls out is a squashed and shining mass.

"Oh dear," he says. "The rain seems to have got to it. How silly of me to put it in the outside pocket."

He smiles, brightly.

"Ah well, bite off the freshest looking lump you can and pass it round." And he hands the congealed food to Nina. She stares at it for a second and then with unrestrained viciousness hurls it into the bog.

"Nina!" cries Gertrud. "We have no more food!"

Tess shakes her head, gets back to her feet and slings her rucksack on.

"Perhaps now we can continue?" she says.

171

After a moment we all reach for our own packs and pull them wearily onto our shoulders.

Tess and Wentworth set off in front and I follow them. Then Nina tags on, but now she has a friend at the rear – Gertrud, who glares steadily at Wentworth's back from deep inside her hood.

*

We slog on across the moor. For every hundred yards we move forward we expend about three hundred yards' worth of effort as we climb down and up the winding chasms in the scarred landscape. Going over the top, the heather is spongy and clawing. In the runnels the peat is skiddy and sticky. I can feel molecules of muscle draining from my legs with every step. It's difficult to stay in a line, as we each take slightly different routes around, through or over the obstacles, depending on stride length, confidence or energy. We end up drifting into three parties. Tess and Wentworth are at the front, Gertrud and Nina at the back. I toggle in the middle, trying to stay with both groups, wanting to bring them together without telling Tess to slow down or Nina to hurry up.

An hour or so of this and the ground rises – or rather, the vast landscape tilts – and Nina slows even more. Gertrud's face is marked with lines of concern. Her normally steady eyes are now flicking from her toiling friend to the solid sky to the moor and back again. At last her worry bursts from her.

"Mr Wentworth," she calls into the rain, "how much longer is this going to take?"

"Not far now!" replies Wentworth over his shoulder, and he steps briskly on.

We try to keep a decent pace up, but the ground kicks upwards even more and the gradient is exhausting. Some of the chasms in the peat are now filled with brackish streams. We can jump these at first, then ford them. But after a while they become too broad and hungry. We have to track left or right for some distance along each one looking for a suitable crossing. And still the rain comes down. Visibility is only a couple of hundred feet. By the time we've zigged, crossed, then zagged back again, I can hardly tell whether we're even heading in the same direction.

After another hour or so – though it could be two, because it's so wet that lifting my wrist to look at my watch causes icy streams to course into my armpit – Gertrud walks forward to Wentworth.

"How much longer?" she asks again.

"Not far!" he replies.

"But you said that before!" Gertrud cries.

"Just up ahead, you'll see."

He seems so confident it's absurd. No boot-sucking bog or spirit-sapping detour lessens the vigour of his step and Gertrud wilts in the face of his brashness. She slackens her pace and for a second I think she's going to drop to her knees when a sudden cry from ahead snaps her head up.

"Quick!"

I look round. Wentworth has stopped a few yards away. He's hopping from foot to foot with excitement and jabbing a hand at the heather.

"Come and look!" he cries, beckoning us all forward.

"Is it a nest?" asks Gertrud.

"Might be," I say, and lead her towards Wentworth.

He's peering down into one of the snaking chasms and I can't see what he's looking at until I'm right beside him. Soon as I draw up level I glance down and my blood freezes.

Half submerged in the peaty marsh is a stag. It's clearly dead – its limbs are twisted to hideous angles, like it broke itself struggling to escape, and its hide has been torn open in several places, revealing shining sinews, guts and bone. But there's still something so incredibly alive about it that I am astonished. Muscles bulge. Glossy hair shines with rain. Antlers split the air like lightning. How could a creature so vigorous, alive and... male end up trapped in a bog?

Nina and Gertrud appear at my shoulder. Nina instantly spins away and starts retching. Gertrud stands beside me and stares.

"Isn't this wonderful?!" says Wentworth. "Look, its eyes and tongue have been almost completely pecked out. We're in eagle territory alright! Come on, gang." And he and Tess start to move away.

Gertrud keeps staring at the dead animal. When she looks up from the stag to Wentworth's retreating back I notice her eyes are watery and red. She takes a breath and says in a stumbling voice:

"Can I see the map, please?"

Wentworth stops. Turns. Raises his eyebrows.

"I'm sorry, what?" he says.

Gertrud swallows.

"The map," she says. "I'd like to look at it."

Tess takes a step back towards us.

"Why are you wasting time?" she asks. "We are so close now."

Gertrud turns to Tess.

"I think we should head for the nearest road," she says. And she can't help looking back down at the carcass. "We're putting ourselves in danger out here," she adds.

I also look back down. And instantly my knees turn into two marshmallows and I almost stagger into the hole. Because I don't know how, but I have the sudden, horrific conviction that this is the same stag I saw in Drymen. It's impossible, I know – deer don't range that far and how could I tell one apart from another and the coincidence would be too much – but nevertheless… I know for a fact that it's the same creature.

I look up.

Tess is staring at me, her jaw slack with shock, her eyebrows steepled in sadness, like she too has seen the truth through my eyes. And for the first time since I met her, I see doubt on her face.

"Let her see the map," Tess says softly.

"But of course," says Wentworth. "Whatever you like." And he reaches inside his waterproof and hands Gertrud the map.

Gertrud's arm flies out so fast I recoil. She grabs the map, tears it open and stares at it, eyes blazing. Suddenly she cries out:

"Min Gud! I am right, look!"

Nina and Tess peer over her shoulder.

"Okay," Gertrud says, the rain battering on the paper, "we left the Way at Ba Cottage, correct? Walked east along that path for around three kilometres then crossed the road. From there we walked along the shore of that loch for a couple more kilometres, which must be Loch Ba. Then we walked out onto the moor and have continued for more than two hours, but look! – Tom Dubh Mor is only three kilometres beyond Loch Ba!"

"It's been rather heavy going," says Wentworth.

"Not that heavy!" cries Gertrud. "We should have reached it a long time ago. Tess, we are lost. We must turn for the road."

Wentworth sighs theatrically and rolls his eyes at Tess.

"If you do, you'll miss the eagles."

Tess opens her mouth to speak, then closes it and thinks for a second. At last she says:

"I so want to see the eagles, but we have been walking for a long time. What if we are not where we think we are?"

"There are no other hills around," says Wentworth, "and we're still rising. As long as we're going up, we're getting nearer to the crags and to the eagles, yes?"

The girls stare at him. A gust of wind slaps the rain hard against their jackets.

"Look, ladies," Wentworth continues, "I know it's confusing, but you have to trust me. When it comes to maps and timetables and suchlike I am – if you will permit me the coarseness – the most anal man on the planet. Just ask Tom."

Everyone is looking at me.

Wentworth is calm and expectant. Nina and Gertrud are bedraggled and unhappy. God knows I don't want to upset them... but then I look at Tess – her eyes are wide with hope and desperation. If I call it off now she'll be inconsolable.

I suck in a breath.

"I trust him," I say. "If he says we're close to the eagles, we're close."

A huge smile smears itself across Wentworth's face.

"Come on, then," he says. "Up to the top of the hill. And less talking this time, girls. We don't want to scare those eagle weagles away!"

And once more we plunge into the rain. But rather than striding ahead with Wentworth, Tess is now walking beside the other two girls. I watch her, trying to focus on her beautiful, troubled face, on her now-pale cheeks, on her teeth gnawing at her coral lip, but no matter how long I look at her, all I can see is the stag, his half-eaten eyes staring deep into mine.

*

Tess is far and away the fittest of the girls, but even she is now clearly knackered. All the energy she had has drained from her legs and run off down this never-ending slope. As for the other two, they're practically staggering across the moor.

And Wentworth – well, maybe I'm just hyper-tired, but he's suddenly bugging the shit out of me. Childish I know, but that really is the best way to describe it. The bounce in his walk. The way he hums a tune that is impossible to identify. How can he be so bloody jovial? Didn't he see the stag? A beautiful creature torn apart by the wilderness that once protected it – and he is singing. Doesn't he understand? It's life and death out here!

"The light is fading," says Gertrud.

"The rain is getting heavier," says Nina.

"And we're going down," says Tess.

Huh?

"Look!" cries Tess, shaking my arm. "The land is sloping downhill! And he said we must continue uphill!"

I have to admit, it does feels like we're starting to descend. I glance at Wentworth but he continues to stride confidently ahead.

"Maybe it's just a dip in the contour," I say, but my voice doesn't sound very convincing as it echoes round my hood. "It'll probably rise again in a minute."

But it doesn't rise again. It keeps dropping. Steeper and steeper.

Tess turns and yanks my sleeve. Her eyes are wild.

"Where are the cliffs?!" she cries. "You must do something!"

And the desperation in her once-strong eyes makes it clear that if I don't do it now, she won't give me another chance.

I nod numbly and walk forward.

"Wentworth," I say, tapping him on the shoulder, "the girls are wondering why-"

"Nearly there, just a little further…"

But he isn't talking in response to my question. He's muttering to himself, eyes wide and lip quivering as he stares eagerly into the rain. There's something terrifying about his panting, trance-like stare, and I suddenly have the plummeting feeling that we're in the hands of a madman.

Panic seizes my throat like a wolf.

"For God's sake," I choke, "can't you see what's right in front of-"

But I don't get to finish my sentence because Wentworth suddenly stops.

I halt beside him. A second later, the girls are by my side. And we're all staring, wordless, because right in front of us is–

Water.

For a second I think it's just another lochan or stream, but then, as we stand there staring, a severe gust of wind tugs the rain away like a curtain and the stunning panorama it reveals stops my heart and slams my belly down to hell.

A vast body of water stretches left and right as far as we can see. The opposite bank is at least half a mile away. Beyond it rise huge mountains, snow-capped and serious.

"Ee-aargh!" Nina lets out a strangled cry and falls to the ground sobbing.

"Gud i himmel!" says Gertrud and clasps her hands to her face.

Tess turns to me. Glares hard for a second. Then she tenses her body and punches me in the guts as hard as she can.

It's not the blow that hurts – although her knuckles drive so deep I swear I feel them grind against my spine – it's the fierce rejection in her eyes.

I stagger back, gulping for air, my eyes whipping around, frantically searching for some sanity. But all they see is Wentworth.

He's staring out across the water with a look of quiet triumph on his face. Like we have in fact arrived. He lets out a peaceful sigh and suddenly his calmness is a target in front of me.

Pain boils in my belly like lava, and as I regain control of my muscles it heats every atom of air that I suck in to my lungs. When I finally manage to speak, the words spit out like white-hot rivets:

"Went… worth," I say through grinding teeth, "where… the fuck… is the fucking… mountain?"

He gazes dreamily out across the water.

"Do you know," he muses, "I'm not entirely sure."

"Not… sure?" I can sense the girls staring at me, fascinated by my rage. "You said there would be a hill," I go on. "You said there would be cliffs. You said there would be eagles. But there isn't any of that shit. What there is, instead, is a ten mile long fucking loch!"

"I knew that wasn't the translation," says Gertrud.

I turn to face her.

"What's that?" I whisper.

"Tom Dubh Mor," she growls, her red eyes fixed on Wentworth, "means 'big black hill'. There never was an eagle crag."

Slowly I swivel back round to face Wentworth.

"Is that true?" I ask.

"Eagles have to live somewhere–" he starts.

"W-w-w-w–wait a minute," I interrupt. "Let me get this straight. I stuck my neck out for you. I trusted you. I vouched for you. And you made this up? Why would you do that?"

He's staring at me with a hopeless look in his eyes and a nervous smile on his lips, which I presume is intended to make him look endearing and vulnerable. But the fire in my belly isn't buying it. Every second I look at his helpless pudding face, I want to smash it more.

"I thought–" he starts, but I take a breath and unload a volley:

"Are you that desperate for attention?" I say. "So jealous of Macrae? Or just so spiteful that you want to watch us suffer?"

The sneer in my voice hits home like an arrow.

"Oh, Tom!" he cries, "I would never do anything to hurt you."

"Apart from dragging me into the middle of nowhere to see eagles that don't exist, you mean?"

His eyebrows crash together in confusion.

"Why are you getting so upset?" he whines.

"Why indeed?" I reply. "I'm sure we can find something equally imaginary to get us out of here." I point my arm at a shallow patch of water on the bank. "Why, I'll bet this puddle is magical gateway that will transport us all to Narnia. Come on, everyone, let's go!"

And I leap into the puddle, splatting a couple of inches down into the peaty treacle.

"Shit," I say, looking around, "no sign of Aslan. Maybe we should call him. Aslan! Aslan! Come and take us, please!" I yell, hopping from foot to squelching foot and waving my arms. "I want to be a faun in your heavenly animal kingdom!"

"Tom, please stop!" he wails, his lower lip quivering.

"Why would I stop now?" I cry, "I'm just getting going. Aslan's obviously gone to the pub, so let's try Gandalf. Gandalf!" I scream into the rain. "Oh,

Gandalf, darling! Carry us aloft on your giant eagles! There's a good wizard!"

"Why are you doing this?!"

"Because, Wentworth, someone has to do something to get us out of here. We've exhausted all other possibilities, so I'm giving Gandalf a go. Unless you have a better idea?"

"Yes!" he cries, stepping towards me and clasping his hands together in front of his chest. "We camp here!"

I curl my lip and recoil from him.

"George, we have two one-man tents. What are the girls going to do? Click the heels of their ruby walking boots three times and wish themselves to Kinlochleven?"

"They can walk back to the road."

"Wentworth, I'm not leaving them alone on Rannoch Moor in the middle of a monsoon! What the fuck are you thinking of?"

Wentworth freezes – like the piece of grit that causes ice to form, the swearword crystallizes his face as soon as it leaves my mouth. I feel I've crossed a line, but I don't care. His face reddens, his eyes narrow, but I press on even more forcefully:

"We have a fucking responsibility here. We have to think about the girls!"

That's it. Wentworth gathers himself up and takes a breath so big I think he's going to burst.

"Why?" he barks, his face fierce and puffy.

My belly wobbles. I hadn't expected that.

"Uh, what?"

"You lot are always thinking about women and not one of them ever made you happy, not ever!"

I feel like the conversation is dragging me to the edge of some hideous precipice. I know there's dreadful danger ahead, but I can't stop myself going along.

"What are you talking about, George?"

He wafts a fat paw dismissively at the staring girls.

"Why do you even bother?!" he sniffs. "You'd be much better off without them. Spending your time with someone who actually cares about your happiness."

179

"Like who?" I spit back.

And then he says these two words like they're huge and heavy. Like anchors on his tongue:

"Like me."

And everything stops.

Even the wind and the rain disappear. There is just Wentworth and me in a bubble of black silence in the wilderness.

I stare at his pudgy schoolboy face as it hangs there, lost in the void, and for a second I see straight through his eyes, deep into his soul, and I suddenly realise...

"George. Have you dragged me out here to tell me you're gay?"

"I don't know… I mean…. that is… yes, no…" and then he yells: "I JUST WANT TO BE WITH YOU!"

And he turns and runs and as suddenly as it came the bubble is burst and the storm is roaring around me.

And I drop my head into my hands and breathe out hard.

"For. Fuck's. Sake."

Then I turn to the girls who are looking at me with eyes wide as oyster shells.

"Can you please wait here for a second?" I say, then shrug off my rucksack and tear into the teeth of the gale.

★

"Wentworth! Where are you!?"

It's almost dark now and the peat hags loom at me like ghouls.

I run over them, round them, into them, my blood pounding and lungs heaving. He can't have got that far, can he? He's just a big old lump. But he's a determined son of a bitch, too. My heart flips and I double my pace.

"Come on, mate, don't do anything stupid!"

But there's no sign of him, just the waves of rain sweeping in over the loch and the endless slopes of the hills.

"Please, Wentworth, let's have a chat!"

But all I get is a wall of rain in my face. Now I can barely see two yards in front of me. There's no point in running – I don't know if I'm going in the

180

right direction.

"GEORGE!!" I scream in final desperation into the blackness.

My breath hangs in coils for a second before the machine gun rain blows it to hell.

KRRSPLSH-OOOW!

To my left – a definite splash followed by a startled yelp.

I dive off sideways into the mist. Suddenly I'm right at the shore. I can't see more than twenty feet out. I scan the black water. Left, right, left, right again… but nothing.

Shit!!

And then – there is something, right out at the edge of my visibility. Nothing more than a bunch of lines… angles that look wrong on the water…

"George, is that you?"

The lines twist, then pause, then start to move.

Jesus Christ, it's him!

I wade into the water. I have never, ever, felt anything so cold. A great stone vice seizes my body and crushes the breath from it.

The bottom drops away sharply from my feet. Suddenly I'm swimming. I thrash as fast as I can, but my limbs start to seize before I've gone five yards.

Just got to keep going. I can't feel my hands or feet, but I keep my shoulders and hips moving.

The strange lines are approaching. Something is bobbing in the water.

Wentworth.

He's still wearing his rucksack, and is splashing slowly out into the loch. His face is shock white and his eyes wildly round.

I gulp in some needle-cold air and thrash on towards him.

He sees me coming. Turns. Utters a small squeak and tries to swim off. But I have more strength than him. I reach out and grab one of his rucksack straps.

He shakes his head and splashes a feeble hand at me.

"Leave me be!" he wheezes, "I'm not worth saving!"

I try hauling on his rucksack, but he's too heavy for me to pull in. In fact, he's starting to go under. Another few seconds and he'll be gone forever.

His mouth drops under the surface. Bubbles blow up past his startled eyes.

Shit! Think fast…

I reach down and unclip the straps of his rucksack. Tear it off. Kick it free of his body.

It sinks. He rises.

"My kit!" he moans. "Oh Tom, my lovely kit!"

"Fuck your kit. Swim!"

And I grab him by the collar and kick for the shore.

He resists at first, trying pathetically to hit my hand away. Then he seems to come to. He realises what I'm doing.

"You're saving me," he whispers, as if he can't quite believe what he's seeing.

"I'm trying," I splutter, still kicking furiously at the water.

He smiles.

And he kicks for home.

We get near the shore. My feet scrabble for purchase, fail twice, then get a stance. I haul Wentworth free of the water.

We collapse, soaking and exhausted on the heather bank. Great shivers rack our bodies.

He rolls onto his side and vomits up some water. He rolls back to me. With his slicked hair and mournful eyes he looks like a very naughty seal.

A smile flicks across my lips. Then I realise the seriousness of the situation.

"Come on," I say, "we have to get going or we'll freeze to death here."

I start to get up. He doesn't move.

"I'm sorry," he whispers.

"You don't have to apologise-"

"Oh, I do. I'm sorry I caused such a bother. Sorry I dragged you all out here. Sorry I made you made you risk your life, Tom. For nothing."

"You're not nothing-"

He lifts a hand.

"Please. Listen. You know I don't care about girls-"

"George, I-"

Again, he waves a hand to shut me up.

"You've always known. Alan has too, in his way. But you never talked about it. Never judged me. Which was what made you special. Tom, I didn't bring you out here to... declare love or anything so frightfully dramatic... I brought you out here because I just... wanted things to... stay as they were."

He's shivering so hard. His rambling scares me. Is he fading? He goes on:

"Oh Tom," he cries, "I hate my life! I hate my job, I hate staying in that vast house on my own..." There are tears in his eyes. "I know I should be grateful, I remember the looks in people's eyes when they heard I'd inherited a whole townhouse. But I grew up there, and I can tell you it can be hard to fill a house that size with love. Particularly when there isn't much love to start with. Between boarding school and coming home to that place..." he sighs and looks down at the mud. For a second he gathers his thoughts then looks up at me, his blue eyes shining. "You have to understand, when I went to college and met you – and yes, Alan too – it felt like I was starting out on a fabulous journey. I couldn't wait to explore the world. Possibilities lay like treasure in the street. But it was such a few short years...

"And when we left, things were different. With every year that went by another path closed off. Every choice I made narrowed the road. The journey wasn't fun any more and worst of all, I knew the excitement would never come back. That loss was physically painful to me, like ice in my belly. I suppose I missed being young.

"But when you and Judy split up and you came to stay, it actually felt like we'd gone back to the start. I know we hadn't. But it felt like it. And so although I knew it wasn't true, I gave into that feeling, luxuriated in it – because it was so much fun. It made going to work bearable, knowing I had you to come home to. To cook for and console and talk about poetry with."

He coughs, and his eyes seem to fade a little. For a second I panic – is he drifting away? Then he gathers himself and goes on:

"I didn't want to come on this trip, but when we got out here..." he waves a shaking arm round at the hills, "...I thought I'd discovered the perfect place. An absolute wilderness. Complete freedom. That's what I had you traipsing into the darkness for. To find somewhere you and I could just be. I was deluded, I see that, and I am sorry. But at least now I can die in peace, knowing that I have truly had an adventure."

His pudgy face is ghost-pale and his blue eyes have dulled to wet grey. His spirit seems truly beaten. Another minute and his light might go out entirely.

But there's no way I'm going to let that happen. I seize his hand and yank it towards me.

"Die?! What are you talking about, you great lump? Nobody's dying today! This isn't the end – this is the start for you. By just saying this stuff you've opened up a whole new bunch of paths, and damn me if you're not going to walk them."

And I haul him to his feet.

He stares at me like he can't believe what he's seeing.

"Come on, my friend," I say, "we'll take the first steps together. Like in the old days."

And I throw both my arms around his shoulders and hug him till I feel the warmth return to his big polar bear face.

★

The girls are still lined up on the bank, three drookit water rats huddled together.

Nina and Gertrud welcome us, leaping to their feet and gathering round to hug Wentworth. Tess stays sitting down, coiled and glaring like a kicked cat.

"Are you okay?"

"My God, what happened!"

"We thought you were drowned!"

"We're okay," I say, "but we must get moving before we freeze. Let's look at the map."

"Um, I put the map back in my rucksack," says George. "Sorry."

"It's okay," I say, patting him on the shoulder.

"We're not getting out of here, are we?" says Nina, her upper lip quivering.

"Course we are," I say. "A quick call to mountain rescue will sort us out."

I delve into my pack and fish out my mobile.

"Shit!" I say. "No signal. You girls got anything?"

Nina pulls out her phone.

"Sorry, it is wet."

"My battery's dead," says Gertrud.

I turn to Tess. She shrugs.

"Eagles don't need phones," she says.

Something about her tone is intensely irritating. My belly still twinges from her blow. I decide to ignore her.

"Right," I say. "We need to think. This must be the Blackwater reservoir that Macrae talked about. Wentworth, you're the brainbox, do you know anything about it?"

"It was built in 1907," he says.

"No good," I say, shaking my head.

"It powered the aluminium smelting plant at Kinlochleven," he says. "But that's closed down. I think they turned it into a climbing wall."

"More interesting," I say, "but still not useful. Come on, think."

"Um, I believe people mostly use it for fishing nowadays."

I half turn away in frustration – then stop.

"So if they fish in it," I say, turning back, "there must be a way of getting up from the village. A Land Rover track or something, Let's have a look – hang on, which way?"

"Kinlochleven is west," says Wentworth. "That way." And he points to the left.

"West it is," I say. "Come on everyone."

Nina, Gertrud and George turn with me. Tess still slumps on the ground.

"You coming?" I ask her.

"What's the point?" she snaps. Again, the feeling of irritation stabbing into my chest. "Your friend dragged us out here," she continues. "And now you're going to let him get us into more trouble."

I bend down towards her and notice that when she frowns she looks old.

"Listen up," I say, "it wasn't George that got us into this mess. It was me. And I'm going to get us out of it. But I can't do that alone. It's not about egos out here – the moor simply doesn't care. We have to work together if we're to make it. And that means I need your help – everybody's help. Now you can sit here on your own in the mud or you can wipe that sulk off your face, get on your feet and do your damn best to get us to Kinlochleven."

Her lip curls. Her eyes blow wide. For a moment she just stares at me.

Then she slowly gets up, pulls on her pack and falls in line.

★

185

We charge over heather and through streams, briefly invigorated by the hope that being back together brings.

But it's properly dark now, the rain isn't letting up and fundamentally we're shattered; after half a mile or so we have to stop. We stand in a circle, panting. Each looking round the others to see who will say what we all want to express, but don't want to hear:

There is no path.

There are just the endless wilds and the loch stretching out beside us like a reclining tyrant.

I want to say something hopeful, but the words are dead in my throat. Wentworth is even paler than before. He shivers like two giant hands are on his shoulders, shaking his body. I really don't know how much more of this he'll be able to take-

"Look!" Gertrud cries.

I glance round and follow her pointing arm.

It's a canoe. Drifting past us, a few yards out from the shore, its rope trailing in the frothy water.

"The wind must have blown it free from its moorings!"

"Quick, grab it!"

"You have to be joking," I mutter. "Not another bloody boat."

Then I wade out, take hold of the rope and haul the canoe in to the shore.

★

There's a bench in the stern with a paddle propped against it. Some fishing gear sits in the bottom in padlocked boxes. I use the paddle to help the girls and George on board. I lob the fishing gear into the loch.

George flumps down on the damp boards. His face is shock white.

The girls sit around him.

"Hold on," says Nina to him, "I'm going to look in the rucksacks and get you some dry clothes."

I nod at her and she starts rummaging.

I open the top flap of my rucksack, pull out my headtorch and start to put it on.

"I'll wear that."

I look up. Gertrud is holding out her hand.

"I'm taller. I'll get a better view than you."

"Uh, okay," I say. "Sure."

She straps the torch on her head and looks out to the front.

I glance at Tess. Her brown eyes hold mine for a second, then she looks away.

I pick up the paddle, take a breath, lean over the side and get to work.

★

I paddle west, directly into the prevailing wind. Rain blatters in our faces. Waves slap the canoe. My arms are soon screaming. Hot sweat and cold rain stream together on my face. Every breath sucks more needles into my lungs.

Nina has wrapped some dry clothes round George, but he doesn't look good. His eyes are weak and yellow. The pale flesh around his chin sags as his head lolls. I'm just wondering how long we've got before he gets hypothermia when-

"Look!" cries Gertrud.

I follow her pointing finger. There isn't a lot of light, but up ahead I can make out an unnaturally straight line coming out of the hills just above where the horizon should be.

"Some sort of wall..." I mutter.

"The dam," murmurs Wentworth. "Head for the end. There'll be an access road that leads down from there to the village."

"Thank God for that," I say, and steer the boat slightly out of the wind.

Suddenly Nina says:

"Hey, you notice that?"

"What?"

"The rain."

"What about it?"

"It's stopped!"

My face is so wet that I can't tell whether it's raining or not. I pull my paddle from the water. Wipe my forehead on the back of my glove.

Shit. So it has.

"The wind has dropped also," adds Gertrud.

She's right.

"And look at the sky!" whispers George.

We all stare upwards – and gasp.

The clouds have shredded, revealing depths so sudden and vast that my head lurches.

I've never seen the stars so clear. Orion's belt gleams like celestial bling. The Great Bear is so close it's scary. And the Milky Way is a spill of icing sugar, its billion granules glistening white and sweet.

After the first wave of fear, a profound sense of calm floods over me. I sit back, the paddle cradled in my lap. I look down and-

-another wonder snatches my heart.

Right behind Tess's head, low and beautiful over the top of the dam, the moon is rising.

As I stare, jaw hanging, Tess looks down from the stars. She turns to me. Her face is flooded by moonlight. For one still second all the frustration and exhaustion is washed clean away by the magical silver glow.

She looks young, like-

"Why are we speeding up?" interrupts George.

Huh?

"You've stopped paddling – but we're going faster."

I peer over the edge of the canoe. We are indeed moving quicker. The water chuckles around us.

"We're in a current," I say.

"Where has the dam gone?" asks Gertrud.

Now we all look up. The black wall sheers across from our left, but just before it reaches the tumbling hillside, there's a gap. And there's something about the way the horizon ripples there that makes me shiver.

"I think you should paddle the other way," says Nina.

"I think you're right," I reply, and dig the blade hard into the water.

But I can't get any purchase. The water is moving too fast. Very fast now. The surface is boiling around us. Huge black muscles tensing beneath the skin.

Faster and faster we cut through the water. I slash the paddle in a frenzy. It breaks. I topple backwards. We stare at the fractured stump, horrified in the moonlight.

A shadow falls over us. The dam looms on our left, a vast concrete mountain. And then we're passing it – how can that be? But there's no time to understand because now-

Our canoe is tipping.

A hideous, unnatural movement that sickens me in an instant. Hands snatch at wood. Eyes blow wide. Knuckles crack white. But there's no escape.

Just an eerie moment of silence as for one calm second the whole landscape is laid out before us – moonlit mountains, a shimmering sea loch, a town nestling among the trees.

Then we skew a little further and the view changes. In front of us now is the foaming insanity of the dam's overflow conduit, a concrete channel of roaring water that plunges first to the right, then yanks back to the left before crashing headlong into the rapids of the River Leven, hundreds of miles below.

"Get down low!" yells Nina.

Huh?

"Everyone!" she screams. "In the bottom of the boat. Keep our centre of gravity as low as possible."

We throw ourselves to the boards. The boat tips even more. I'm on my back, the stars spinning above me.

Then reality falls away.

I suck in a breath.

Try to scream.

But all sound is lost in the hurricane of water that roars around us.

*

Freefall.

No up, no down, no left, no right – only speed.

And violence. Relentless shocking violence.

Towers of spume rise up and smash over us. Rocks loom out of the night and crunch us sideways. Tree branches swipe at us like claws.

Rapids jerk my limbs and jam my spine. We plummet over weirs, rocket through gorges, flail over waterfalls.

Wave after wave. Plunge after plunge. Mile after mile. And through all of it, we cram together in the bowels of the boat, each of us holding onto another, as dear and as precious as ourselves.

★

Then, as soon as it started, the violence stops.

The water is again chuckling below us, not roaring above.

We're drifting under calm trees, not ducking savage branches. The moon is no longer whanging around the sky.

We look around at each other. Everyone seems okay. Clattered, battered, splattered and bruised – but alive.

Wentworth looks up at me and says in a cracked voice:

"Well, at least it beats walking."

And he smiles at me. I have to hand it to him. He has spirit. I smile back.

We look around. On the left bank there are nothing but dark woods. On the right hand side of the river, set back through the trees, are some houses. Most of the lights are out, but a few windows glimmer.

"Kinlochleven," I say.

"Oh no, look!" cries Gertrud.

She's pointing to the river ahead of us. Six huge pipes, each two metres in diameter, are spewing jets of torrential water into the river at head height just a few yards away. The canoe will be instantly swamped.

"The turbine pipes from the old smelter," says George.

"Head for the bank!" I shout, and plunge my hands into the icy water. I try to paddle, but the boat is far too heavy. The jets roar nearer.

"The tree," says George, pointing above my head.

I understand. I reach up and grab hold of an overhanging branch.

"Hold me!" I say.

Nina and Gertrud each grab a leg. Sopping moss squirms between my fingers. I heave on the tree and pull us in towards the shore.

We haul our aching bones out of the canoe. As we slump onto the bank, the canoe drifts downstream – and is pulverised by the jets. It shatters and tilts and promptly sinks.

We turn round. The lights are across the water. We're on the wrong side of the river. There's no bridge.

"Shit!" I curse. "So close–"

"Wait."

I look round. It's Tess. The first word she has spoken in hours.

She has her head on one side and is holding up a finger as if conducting.

"You hear it?" she asks.

"Hear what?"

"This way," she says, and sets off deep into the woods behind us. We look at each other for a second then skip after her.

The night is clear but snapping cold. There's a smell of winter in the air.

"Where are we going?" I ask.

But Tess says nothing, just gallops on through the forest.

Suddenly, a vast building rears up from the shadows. Tumbledown brick walls and scattered piles of ironwork –

"The old aluminium plant," says George.

Holes in the walls like vast eyes. Broken chimneys. Heaps of slag and waste. The building is hideous. It rots in its rubble-strewn ruin like a slain dragon.

I shiver.

"There's nothing here," I say, turning to Tess.

"Sh!" she says. "Listen!"

And she cocks her head on the other side and sets off round a corner of the plant.

I run after her, wanting to catch her, stop her, shake her, when I turn the corner and–

See the dragon's treasure.

Nestling neatly by the chaotic plant is a little stone building.

Smoke curls from a chimney. Flowerpots dangle from the eaves. Two bottle-glass windows glow on either side of a smart green door. Above the lintel is a neat sign: 'Kinlochleven Village Hall'.

Tess leads the way up to the stone doorstep. We press close behind her. She grasps the handle, turns it, presses the door open. Light floods her face as she reveals–

–the most welcoming scene I have ever witnessed.

191

A long, low room with a wooden floor and rafters. Along the sides, tables and benches and a makeshift trestle bar. Tartan tablecloths. At one end, flames crackle in a large fireplace. Opposite that, and raised slightly from the floor, a small platform. On this stage are four men with chunky white sweaters and even chunkier white beards. One plays a fiddle, one an accordion, one a bass guitar, hammering away at their instruments like demented elves, filling the air with magical music. The fourth bearded guy is bellowing dance moves into a microphone: "Forward 2 3 4... turn back 2 3 4... turn the lady, dance around and forward 2 3 4..."

Because in front of the stage, filling the floor, are a dozen couples dancing the Gay Gordons. More people cluster round the bar and sit at the tables chatting and laughing.

A bloody ceilidh.

Tess is at my side.

"Like you said," she whispers, "we work together."

And she smiles at me, and for one perfect second, I know that everything is finally going to be okay.

"Well, look what we are having here."

My spine turns to ice.

I know that voice.

I turn.

Sprawled at a table by the door are Wassily, Uzeyir and Zinaida. A couple of nearly empty whisky bottles stand in puddles on the table between them.

Wassily leans forward, waving at me with a seasick hand.

"Come and join us."

"Over by the fire," I nod to George, and start to lead the way across to the opposite side of the room.

"You ignore me!?" says Wassily, staggering to his feet and stepping quickly out in front of me.

"We don't want any trouble-" I start.

"We did not want any trouble either," says Wassily, swaying. "But we were arrested. Spend all day explaining. Pay fine for something we not do. So maybe the thing about trouble is that it..." He leans in really close. I can smell his whisky breath. See the vessels in his bloodshot eyes. "...finds you."

"Listen," I say, raising my palms. "We're sorry about before. Really we are. But you wouldn't believe what we've been through. We only want to sit down and get warm."

"Of course," Wassily grins. And he lets me past. But as soon as I've gone, he puts his arm up to stop Tess moving.

"Hey!" she cries.

At her shout, the music stops.

The room goes quiet.

Everyone is looking at us.

"Come on, baby," leers Wassily, "just a little dance."

She recoils from his face.

I turn.

"Haven't you got the message?" I say, stepping towards him. "They don't want to dance with you-"

-a flashbulb goes off-

-and I'm staring very closely at the parquet flooring. A drop of blood falls from somewhere onto the worn fibres of the wood. Then another. It's fascinating how it just soaks in. And then – my cheekbone starts to scream.

I swivel my swaying head up. Wassily looms above me, fists clenched.

"Anyone else want to stop us dancing?!"

The band stare, eyes wide. The villagers press themselves up against the walls of the hall.

"Good. Then start up the music once again. And do not stop it until I say."

The band launches uncertainly into the Dashing White Sergeant.

Wassily sneers in black triumph and grabs Tess into the middle of the room.

I stare at her terrified eyes, longing to save her but unable to move. The pain inside is worse than the pain in my face. I can't believe we could get this close and still lose. And as he spins her round savagely amid a sea of fearful faces, I realise there is nothing I can do.

My defeat is total.

-then we hear it.

The voice.

Deep, black and rolling, it surges from the depths like a tidal wave, drowning the music and filling the room with its unmistakeable intention:

"IF YOU WANT TO DANCE, DANCE WITH ME."

And the room turns as one to see Alan John Macrae in the doorway, a corner of the night still cloaking his shoulders, a ginger cat crouching ready by his side.

Ceilidh music bounces incongruously.

But Macrae doesn't care. He simply walks across the room. Slowly. Eyes fixed. Barely breathing. Unemotional, but with total intent. Like Scotland coming out against England at Murrayfield in '90.

His boots move on the beat of the music.

The air crackles.

Wassily narrows his eyes.

Uzeyir cracks his fingers.

Zinaida rolls his head from side to side.

Everyone in the room knows words are useless now.

This is a battlefield.

Macrae walks steadily up to Wassily. For a moment I think he's going to walk right into him. Then, a foot before he does, Macrae stops.

Utterly still.

Wassily grins.

Macrae waits.

Wassily smirks.

Macrae waits.

Wassily snorts.

Macrae waits.

Then Wassily makes his mistake.

He throws a punch.

What happens next is not like anything I've seen in any movie. The violence is both faster and slower. It's fluid and sharp. Aggressive and calm.

One second Wassily is throwing a punch. The second after that, his flying fist is moving off target. Macrae has caught his hand, turned it and is holding it down towards me. It stops an inch from my nose. The three of us stare at it as if inspecting some curious museum artefact.

Another second passes.

Then Macrae pinches the web of skin between Wassily's thumb and forefinger – extremely hard.

Wassily's mouth flies open. His eyes roll back in agony. His knees sag. Macrae jabs two fingers of his other hand deep into Wassily's kidney and steps back as the Russian falls away, twisted and useless.

Uzeyir is on him instantly. And man, does he know some moves. He sends karate chops at Macrae like a snowstorm.

But Macrae bats the blows away like a cat might bat away moths.

After a dozen perfectly countered moves, Uzeyir stops and stares, amazed at the cheek of it. Before this half second of doubt has elapsed, Macrae has dropped to one knee and plunged his fist smartly into the Russian's groin.

Uzeyir's lungs implode and he topples over.

And now here's Zinaida.

The giant growls and surges forward. He's a whole foot taller than Macrae and twice as broad. He doesn't attempt subtlety. He simply pulls back a granite fist and launches it. The power is horrific. Half a connection would fell a bull. But Macrae doesn't duck.

He moves nearer.

Right inside Zinaida's arc. To get to this new position, he has to lift one foot up. When he gets to where he wants to be, he simply puts the foot down again. On its way to the ground it happens to meet the inside of the Russian's knee, which it pushes out of the way with a dismissive crack.

Zinaida's massive blow instantly veers off axis, rocketing now towards the ceiling, and the shift in his weight starts to take him down.

But Macrae isn't letting gravity have its fun yet.

He extends an arm, as straight and hard as the gun on a tank. The heel of his hand takes Zinaida plumb under the chin and lifts all seventeen stone of him three inches clear of planet Earth.

Ceilidh music twinkles.

Zinaida reconnects with timber, shaking the bottles on the trestle bar.

It's at this point that Jones pads over and pees on his crotch.

Macrae then does something odd. He walks to where Wassily lies, drops to one knee and speaks softly into his ear.

"That's it now," he whispers. And he pats Wassily on the shoulder.

The Russian stares blankly at Macrae, his mouth still frozen wide in pain. Then he seems to understand. He closes his lips. Nods his head. Hauls himself to his feet. Then without another word or look, he gathers up his friends and they stagger out of the hall.

Thirty astonished teuchters are gaping at Macrae.

He is looking at me.

"Well I don't know about you jokers," he says, "but fuck me I fancy a pint."

And he winks and walks over to the still-trembling bar.

★

He stands in front of the trestle-table bar. The girls flock round. Saying thank you. Kissing his cheek. Nina's hand is drifting onto his bum. George is gabbling an embarrassed apology, Macrae is embracing him.

My heart lifts at the scene – but I don't move any closer.

I'm sat a few yards away on a bench at the end of the bar, some ice from a Famous Grouse bucket pressed to my cheekbone.

I want to walk along and join the group, but I feel a little dizzy. No, it's not really dizziness, it's more a feeling of -

"Hey."

I look up. It's him. Sitting down beside me on my bench.

"That looks sore," he says.

I look at the floorboards.

"Don't you dare be cool about this," I say. "I was a total dick to you on that moor. It's my head you should be knocking off."

He smiles. Says:

"You remember I said that when this thing is decided, it will happen quickly?"

"Uh, yeah-"

"Well, look." And he lifts my chin up and points it towards the girls. They are standing at the bar, watching us. Their eyes are wide and shiny. Nina is rubbing one knee against the other. Tess is nibbling a glass of wine.

"We have to move fast," he says.

I slowly shake my head.

"Listen, I don't feel that good-"

He nods.

"Don't look too great either. Very peaky." And he starts fishing about in one of his pockets. "Good job I brought my first aid kit." He pulls out a yellowish tablet and holds it up to my mouth.

"What is it?" I ask.

"Medicine," he says. "For the pain. Stop you shivering. You guys have been out in the cold. Probably running a temperature. Come on, gobble gobble." He nods over his shoulder to the girls and George. "I've given them to everyone else."

I nod. Open my mouth.

He puts the tablet on my tongue.

I close my mouth. The tablet tastes very dry and bitter.

"You got anything I can wash it down with?" I ask.

"Sure," he replies, and hands me a paper cup of liquid.

I take a slug – and gag.

"What's this?"

"Lemsip."

"Doesn't taste like Lemsip."

"New flavour. Do you good. You drink it all up now."

"It tastes like vodka."

"That's the new flavour."

I smile. It's like arguing with an avalanche. Better to turn and go with the flow.

I chin my medicine.

"Good lad!" he says, and slaps a brawny arm round my shoulders, making me cough.

"Excuse me."

We both look round.

It's the Caller from the ceilidh.

He is stepping nervously from foot to foot. He chews his beard. Then he gathers himself up, nods respectfully at Macrae and says:

"Er, thank you for sorting that… wee problem out."

"Anytime," smiles Macrae.

The Caller goes on:

"But we've decided to wind things up a bit early. Nobody is really in the mood anymore."

"Of course," says Macrae, patting him on the shoulder. "But would you mind if we stayed on a little after everyone else has gone?"

"Um-"

"My friends have had a long day in the hills. Raising money for kids with manky legs. And if they could warm themselves by the fire for an hour or so that would be fabulous."

"I suppose... as long as you close up when you leave. The janny gets uptight if-"

"Thank you so much. One more thing."

"Y-yes?"

"Could you ask the bass player to leave his amplifier behind?"

"His what?"

"Amplifier. Please. For me."

And Macrae very subtly, but very definitely, flexes one of the sinews in his neck.

"S-sure," nods the Caller, backing away. "I'll see what I can do."

"My man," says Macrae, winking.

As soon as the Caller has gone, Macrae spins to me.

"Okay, let's pick it up double time."

"What? Why?"

"We have to clear the bufties from the dancefloor, get the bar moved into the corner, make some kilts from those tablecloths, sort the lights out and somehow get your iPod jacked into that amp – all before we start coming up."

"Right. Before we start – what?!"

"I hope to fuck you've got some decent dance music loaded on that thing."

I grab his arm.

"The medicine was Ecstasy?"

"For someone who's known me as long as you have, I can't imagine why you're surprised at that."

"But you gave one to the girls!"

"Yes."

"To Tess!"

"Indeed."

198

"You gave one to George!"

"No I didn't."

"Thank God!"

"I gave three to George."

"What?"

"He's a big lad. It's his first time. I didn't want him to be disappointed."

"Disappointed!?!"

"As the French say, 'Pas de drugs – beaucoup problems. Beaucoup drugs – pas de problems.'"

"The French don't say that!"

He leans towards me confidentially and waggles a finger. "When it comes to a party, you should always, always, err on the side of recklessness."

I stare at him.

"You crazy crazy fucking bastard," I say.

I stare at him a little longer.

Then I smile.

"Missed you," I say.

"Course you did," he smiles.

And we slap our arms round each other.

"Now finish your Lemsip," he says. "And we'll clear these old farts out of here and pull the fucking pin."

★

We walk back over to the others.

"Give us a hand with this, George," says Macrae, taking one end of the trestle, to the elderly barmaid's surprise. "Ladies, you want to move those benches back?"

"What are you doing?" asks George.

"Sorting things out for our ceilidh,"

"I'm not sure I have the energy to stay up much longer-"

"Oh, you'll have the energy alright."

"What do you mean?"

Macrae smiles at me. I frown back.

"You have to tell them," I say.

"Best not to."

I turn to George and the girls.

"Listen. That medicine you took wasn't medicine, it was-"

"Ecstasy," says Tess.

"You know?"

"We're not stupid," says Nina.

"Nor square," adds Gertrud, pulling off her glasses and shaking down her hair.

"Oh. Right."

"Hold on," whispers George, wide-eyed. "You have given me... narcotics?"

"Listen, George, it's all perfectly natural," says Macrae. "If God hadn't wanted us to take drugs he wouldn't have created dealers, would he?"

"I'll handle this," I say, shooing him away. "You go and sort the music out."

I put my arm round George and sit him down on a fireside bench. The flames are painting a rosy glow back on his cheeks. I lay my hand on his thigh. Take a breath. Say:

"George, you are about to have what can best be described as... an experience. At first it may feel overwhelming. But you're best not to fight it. Go with the flow. Imagine it's a wave. Don't stand against it; turn and ride it like a surfer. And always remember, you're in a safe place with friends. We all care for you, in a spiritual, gentle, loving way-"

BAWWOOOMMMMMM!!!

A huge bass pulse throbs into being and swells to fill the room.

"Yeeaargghh!" yells Macrae behind me.

I turn.

He is wearing his makeshift tablecloth kilt. He leaps on top of the speaker and tears his shirt off.

"Let's go fucking mental!" he roars.

I sigh.

"This doesn't sound like ceilidh music to me," says George quietly.

"Course it's a ceilidh!" cries Macrae. "It's just got completely fucked up!"

And as the song kicks in he leaps from the speaker, his kilt flying to heaven.

PLAYLIST FOR AN ALL-NIGHT CEILIDH THAT'S GOT COMPLETELY FUCKED-UP

Big Time Sensuality (The Fluke Minimix) – Björk
Open Up – Leftfield
King Of My Castle – Wamdue Project
I Feel Love – Donna Summer
2 People – Jean Jacques Smoothie
Blue Song – Mint Royale
Take Me To The Clouds Above – LMC & U2
Surface To Air – The Chemical Brothers
Love Don't Let Me Go (Walking Away) – David Guetta vs The Egg
Heartbeats (Rex The Dog Remix) – The Knife
Sweet Dreams Are Made Of This (I've Got A Life/Sweet Dreams Remix) – Eurythmics

FROM WENTWORTH'S NOTEBOOK

I suppose one should try most things in life at least once. Bestiality and McDonald's excepted, obviously.

And since I now find myself in the situation where I have to try something, I fully intend to make the best of it. As the greatest drug experimenter of them all, Huxley, wrote: "Experience is not what happens to a man; it is what a man does with what happens to him."

My pen is in my hand. My mind is open. My heart is willing.

FROM MACRAE'S NOTEBOOK

Thought the birds might be a bit ticklish about the whole drugs gig but fair play they're well up for it.

Look at them dancing away over there. Gertrud is getting a right wiggle on trying to get George on his feet. He's not feeling it yet but his face is starting to go a bit red. Another couple of songs and I reckon he'll be off like a rocket.

Tess is putting on a bit of a show for Tom and man you can tell she dances for a living. And she's so into him right now even he can't fuck it up from here. Stay on target Luke!

As for Nina God she's hot. More than that she's beautiful. Look at the sweat on her body glistening in the firelight and the way her breasts bounce doubletime to the music and her lower lip that hangs so low and full and her eyes…

She's special. Unique. She goes beyond everything else. What's that word… transcends? That's it that's what she does she transcends the ordinary. She's the first slug of cold beer on a hot June day. A shower after a week's exercise on Dartmoor. The first flower of spring when all the snow has melted.

I am so going to pump her.

FROM WENTWORTH'S NOTEBOOK

Little to report so far. The others seem to be enjoying themselves, and there is a certain pleasure in observing that. But as to any psychokinetic effects in myself, I have to say I am a little disappointed.

The music isn't particularly inspiring either. Some rather fragile-sounding young lady yelping about something important being about to happen and how it takes courage to enjoy it.

I'll try my dear, I really will. But you'll have to make it happen a little sooner.

FROM FITCH'S DIARY

Great little set-up we got here. The locals have gone, the floor is ours.

Bass lines twist and slide through my body like silicon sinews. The fire paints us with splashes of savagery. We each dance differently – but all together.

And in front of me, Tess.

The greatest dancer ever to move.

Her limbs are the purest poetry, writing out rhymes in the air in front of me. Telling the story of our togetherness, how she and I are the only humans on the planet. Or not even humans at all – animals in the wild forest. No, we're the spirits of the wilderness and the music is our forest. Yeah. And now, tonight, we will teach the world about ourselves. Write our legacy of beauty.

Create a new generation.

FROM WENTWORTH'S NOTEBOOK

I think Alan might have overstoked that fire somewhat. It's getting jolly warm in here. They must feel it too with all that dancing they're doing. I wonder if anyone will mind if I open a wind-

Oh.

How unusual, my spine feels a little tingly. And blow me if that wall isn't tingling as well. What a bizarre trick of the light. Must be the way the logs are stacked on the fi-

AAAYYYYAAARRRR

Golly.

Something very strange is happening to my neck. It's getting longer, like my head is trying to escape. And my heart – it seems to be beating in time to the music. My blood is flowing like the melod

EEEEEEEEEEEEEEEEEEEEEEEEEEEEE

Goodness.

This is all a little unexpected.

*I wonder if I should try a spot of danci-*NNNNNNNNNNNNNNNNNNN
NNNNNNNNGGGGGGGGGGGGGGGGGGGGGGGGGGGGGGGGGGGGGGGGGG
GGGGGGGGG

FROM FITCH'S DIARY

I had forgotten what an absolutely sensational dancer Macrae is. He cuts old school disco moves with highland dancing twirls and Goa trance bouncing and somehow it all comes together. He is completely in his element and it's hard not to just stand back and admire his muscled body at work. That's certainly what Nina is doing.

"Holy fuck look at that!" he suddenly cries, jabbing a pointing finger over my shoulder.

I turn.

George has shot onto the floor. Hands tucked into his armpits, he is waggling his arms and running rapidly round the room.

"Man, look at him scoot!" says Macrae.

"Why's he dancing like a chicken?" I wonder.

"Chicken?!" says Macrae, as if a child could understand. "He's buzzing. He's a bee."

"You think?"

"Damn right. Look, he's visiting flowers."

George is bent over, buzzing and sniffing at something imaginary on the floor. Then he suddenly jerks his head up and, still buzzing, zooms five feet to the right and bends over again.

"George!" says Macrae. "Over here! Pollen!"

George looks up, eyes huge and buzzes over to Macrae, who puts an arm round him and says:

"Listen, you got a grade A rush on, Georgie. But that's cool. Just dance it up and get to your happy place."

"Bzzzz!"

"I know, you're a bee, a lovely big bumbler."

"Bzzzzzzzzz."

"But it's only by dancing that you can make honey."

"Bzz?"

"Come on, baby bee, I'll show you."

FROM WENTWORTH'S NOTEBOOK

BZZZZZZZZZZZzzzzzzzzz
bzzzz

Oh goodness, what happened there?

"Hey, George, you're back with us!"

It's Alan. He's dancing in front of me. Hold on – he's dancing with me. Which must mean that I'm dancing...

"W-what's going on?" *I ask*

"You came up, baby! How you feel?"

"I feel... good!"

"Thassaboy!"

"And this music is... beautiful!"

"Pretty good, huh?"

"I've never heard anything like it! Who is this?"

"Donna Summer."

"It's so... beautiful – oh goodness, listen to the bass!"

"I hear it."

I throw an arm round Alan's shoulder. I have to make him understand.

"No, listen," *I say.* "How it pounds along down there and loops around the melody up here at the same time... like they're two birds flying together... they drift off and then suddenly swoop back in again and take it to a whole new level..."

"I'll put it on your computer when we get back."

"You'd do that for me?"

"Course."

I throw my arms round his shoulders and hug him tight.

"You're BEAUTIFUL," *I smile.*

Because he is.

FROM FITCH, MACRAE & GEORGE'S NOTEBOOKS

                                            dancing together

     firelight

shining on the floor

we're in a circle

               all friends

                              all understanding

Jones in front of the fire

                        bathing in warmth and love

beautiful puss!

                  O, feel his fur!

                       he's purring in time with the music

isn't that beautiful?

                it's beautiful

                     arms round shoulders

       hugging

             kissing

                        faces warm

happy

          spines rippling with electricity   *the flames*

dancing

          in our souls

                    love you guys

I love you

          yes

                you don't understand

I do

        you love me

             no

             I love you

isn't   THIS

                BEAUTIFUL

Gertrud and George are jiving – a melody of twirls and smiles.

Nina and Macrae are twisted together into one shining panting creature, their legs and arms writhing around each other like eels.

Tess is just in front of me, her huge dark eyes shining in the firelight.

"Look outside!" she suddenly cries.

I turn.

"Is that… snow?"

We groove over to the window.

The flickering fire illuminates dozens of dancing flakes.

"They're falling in time to the music," breathes Tess.

She grabs my hand.

"Let's go out!"

"Sure."

She leads me to the door.

"Miaow!"

Jones is at my feet.

"You want to see the snow, too, puss?"

I open the door.

Jones bounds out into immaculate whiteness. A trail of little pawprints follows him. After a few yards he stops. Sniffs the air. Turns his head. Sniffs again. And trots sharply off to the left.

"Where's he going?"

"Dunno. Let's follow him."

We follow Jones's prints through the snowy ruins. The music beats time to our steps as we pass under mossed archways, round fallen walls, over piles of rubble. Around us, the jagged shadows have softened into pale beauty.

Suddenly Jones jumps up onto a kind of concrete ledge three feet high. This extends back ten feet to a pair of open doorways with 'In' and 'Out' painted in faded white letters above them. A corrugated roof shelters this ancient delivery bay from the elements. A little patch of grass has grown on the concrete.

Jones stops and looks back at us. Seems to say, 'here'. Then he walks on into the darkness of the 'Out' door.

"Where's he going now?" asks Tess.

In the shadows, I think I glimpse another pair of shining eyes.

"He wants someone to dance with, too," I say.

And I turn to look at her.

Snow falls on our faces.

I lift my hand to her cheek. My skin tingles where we touch. I can feel her heart beat, pulsing and rising like the distant music. She opens her mouth a little, but I speak first.

"I'm sorry you didn't see an eagle," I say.

"But I did," she smiles, her wide eyes blown even bigger.

"Huh?"

"He flew me down the rapids. Sang beautiful music to me. And now…"

And without another word she pulls her top over her head.

I gasp in surprise at the sudden exposure of brown flesh.

"A-aren't you cold?" I ask.

She laughs.

"It's time for your world premiere, baby," she says, and pulls me to the patch of grass.

I drink in the goosebumps on her taut body. Her dark, contracted nipples. The smooth movement of her thighs against mine.

A blown snowflake alights on her naked breast. I lick it off as it melts.

She gasps.

"You're so… beautiful," I say.

She laughs. Slides her hands under my shirt and down the skin of my belly. We make love.

It's fabulous.

And yet – intense and passionate and loud and wonderful as it is, I feel somehow removed from the experience. Like there's a lens over all my senses.

It must be the drugs. They're really strong. Must be. Because, despite the flawless, sensual woman arcing beneath me, all I can see as I lose control is Judy's brilliant smile.

DAY 6

KINLOCHLEVEN TO FORT WILLIAM

Summary:
- *Distance: 22.5km (14miles)*
- *Estimated Time: 4-6 hours*
- *Height Range: 1800ft ascent*
- *Terrain: Very good paths at this last stage, there is a steep climb out of Kinlochleven, then there are no more serious gradients, the path through Nevis Forest is a bit rough before tarmac takes you down into Fort William.*
- *Accommodation: Kinlochleven, Glen Nevis, Fort William, Lochaber*
- *Refreshments: There is no place to stop for refreshments until you reach Fort William.*
- *Places of Interest: The way goes through Lairigmor, this section of the walk boasts 11 Munros (mountains over 3000 feet).*

Description: A fitting end to the Way, this final stage traverses a magnificent glaciated glen before winding through mature forests and coming out in front of the stark cliffs of Britain's highest mountain, Ben Nevis.

FROM FITCH'S DIARY

Whoop whoop!

Whisssssssstleeeeee!

Fffwwweeep! Fffwwweeep!

"What the fuck are youse doin' here?"

We turn. A tweed-hatted dude in overalls stands in the doorway, the sun flooding in behind him.

"Hey man, join the party!"

"Yeah, dance with us!"

"Fuck off oot of it! Go on get oot. Ah've got tae clean this place. Fuckin' bawheeds. OOT!"

*

We score some snacks from a terrified old lady in a grocer's shop. Macrae persuades her to sell us a couple of bottles of sparkling wine. Wentworth steals some Pepperamis.

Spicy sausage and cava for breakfast. Delicious.

We groove along the main street of the village. The houses sit snug in coats of white fur. The rising sun glows in our hearts. Macrae still has his top off. We drift through Kinlochleven in a mellow dream.

It's only when we're about to turn off the road up the track that takes the Way back into the hills when suddenly I realise that Jones isn't with us.

"Jones! Puss, where are you!?"

Everyone looks around – no sign.

My heart hammers at my ribs. Then suddenly he pops out of the woods in front of us.

"There you are!"

"I see our General has met himself a lady," smiles Macrae.

"You think?"

"Oh yeah, look. The boy's in love."

Maybe it's the drugs still flowing round my system or the cava bubbles popping in my brain, but my cat does indeed appear lovelorn. There's a heaviness in his normally graceful tread and he keeps looking back over his shoulder at the trees.

But reluctant though he seems, he walks with us, and together we rise through the snowy forest.

After a mile or so we pop out of the woods into an exposed glen. It's heart-flippingly beautiful. High hills shoot up on both sides. With their immaculate white torsos and jet-black ravines they look dressed for dinner. But the deeper snow is hard going and it's lucky for us that the path joins a Land Rover track – a vehicle has cut a pair of miniature canyons through the drifts. We walk along, girls in the right hand track, boys in the left, the sun scattering diamonds on the snow between us.

The speakers attached to my rucksack are laying down a very mellow Dusty Springfield vibe. We rise through the glen in harmony.

George is paired with Gertrud. I've never seen his cheeks so rosy.

"I can't believe we haven't slept," he says, "and yet I still feel marvellous."

"You look very well, also," she replies.

"From my previous research I would have expected some sort of come down cold turkey."

"Yes, but one gets such a biased view of these things in the media."

"Indeed, one truly does…"

Macrae is talking to Nina.

"It was a morning like this that I had my business idea," he says.

"You had a business idea?" she asks.

"A belter. Okay, you know if you have to leave a party and go home. Or if you're the only one left up and you've still got a buzz on?"

"Yeah…"

"It's kind of lonely."

"Of course."

"Well, my idea helps with that. It's an online chatroom, right, but it's only for people who're on drugs."

"Wow."

"I know. I've got the name and everything 'www.imfuckingmashed.com'."

"Very memorable."

"Which is important, given our target audience. There's gonna be different rooms for different drugs so the speed freaks don't upset the stoners. And we could get Pot Noodle to advertise on it."

"You're such a clever bunny."

"Takes one to know one."

As for me and Tess, well.

We're not talking.

Not because we've fallen out, or we're too spaced or anything.

It's because we're beyond words.

Why do I need to hear her voice when I can feel her soft hand? When I can smell her sweet hair as she steps into my track and nestles into my shoulder. Taste her kisses. See her once wild eyes now smiling up at me - peaceful. Calm.

Tame.

I swear, I can almost feel her purring.

And there's something about her sensual submission that makes me finally feel like I'm in control of the world. Together we create a forcefield, a bulletproof bubble where nothing can touch or hurt us. It's eternal summertime for us despite the snow. We cannot feel the cold of winters past or future, just the everlasting warmth of the present...

And then-

-the music stops.

The suddenness of it startles me. I hear our bubble pop and the outside world come rushing in. I shiver. A sudden cloud scuds over the sun.

Everyone stops on the track and turns to me.

"Must be the battery," I shrug.

"Do you have a spare?" asks George.

I shake my head.

And as I do, something comes loose deep in my brain. A catch on a door to something that sits the darkness. Something that has always been there and now wants to come out. I don't know what it is, and I don't want to. I slam the door shut and turn to Tess.

"Nevermind," I say, "I'll sing!"

And I launch into the cut-short chorus.

But, although I can hold a tune, I'm no Dusty. My voice is lost in the huge wilds of the glen. And I can see the roses in George's cheeks grow dull.

I stop singing, and we walk on in silence.

★

The music may have stopped, but at least Tess is still by my side. Hand in hand we follow the rising path for an hour. In my other hand is a bottle of cava which I pass in turn to our lips.

The track levels then drops away. We pause at this crest, the watershed of the glen, for a breather. Ahead of us, a near mirror image of the glen we have just walked stretches away. The path wobbles along the flanks of the hills, before swinging round a far corner out of sight.

I lift the wine bottle to Tess's mouth.

"It is empty," she says.

"Hey mate," I say to Macrae, "dig out another bottle will you?" I say.

We take in the view as Macrae rummages in his pack.

An ancient stone farmhouse sits just off to the side of the path. The far wall is still intact, but the roof and most of the other walls have fallen into the central space. A few sheep stand dozily around the ruin.

Nina is staring at it, her mouth slightly open. There's a feeling in the air I don't like. Something about the tumbledown hut that seems to drain the energy from the air between us.

Tess's hand drops from mine and she walks over to join her friend by the old house. She runs her fingers over the moss of the fallen walls, like she's in a trance.

"The only house in this whole glen," Tess muses out loud. "I wonder who built it? Who brought the stones all the way here? Cut them. Shaped them. Stacked them. Finished it and stood back proudly. You think if he knew that his house would end up like this he would have bothered?"

There's a sadness in her voice that I don't like the sound of.

"It's a nice spot, though," I say. "So quiet and–"

Suddenly, as if on cue, my words are obliterated by the roar of a helicopter. It rips into existence over the watershed and clatters low overhead, its twin rotors whumping the air.

We stare up as it passes, cowed and fearful like little creatures watching an eagle. In the corner of my vision I notice Macrae ducking into the farmhouse doorway.

"Who is flying that horrible noisy thing here?" asks Tess when the helicopter passes, banking through the glen towards Fort William.

"Mountain Rescue," I say. "Probably on a training exercise."

"I don't know," says Wentworth. "There were some odd-looking fellows in uniform inside it."

"What do you think, Macrae?" I ask.

Macrae looks at the ground and shrugs.

"Didn't really see it," he says.

I swallow. My throat is dry.

No one seems to be looking anyone else in the eye.

The door in the back of my brain rattles menacingly.

"Hey mate," I say, "what happened to that fizz?"

"None left," says Macrae. And he slings his rucksack back on and leads the way to the tracks of the Land Rover, fresh-cut in the pristine snow.

He looks tired.

I reach for Tess's hand. She lets me take it. But her flesh feels odd against mine. The warm tingle of before is gone.

I let her fingers drop.

★

We round the corner of the hill and the Land Rover track parts from the Way which rises into some woods. The going is easier here – the densely packed trees have sheltered much of the ground from the snow.

Moss verges the path, soft and green. Beneath the trees, brown earth is fragrant with needles. On the upper branches and in the clearings a little snow creates a white counterpart to the moss.

Thick silence has settled on everything.

"Hey girls," I say. "Looks like we found Narnia after all!"

They nod at me, but there's no softness in their smiles. And the door in the darkness rattles again.

The path winds and falls deeper into the sleepy wood. Every step seems to take us deeper into some kind of trance. In the thin gap the path cuts on the horizon, I see a sliver of a vast snowy mountain, its head and shoulders sulking in a hood of mist.

I turn to the girls.

"Come here," I say, and I lead them to a rise in the path, where it's easier to see the hill.

"Look!" I say. "Ben Nevis. Highest mountain in the country." I point to an area in the middle of the mountain. "You see that tiny line, zigzagging up beside that stream? That's the path. This time tomorrow, you'll be up there."

Gertrud flicks her eyes at Tess.

"But–" she starts.

And that single syllable rattles the door like a road-drill.

"What?" I ask.

"We are getting the train back to Glasgow tonight. Tomorrow we fly home to Sweden."

BANG BANG BANG

"But we have to climb the Ben!" I say. "It's the climax of the Way!"

I turn to Tess.

"You're not going with them?" I ask.

"Oh no," she smiles. "But I must press on further north. I have to hitchhike up Loch Ness then through Sutherland to Thurso. From there I will head onto Orkney and Shetland. Then I will take a ferry to the Faroe islands before finally sailing to Iceland and the Reykjavik Dance Festival where 'Fly Eagle Sing Eagle Fuck Eagle' is booked to make its international debut."

The banging is so loud I can barely think. It takes every ounce of my will to shut it in and spread a thin smile on my face and say:

"What are we talking about this now for? We still have plenty of walking to do." I laugh. "Don't you know that time stands still in Narnia!?"

And my words have barely hit the air when I look around and see that–

–the woods have gone.

One moment we are cloaked in the order of nature. Then we turn a corner, and raw destruction screams at us.

"They chopped the forest down," whispers Nina.

She's right. Rotting stumps pepper the snowscape. Lopped branches, stripped of bark, lie around us like discarded bones. They're unmistakeable signs of violence and they give the glen the feel of a battlefield.

The path files quietly through the middle of the carnage and joins a road.

George sighs. "It was a plantation," he says. "A crop like any other."

I shiver.

And there's a final horrendous bang and the thing in darkness comes crashing out, like a truck through a shop window.

I can't ignore it. It's right in front of me. The ugly grey houses littering the bottom of the glen. The roof of the woollen mill and factory shop. The tarmac road just below us. The cars.

It's Fort William.

The end.

I suddenly realise that every step has only served to bring us to this point. And I don't want to take another.

"Captain Macrae."

Huh?

We turn.

Three enormous men and one sharp-faced woman in green uniforms are standing by the path on our right. They wear red berets and have 'MP' written on a tan flash on their arms.

The three men fan out in front of us. The woman, a sergeant, steps forward. She has piercing blue eyes. She lifts a pair of handcuffs up in front of those eyes.

"Come with us, sir," she says.

And Macrae holds out his wrists.

FROM WENTWORTH'S NOTEBOOK

The appearance of the military police was clearly expected by Alan. Head down, he stands quietly, like a 50s schoolboy caught with stolen apples.

It's more of a surprise to me, but after a few moments I can understand it: Alan is clearly absent without leave.

Tom, however, has been shocked into pale astonishment.

"What's going on?" he whispers, as the rather vicious-looking sergeant places her

handcuffs on Alan.

"They wouldn't give me leave," says Alan softly. "I had no choice."

Tom stares at him, eyes wild, bottom lip visibly quaking.

"Choice?" says Tom. "What are you talking about?"

Alan takes a breath. "When you texted me. I could tell you were in a right state and you weren't picking up your phone. I had to do something."

"You deserted the marines to take me on holiday?!"

"To get you laid," he corrects.

"That's why it took you nine months to get to me," mutters Tom. "You've been on the run."

Alan nods.

"But your career!?" cries Tom.

Alan lifts his head and looks across the glen to the high shoulders of Ben Nevis. He thinks for a second. Then he says:

"No more mud and blood and early mornings and marching and banging guns and kicking the shit out of people. Ah well," he smiles. "I suppose all good things must come to end."

"Now, sir," says the sergeant. "We have to go."

Tom looks like he's about to collapse.

"I can't believe you're going to jail for me," he says, voice cracking.

And what I have to do occurs to me in an instant.

"He's not going to jail," I say, stepping forward.

"Who are you?" snaps the sergeant.

"Captain Macrae's defence counsel."

"This is a military matter."

"On the contrary," I say. "A defendant is entitled to a civilian lawyer even in a military court. And," I add, turning to face Alan, "since I am no longer convinced that the ne-erdowells of Edinburgh should be my focus in life, I hereby offer to take your case. On a pro bono basis, of course." And I give him a little wink.

"Why, counsel," replies Alan, "I believe I will accept your kind offer."

"Jolly good," I say. "Then I find it necessary to point out to you, sergeant, that according to section 28 of the Police and Criminal Evidence Act 1984, you not allowed to handcuff any suspect until you have read him his rights."

The sergeant swallows.

217

"And as his counsel," I continue, "I have a right to know where you will be holding him until the Board of Inquiry."

The sergeant stares at me in fury, her jaw grinding.

"We're taking him back to Poole," says the man-mountain on her left.

"Ah, Dorset!" I say. "Home of Hardy and the pilgrims of palaeontology. Well, Alan, I doubt your friends here will have room for me in their gyroscopic device, so I shall hurry to town and take a cab on to Inverness and catch the first aeroplane to Bournemouth – where I shall meet you in the guardhouse, briefed and ready to do battle."

The sergeant snatches at Macrae's hands and pulls him away.

I turn to the others.

"Ladies," I say, "it has been a profound pleasure to walk with you. But now I must excuse myself. I'm sure you understand." I step forward and shake each of their hands in turn. When I get to Gertrud I kiss her softly on the cheek. "Tom will pass you my details. You must visit us at home."

"I will hold you to that," she says. "It has been a great pleasure to talk with you."

Whereupon she kisses me on the lips and causes me to blush.

I smile and bow to her once more. She smiles and bows in return and an odd surge of warmth in my intestines tells me that I have made a friend for life.

I turn to Tom. He looks so upset. So ill. I don't want to leave him. But I can't look after him all the time.

I pull my Moleskine notebook from my pocket. It is still rather damp from my little dip in the Blackwater. With my cuff I wipe the moisture from its leather and pass it to Tom.

"This is yours," I say. "Keep it safe and I'll see you back at the house in a few days to help you type it up."

And I have to give him one final hug, because I don't want him to see the lie of those words in my eyes.

FROM MACRAE'S NOTEBOOK

Those redcap pricks aren't as stupid as they look. I knew they were on to me soon as I saw that chopper go over. Maybe the cops got my mug from Tiso's security camera and clocked the AWOL bulletin or perhaps the hostie tipped off the Foreign Office. Hell, that dealer in Delhi could have sold me out.

Ah well. Fuck it. Had a good run.

Besides, George will get me off – he's already made this bitch sergeant brown her khakis and he shot off down towards town like a man who means business.

So it's not what's happening to me that's bugging me as they drag me towards the chopper it's just that I'm looking back at Fitch and the poor bastard looks so fucking lost.

Which is why I elbow the nearest redcap in the belly and run back towards him.

I seize his arm. Look up into his wide blue eyes.

"Tell her!" I hiss. "Tell her everything."

And I stuff my notebook into his hands and fling my arms round him one last time.

Then I jump over to Nina.

"As for you, gorgeous…"

And I kiss her beautiful plum mouth.

Which is the last thing I have a chance to do before a baton brings night crashing down on the whole world.

FROM FITCH'S DIARY

I'm standing on a road outside Fort William and my friends are gone.

What the hell happened?

I feel like gravity is failing. Any second I'm going to float clean off into space.

Tess is standing a few feet away with Nina and Gertrud.

"Grönt lys. Jag vill följa," she says quietly to them. They start to move away up the road. Tess walks back to me.

"I was thinking," I mumble. "Maybe I can come to Iceland with you–"

"Come over here," she says, and takes my hand. She leads me over the road and into a wood. We pace silently between black trunks then suddenly step out into a clearing.

Muddy slopes slide to a crashing, steel-grey river. Just to our right, a large flat rock slants down to lie half-in, half-out of the maelstrom. It reminds me of the one I was sitting on when we first met. But this river is too cold and wild to bathe in.

Tess points to the stone.

"Sit down," she says.

Wet grass sops my trouser legs as I walk across to take a seat on the rock.

Tess sits beside me. She looks very serious.

"There's something you must tell me," she says.

"I don't know what you-" I start.

"What did Alan mean when he said 'Tell her'?"

"Not much Alan says actually means anything-"

She holds up a hand to stop me.

"He gave up everything for you," she says. "It meant something. And now you will tell me what."

I stare at the tumbling water.

I don't want to tell her anything. But then I think about what Macrae has done, how much he has sacrificed, and though I don't know where they're coming from or where they're going, words begin to flow from me.

"It's ancient history, really. Seems silly to tell you."

"Go on."

"But, well, I used to go out with a girl. Judy."

"How long were you together?"

"A long time. Since university. Nine years, give or take. We were going to get married. I mean, we never really framed it in those words…"

The river clatters round our rock.

"…but I wanted to ask her. You know, do it properly. But it always seemed like something was in the way."

"So why did you split?"

"Well, Judy got pregnant – that's not why we broke up. God no. Her getting pregnant was brilliant. We were both up for it. Our parents were cool. It was all okay…"

"So what happened?"

I shrug.

"Nothing. There was no sign that anything was wrong during the pregnancy. Scans, weight, classes together, it was all hunky dory. It all went so fast we didn't get round to the whole marriage deal.

"And then the birth. Well, that was amazing. Twelve hours of screaming and astonishment and at the end of it, a little person. We called her Rowan. After the tree."

I smile at the memory.

"We took her home. And I can genuinely say, everything else aside, that evening was the happiest of my life. By a country mile. You could stack up all the mountains in this country and I would still have been higher. I floated over the whole world that day.

"But then, in the middle of that first night, Rowan got the hiccups. Or so we thought. We figured it was just something to do with us winding her wrong or something. The midwife was coming in the morning. We'd ask her.

"We were worried, but we just thought it was one of those little sounds they make, you know?

"In the morning, the midwife came and she was so friendly and nice, I can remember her face beaming in at the door. She came in to the flat and picked Rowan up to check her. Our little girl went all stiff. Her hand clenched. The midwife said she was having a fit. And that friendly face was so… transformed it was terrifying."

I take a breath and throw a stick into the river.

"From that moment on, it felt like I was swimming in a deep dark lake, with doctors, nurses, machines, tubes, wires all floating around me in the chill of the blackest depths.

"At some point a doctor took us to one side and said very clearly that Rowan had a rare infection. Group B Strep it was called, and it was caused by a bacteria picked up in the womb during labour. If the hospital had known Judy was carrying the bacteria, they could have given her antibiotics, but they don't normally test pregnant women for it and-"

I kick my foot against the rock we're on and look upstream.

"Well anyway, that didn't matter. What mattered was that Rowan couldn't breathe without a ventilator. We spent the next day with our girl, saying goodbye and then we held her as they switched off the machine. She was already unconscious and not in any pain. She just drifted away. Two days she was on this earth, then she was gone. Last September. In fact, that was one year ago this week."

I sigh.

"At first I wondered if Rowan was just a dream. But the reality of it all came soon enough. And Judy and me... well, whenever we looked at each other it was like the biggest glen in Scotland had opened up between us. A wilderness we couldn't cross. I was a teacher and for some reason I just couldn't face going in to school. I got a bit... confused and lost my job. Things got weird between us. I left Judy in our flat and I moved in with George. It was only meant to be temporary, till I felt a bit better. But life froze somehow and time kept passing, and now she's met someone else. And here I am saying goodbye to you. So I guess this is how the story ends."

I look up.

At first I think it must be raining. But then I realise that it's tears that are soaking her cheeks.

She throws her arms wide and dives towards me.

She squashes me against her in hug so tight I feel like I'm part of her.

Her body bucks in sobs. But I am strangely unmoved. I know what's coming.

After a long time she pulls away. Wipes her eyes. Says:

"About Iceland," she starts. "'Fly eagle...'" But she gets no further – the words choke in her throat.

"It is a solo show," I finish for her. "I understand-"

"No you don't!" she whispers, and she lunges forward and seizes my hands. I'm looking right into her tear-wet eyes. She goes on: "Listen to me now, because this is very important. At the start of this trip, 'Fly Eagle' was nothing more than a collection of moves. But now it will be a real ballet. With soul. And the reason... is you."

I blink.

"Tom," she says, "the way you care for your friends... the love you bring to the world... your creative spirit – you have been my wings! You have lifted me higher than I have been in a long, long time. And wherever I fly from now on, you will be there with me. I want you always, always to remember that."

She wipes her eyes again. Takes another breath.

"The reason you cannot come to Iceland is not because I don't want you with me." She rubs my hand with hers. "I would love to take you. It is because your journey is not over. You came on this walk seeking an answer and you have not yet found it. In your heart you know this."

Then Tess pulls back. Wipes her damp hair from in front of her beautiful brown eyes.

She stares at me for a year or so.

Finally she leans forward again. She hugs me hard, releases me and smiles.

"But you are so close," she whispers.

And she kisses me gently on the forehead and walks out of my life.

★

"Just you and me, then, Jones." I say, looking down at my final friend.

He sits halfway between me and a dense copse, his tiger-orange fur bold against the snow.

He stares at me for a second with that look of blank wisdom that cats are such masters of.

Then he turns his head and miaows over his shoulder at the trees.

For a second nothing happens.

Then another cat steps out of the forest. It looks a little like a large tabby, but it has wicked tufts on its ears and a bushy ringed tail. A wildcat.

Approaching very slowly, tail whipping from side to side and black eyes glaring at me, the wildcat eventually reaches Jones and sits beside him.

Jones turns to it and utters a short 'miaow'.

Reluctantly, the wildcat gets to its paws and edges a little further forward, as if presenting herself to me.

I drop to my knees.

"Pleased to meet you, miss," I say.

"MEERROOW!" replies the wildcat and, duty done, whirls round and skips back to a less intimate distance.

Now Jones walks forward and sits by my knee.

"She's very beautiful, Jones," I whisper to him. He slowly closes his eyes and purrs a little. I swear he looks proud.

"You'll be very happy together," I add. Then for some reason my throat clogs up a little and it's difficult for me to get these words out: "But I will miss you very, very much."

And it's so silly, but a tear rolls down my cheek and drops onto his fur.

He puts his paws on my thigh and butts me once on the chin with his nose. As if trying to kiss me.

"Goodbye my little puss-man," I say.

Then he turns and paces back to the wildcat. She rises as he approaches. They touch noses and the two of them walk away towards the copse.

I watch them all the way to the trees. They pause at the edge of the darkness and, for the briefest of moments, Jones pauses. He looks back. Then he lifts his paw to his ear in salute.

And now I laugh and the tears flow down my face like the river by my side.

When I clear my eyes they have gone. Or nearly – through the trees I think I see a pair of tails, one striped and the other orange, twining together.

Then Jones and his bride are gone forever into the hills.

★

The physical shock of being on my own is almost unbearable. My whole body is numb with it. I stare at the river for quite a while, thoughts running through my brain like the icy water at my feet.

It's over. The walk is finished. All my friends are gone.

Why is that so hard to believe? What did I think would happen? We'd keep walking forever? That I'd spend the rest of my life shagging a hot European girl in a tent? Of course I knew it had to finish. But it's the coldness of the ending that really hurts. The hot happiness of last night is so close it makes my solitude a million times worse. I can still remember the intoxicating warmth of the drugs. Can see Macrae's beaming face right in front of me. Feel Tess's flaming passion on my skin.

All so close and yet gone forever. Those sensations will fade from me now, like a mountain being covered by the new winter snow. I feel colder than I ever did in Wentworth's basement.

An icy wind whips the first flakes of a fresh snowfall at me. It's getting dark. Need to get some shelter. Through the trees I can see the faded grass rectangles of a campsite. I drag myself back to the road and head for the little bridge over the river.

As soon as I step in the reception cabin I recognise it as the campsite Judy and I stayed at when we bunked off uni all those years ago. I shake the snow from my Goretex and shiver at the irony.

The manager is preparing to close the site for the winter. This is the last week it's open. I ask to stay for the night. He looks at me like I'm crazy.

"You sure?" he asks. "There's a storm coming. Might get a wee bit blowy later."

"There isn't anywhere else," I say, and throw my money down.

Then I wander out of the cabin and search for a snow-free plot.

I pitch my tent and climb inside my sleeping bag. It's damp and my skin chills to its clammy touch.

The tent flap is still open and some snowflakes whirl inside, but I don't close the zip. For a while I just lie in my bag like a caterpillar, looking up through the open flap at the blank immensity of the hill opposite.

I wonder what Judy is up to right now? Probably lying in bed in our flat. I think of the thousands of nights we have lain together over the years. So many different places – college dorms, Italian villas, open dunes, and right here in this campsite, all those years ago. When we lay together back then the warmth between us seemed to create life of its own. The world was full of things, people, possibilities. It's like Wentworth said – there was treasure everywhere.

But now she's lying with someone else. Warming him as I lie here in a damp sleeping bag in the shadow of a snowy mountain.

It suddenly seems savagely unfair. Anger surges in my throat, hot as vomit. Why should he share her warmth? What has he done to deserve that? Why am I the lonely one? I bloody tried, didn't I? Do I really deserve this?

I feel like running out into the night and screaming at the unjustness of it all. I start to rip my clammy bag from my bones, insane rage pounding through my muscles-

And then I see it.

For a moment the snowfall ceases and the clouds part. Stars appear. Then the full moon rises over the shoulder of Nevis, splashing light like paint all over the vast snowfields. It also illuminates, as fragile as a vein under skin, a path winding into the snowy heavens. Up there, the moon seems to say. That's where you'll find your answers.

My anger subsides to a low boil in my belly.

I pull the zip on the tent flap down and shiver myself to sleep.

The walk isn't over. Yet.

DAY 7

BEN NEVIS

Summary:
- *Distance: 19km (12miles)*
- *Estimated Time: 7-9 hours*
- *Height Range: 4400ft ascent*
- *Terrain: The 'Tourist Route' curves up the flank of the hill from Achintee in Glen Nevis, steepening before it reaches the halfway lochan. The path then zigzags up the western shoulder before reaching the summit plateau. The route via Carn Mor Dearg is for more experienced walkers only, who are happy with scrambling and quite severe exposure.*
- *Accommodation: Glen Nevis, Fort William, Lochaber*

Description: The rounded bulk of Ben Nevis can seem almost placid at times, but please remember that this is Britain's highest – and one of its most deadly – mountains, and should be treated with respect. You can encounter snow and ice at any time of year, and walkers should take particular care on the summit plateau which is really just a broad ridge. Many good climbers have walked straight across towards the summit and fallen through the cornice into Five-Fingered Gully.

I'm climbing up a glacier. It's a beautiful blue-sky day. I step fast because I can see Judy at the top of the glacier, beside a ski restaurant. She's holding a drink and waving. I wave back and walk even faster.

But suddenly a crevasse opens in front of me, jagged and black. I teeter at the edge of its spinning depths. Judy is on the other side. A giant polar bear with six arms is beside her. He sneers at me. Judy cries for help.

I run to leap the crevasse. In two of his paws the bear holds a hosepipe. He sprays water at me as I leap. The water soaks me in the air, so cold my breath hardens in my lungs. I'm frozen all over, cocooned in ice.

Judy shouts in alarm but the bear just clouts her to the ground with a massive paw.

And I fall into the crevasse, which is now a screaming river, the fastest torrent on the planet. The bear sneers at me as I tumble helpless in my icy prison-

HUH?

I shudder awake. The sweat on my sleeping bag has frozen solid. My teeth clatter together with the cold. I tear the zip open and snatch for my clothes.

Outside my tent I stamp around to get warm, but it's hard – the temperature has plummeted overnight. Every dark tree is tagged with icy graffiti. The glen is still in shadow, but overhead the sky is clear blue with streaks of pre-dawn pink.

So much for the storm. Looks like a great day for a climb.

I fix myself a breakfast of Pasta 'n' Sauce which has somehow survived the journey. Then I pack my waterproofs, my phone and my journal into my rucksack and leave everything else in my tent.

The mountain looms above me. A sneer of determination contorts my lips as I stare up at its arrogant bulk and I swing my rucksack onto my shoulders.

I can't wait to get up there.

A little footbridge carries the path over the River Nevis, swollen to such violent proportions that the water shakes the bridge as I cross it.

I stalk straight up the side of the glen, passing a couple of pine plantations. After ten minutes, the path joins the tourist route from Fort William. The slope is fairly gentle and the track is well maintained – this is easy hillwalking and my pace is fast. Another k of this and the track kinks left into a gully and the gradient increases. The path is still good, with steps laid at the steep sections, but now I can see the hill's haunches extending high above me, the first indication of its true size.

I maintain my sharp pace up the steeper section, forcing my body to work, and it doesn't seem that long at all until I'm coasting over the lip of the gully. Now a lochan opens out in front of me, its iced surface calmly reflecting the stormless blue of the sky. The snow around it is thick and virgin.

Here I pause, blowing quite hard.

Ahead, the tourist route continues on up to the south. It's the way most people go, which is why it seems unappealing. But there's another path leading off past the lochan. That's my route.

Fifteen minutes later the track veers round to the right. Ahead, a steep-sided corrie is slowly opening out. A loud stream crashes down the middle, powered by thousands of spidery tributaries which pulse like veins down huge snowy slopes. The head of the corrie is hidden by the convex mass of the hillside I'm walking on, and as I edge round it feels like I'm entering the wings of some vast theatre set.

Soon the path drops down to the glen floor and crosses over the burn. I glance casually up and realise that I have stepped out onto centre stage.

Towering on my right, sudden as a car crash, massive cliffs rear up into the heavens. The head of the corrie is an almost sheer wall of brutal rock and ice, several thousand feet high. Twisted pinnacles spear themselves into existence between thundering gullies. Huge cornices hang over the precipice. Compared with the rounded slopes I've been on so far, this feels like a violation. It's as if some giant gouged the belly of the mountain away in a frenzy of madness. And here I am, tiny on the glen floor, staring at its savage guts.

Now I realise that the gentle dome presented to the tourist route is just a lure, drawing people to this place so the mountain can claim his fill.

I have to get up there.

There's still no sign of any storm. In fact, the sky is absolutely blue and the air calm. I turn away from the cliffs and track up the sharp slope in front of me.

Now I'm climbing into deeper snow, and the sweat starts to really pour. It smells unpleasantly stale and metallic. The excesses of the week are streaming from my pores. Tiredness drags at my legs like chains. A percussive thump swells my brain. I start to work out how much good sleep I've had recently and the answer makes my mind weary. I'm walking underwater as I trudge through the deepening snow.

And yet, despite the pain, it feels like every step is taking me closer to the top of the mountain. I grit my teeth and walk faster.

★

Eventually I haul myself onto the ridge. The view stops me dead.

Jagged peaks line the horizon. In the middle of them, like a commander amongst his guard, Nevis towers skywards. Connecting me with its heights is a sweeping ridge, its icy blade scything the landscape in two.

I'm still admiring the stark beauty of it all when the first gust of wind hits me. Oddly, it doesn't come from either of the corrie sides, like winds on ridges normally do, it slams straight into me from behind. I try to step forward, catch my foot on some ice and fall face first into the snow.

My heart clatters at my ribs – if I'd fallen sideways I'd have toppled into the glen. Shaking, I haul myself back to my feet. As I do, I glance backwards and my legs almost give way.

A surreal mass of purple and black cloud is rolling in from the north. It boils straight towards me as if from a huge nozzle. My brain is numb, but my sinews twitch – they know I have to move. I struggle to my feet and scramble on.

Wind cuffs me along the ridge like a cat with a mouse. Ahead, the route curves out to the left then back and up to join the giant shoulder of Nevis. Where it starts to rise the arête becomes impossibly thin. There doesn't seem to be room for a single foot to stand.

I pull my gloves on tighter and start along the razor's edge.

Which is when the sun goes out and the storm hits me like a truck.

Screaming wind. Black clouds. Bullet hail.

I can't open my eyes let alone see my hand in front of my face. I put my sunglasses on; the wind tears them off.

But I will climb this bloody hill.

Feet angled and fingertips touching the ground like a sprinter in his blocks, I inch my way up the arête. Every step is bought at the cost of huge amounts of energy. Each movement opens another access point in my clothing for the spearing wind to stab at my skin.

How far to go? I lift my head – the wind pummels my chest and threatens to snatch me into the air. I crouch even lower, virtually lying on the snow. Somehow I crane my neck sideways and shield my eyes with a hand. Through the hail I can just see the line of the ridge curving ahead of me. It rises steeply then flattens – the summit plateau.

I drop my hand onto a lump of icy rock and haul myself on another foot.

Years of crawling take me up the ridge. The climb is unrelenting. My limbs are seizing in the overwhelming cold. Each step takes twice the effort of the last one.

Then, just when I feel like I will be frozen to the rock itself, I feel the gradient change. The slope lessens, the ridge broadens under my fingers, and with a wracking effort I heave myself up onto the summit plateau of Nevis.

Which is when the wind really starts to blow.

It is like nothing I have ever felt. It's not like a wall because I can tell it isn't solid. But it is utterly unstoppable. I can image what it would be like to be on the event horizon of a black hole, to be ripped apart by a force infinitely stronger than me.

I cannot move. Nor can I see. The mountain has totally disappeared. No sensations are returning from my limbs. Nothing is solid. Up and down are irrelevant.

I have never felt so cold. So powerless. So alone.

And then the anger boils within me again. Fury born of savage unfairness burns every nerve and muscle. All my human strength distills into one poisoned second of rage.

I leap to my feet amid the fury of the storm.

"WHY?!" I yell my question into the teeth of the gale. "WWWWHHHHYYYY???!!!!!"

Then, the strangest thing.

For one pure, calm second the air clears and through the eye of the storm I see the summit cairn itself – perfect, sunlit, and so close I can almost touch it.

Then with a hideous crack the cornice I'm on gives way and I tumble and all I can see is a thousand feet of rock and howling gullies.

★

There's no pain at first. Just appalling violence and the occasional crunch.

Perhaps I throw my arms out to stop myself, perhaps my tumbling makes them fly. That could be a rock coming towards me, I could be falling away from it.

What does it matter?

★

After a century, the wildness ceases.

The snow is still falling, and the wind still blowing, but the rocks have stopped whirling.

I shake my head and try to focus on something. After a minute, some shapes start to coalesce.

Rocks. Surrounding me on three sides. On the fourth, an ocean of white stretches into infinity. I'm on a ledge at the bottom of a stone chimney. I try to look higher up to see where I've come from, but there's a curious crunching noise when I do that, so I stop. Looking down is okay, and I can see I'm in a sort of sitting position, with one leg tucked under me in an odd way. I try to get up, but the leg that's tucked under won't obey. If I push too hard with the other one I'm going to topple over, so I remain seated. My rucksack has landed a few feet from me, its contents spewed out. My phone lies just in front of me face up on the snow. Some blood – my blood, of course – is pattered all around me like rose petals on the snow.

Clearly I'm incredibly lucky to be here.

But that's not what stuns me. The most amazing thing here is the silence. Whether it's because the chimney cuts out the scream of the storm or because there's something very wrong with my ears, I can't tell. All I know is that a heavy quiet has settled on me, as deep as a quilt.

I stare out into the void and my soul is totally calm. I no longer feel the cold, because I am almost a part of it. Letting it take me completely now will not be giving in; it will be sweet release. My face cracks into a smile. So this is how I'm going to go. Ah well, I think, there are worse ways.

My head sags onto my chest, pressing the breath from my lungs.

Then I notice my blood. Because those hot red petals are soaking through the snow. And rather than finish me off, the sight thrills me with life.

I laugh out loud. Every cell of my body jolts with electricity. If my legs worked I would leap in the air and yell my joy to the world.

At last I understand.

I have my answer.

MY BLOOD IS MELTING THE SNOW!

I have to tell Judy what this means. I reach out for my phone, but there's something not right with my arms. They're moving clumsily, like I'm operating one of those remote grab machines at the fair. It takes me three attempts just to pick it up.

And now I can't press the buttons. My fingers seem to belong to someone else. I prod at the keypad. Has that worked? I put the phone to my ear, but the silence is so deep now it makes my head swim. The rocks fade and swirl. The snowflakes become feathers that fill the air around me as I tumble backwards into the endless clouds.

And then I see her.

Floating towards me out of the storm, dressed in white, smiling, with the light in her eyes burning like it did when we first met.

Judy.

She opens her arms and I sink into her warm embrace.

*

h

e

H

e

r

e

233

HERE!

I look up into her face again.

But she's gone. She's turned into a bearded man with goggles, Goretex round his face like a cowl. The saint of the mountain.

"Come on, he's over here!" yells the saint.

More saints fan out round him. Is this heaven?

"Jesus what a mess."

"Alive?"

"No, he's gone."

"Shit."

"Wait, I got shallow breathing."

"Quick, get the stretcher."

"Stay with us, pal, we're going to get you out of here."

"What's that? I think he's trying to say something."

"J... u... d... y..."

★

They put me in a machine and I do my fall in reverse. Spinning and lurching through the wildness.

Ah, a helicopter.

★

Lots of people running and shouting. Doctors and nurses and suchlike. They seem quite agitated. Which is odd, because I feel so calm. In fact, the calmer I get, the more agitated they become.

They really are the oddest people...

★

Talking of odd people, have you seen the state of this nurse?

She's wearing a uniform and everything. But she has dragon wings. And she's pudgy like George. She is George.

Oh boy. Here's another one. Oo, she's awfully hairy and not very pretty – shit, no wonder, she's Macrae! What's he doing as a nurse? His marine mates are going to piss themselves when they find that out.

Now here comes a doctor – except it's actually Tess. She looks very stern. That's not like her.

"Mr Fitch," she starts. And now I see she's not Tess at all, but a doctor after all. How confusing.

"You've been transferred to the Edinburgh Royal Infirmary," she says. "You have broken both your legs and one of your arms."

"Oh dear."

"Also your cheekbone, your jaw and your shoulder blade."

"Right."

"And you lost your little toes to frostbite."

"Ah."

"But we did save your fingers."

"Excellent."

★

And now here's a surgeon. Watching me at my bedside. Except it's not a real surgeon, it's Judy, dressed as one. I wish people would make up their minds what they want to be.

"Look, I'm getting a bit sick of this–" I start.

"You want me to go away?" says a honey voice.

Shit, it really is Judy.

"Are you real?"

"Yes."

And I see the smile in her eyes and it's like swimming back to the surface after a dive.

I try to sit forwards to be closer to her.

"Relax," she soothes, and lays a hand on me. I look down. Her fingers rest on a mass of white plaster.

"What are you doing here?" I ask.

"You called me."

"Did I?"

"At first all I could hear was this terrible wind. A really howling gale. And then you started – not talking, just this awful groaning, like you were… it was horrible, Tom." She looks down and her hair flops forward. "So I called mountain rescue. They located you by your phone signal."

I sit back on my pillows.

"You saved me," I say.

She looks away.

"I did what anyone would do," she says.

I don't know if it's the light in this little room or something to do with my injuries, but there's a strange look about Judy. She's here with me, but it's also like she's not. Like part of her spirit is hovering half a step away from her body.

The silence between us makes it so much more obvious. I have to say something.

"I hear my tap dancing career is over," I smile.

She smiles in return, but not because she thinks it's funny. Because she wants to make things easier on me.

"Sh," she says. "Save your strength."

"I want to talk to you."

"Not now."

"About us."

"Please rest."

"When Rowan died–" I start.

"Oh Tom!" she gasps, jerking back like I pulled out a pistol and shot her.

But I have to go on:

"Judy, we need to talk about this."

"No!" she cries.

I lift my head and look at her.

"What's the matter?" I ask.

She's blinking in that really fast way that she does when she's upset, and for a second I think she's going to explode in anger. Then she takes a deep breath, like she's drawing all her feelings into a big pot inside her. Then, the lid on the pot, she breathes out and says:

"Tom, you've been on a journey–"

"Yes I have," I interrupt, "and it's brought me to you!"

"-and I'm happy for you," she goes on, "I really am. I'm sure it all makes sense to you now, but…"

"What?"

She sighs. Looks up to the big window.

"I'm just the same as when you left," she says.

"What do you mean?"

She looks around the room for a while. Finally she lifts her eyes back to mine. They are moist.

"You're going to be in here for a long time," she says. "First let's concentrate on getting you well, okay?"

"And then we'll talk?"

"And then we'll see," she says. And she pats me on the leg and turns away towards the door.

"You going to visit?" I ask.

"Of course," she nods. Then adds in a quieter voice: "As often as I can."

She walks to the door and as she leaves her hovering spirit hangs just behind her in the room. It shines hazily for a moment, like it's trying to say something, then it finally disappears after its mistress.

And I am alone again.

PROGRAMME OF RECUPERATIVE EXERCISES
FOR THOMAS FITCH

<u>Month 1</u>
1 set, twice a day:
5 toe raises
5 finger curls
Head leans – 5 each side
Neck turns – 5 each side

<u>Month 2</u>
1 set, twice a day:

Wrist & ankle rotation – 10 times each
10 shoulder shrugs
Gentle waist bends – 5 each side
Number of sets may increase later in the month.

Month 3
2 sets, twice a day:
10 knee flexes
10 arm raises
Sit forward and back 5 times

Month 4
2 sets, 3 times a day:
Walking round hospital on crutches
10 slow squats
5 leg lifts

Month 5
2 sets, 3 times a day:
Walking without crutches
10 crunchies
10 press ups
Number of sets may increase later in the month.

Month 6
Return to normal exercise where possible.

FROM FITCH'S DIARY

The Edinburgh Royal Infirmary is a big new hospital. I'm in my own en-suite room. I suppose this is a good thing – there's space to fit lots of equipment around me and it is very private. But there's something soulless about the isolation. It's like being ill in a Travelodge.

The hours in here stretch on and on. I can call a nurse for attention, but they only come if there's something to be changed or swallowed or checked. They won't just pop by for a chat.

From my window I can see a large oak tree that stands on a nearby hill.

Day after day, I watch the leaves fall from its branches as my body inches towards recovery.

★

Judy visits, but not regularly. Think she has trouble getting away from work. It's wonderful to see her. Even if she is still in that weird shadow.

I don't raise the subject of… well, of us again. It's a kind of an unspoken rule. As long as I'm in here we talk about other stuff. The weather, films, what's happening with her job. Everything that doesn't mean anything.

When I get out, then we can discuss what we want. But until that day it's the other stuff.

And that's what's so hard. Nurses fill me with drugs to counter the pain of my broken body. But lying here for day after endless day with hope white-hot like a rivet in my heart…

…there's nothing anyone can do to ease that agony.

★

Halfway through my second week of toe raises, I get another visitor.

My door opens and a neat head of blonde hair peers round it.

"George!" I cry. "How the hell are you?"

"Good," he smiles.

"You look great," I say. And mean it.

He has lost weight. Got some new clothes. Gelled his hair. There's a calmness and a confidence about him that I haven't seen before. The ivory paleness of his cheeks has been replaced by a rosy flush. He looks grown up and yet younger at the same time. The man he was always meant to be.

"I wanted to apologise for two things. Firstly, I'm sorry for being such a hideous shit to you all those years-"

I open my mouth to protest. He holds a hand up.

"It's not negotiable, Tom," he smiles. "I was awful, and that's that. I hope I've seen the light, but only time will be able to tell. Meanwhile, apology number two – I'm sorry I haven't been able to visit you earlier," he says, laying a small wicker hamper of fine foods on my bedside table. "But Alan's case went to court martial."

I sit forward.

"How'd he get on?"

"He picked a bad time. There's lot of deserting going on at the moment. The marines wanted to make an example of him. Being an officer and whatnot. Prosecution wanted ten years."

"Oh my God!" I say.

He smiles.

"I got them down to six months."

"Well done," I say. "I'd shake your hand, but…" I nod at my casts. I add: "So, you going to do a bit more of this kind of work?"

He shakes his head.

"It was good to help Alan," he says, "but law doesn't really interest me any more. I think I'm going to try my hand at DJing."

"What?!"

"Yes, it's the oddest thing. I was walking along Broughton Street the other evening and I suddenly felt thirsty, so I popped into this little basement bar for a shandy. Everyone in there was terrifically friendly and I ended up staying for a couple more drinks. There was this charming Spanish fellow working behind the bar and when the pub closed he took me to this club he knew – belonged to some chap called CC. You know it?"

"Heard of it," I smile, thinking of Edinburgh's most famous gay bar.

"Well," he goes on, "they played the most wonderful music and Fangio – that's his name – was friends with all the DJ and he showed me how to mix the tracks together and it was ever so much fun and everyone said I was a natural so I was thinking I might try that for a while…"

He tails off, blonde head bowed, and eyes looking shyly up at me as if for approval.

"George," I smile, "you're going to be a brilliant DJ."

★

My oak tree is completely naked.

Christmas is here and my best present is the removal of my casts. But I'm still full of pins and plates and other chunks of hardware.

Judy doesn't make it in until New Year.

When she does come, she looks weary.

"Hey," she says, walking across the room. "You look better."

And she sits on the chair. Normally she sits on the bed beside me.

"You look tired," I reply.

She nods slowly.

"Been working a lot," she says, looking at her feet. "But I got you a Christmas present." And she bends down, pulls out a wrapped parcel from her bag and hands it to me.

I open it to reveal a book.

"'The Complete Guide to Scottish Hillwalking.'" I read. "Wow. Right. Thanks."

"I thought it might help keep you occupied. You know, maybe planning your next trip." Then she sighs. "I might not be able to visit as regularly now," she continues. "Work looks like it's going to go crazy for a while."

"So come at the weekend," I say.

"I might have to work then too."

There's a shard of something in her eyes that makes me shiver. I hurry to move the conversation on.

"Whenever you can manage," I say. "It's just good to see you."

★

January and February slink by in a grey slop of slush and rain. The surgeons gradually fish out the various artificial bits and pieces that they put in me. They leave one plate in my left arm, I suppose as a kind of memento. It feels oddly heavy and I wonder if I'm going to have fun the next time I go through airport

241

security.

I'm starting to look more like a human again, and not some sort of science experiment. I suppose I should be feeling better. But seeing less of Judy really makes the weeks stretch.

March in particular is bad. I can get around pretty well now and it's getting much lighter at nights. Sitting on my own day after day is unbearable.

I ask my doctor how much longer I'm going to be in here.

"A while yet," she says. "End of the month at least. You're still a sick man."

She leaves with a smile but I curse her behind her back.

★

Sometimes I try to read the book Judy gave me. But I've had my fill of walking for now and I always lay it down after no more than a page.

I begin to watch my oak tree very intently. After a few weeks of daily consideration I become attuned to every nuance of its appearance. I realise that a tree doesn't just lose its leaves and grow them again. It's a constant process of development, the bark crinkling and changing colour.

Like skin does with time.

★

Mid March and it's been more like three weeks since Judy was here last. I'm desperate to know what she's been doing. I'm so intent to see her again that I rehearse what I'm going to do when I get out of here.

The doctor said the end of month, so I start to build towards the 31st. I make a plan in my head: I'll get George to come and pick me up. Then we'll drive home and get changed. Then I'll borrow George's car and go and pick up Judy. I'll take her somewhere special.

And we'll talk.

Properly.

On the 31st. It will be perfect.

So I'm pretty surprised when, on the 27th, out of the blue, the doctor comes in and pronounces me fit.

"What do you mean?" I ask.

"You can leave today," she says.

"I thought you were discharging me at the end of the month," I say.

"It's nice to surprise people," smiles the doctor. "Good luck," she adds with a wink.

She leaves.

I look out at my oak tree and I don't know whether it's the tree itself or the way the light is falling on it, but the bark is looking less black than before.

More browny-green.

I pick up my phone and dial.

"George? Get me the hell out of here."

★

George drives me home in style in his old Daimler.

The city seems alien after my six-month absence, the people somehow unreal. Where are they all going in such a rush?

We arrive back at Great King Street and I step out onto the pavement. With all that time in the bandages and the constant warmth of the hospital, my senses have missed a whole season. The spring air feels like champagne on my skin.

I start down to the basement.

"Where you going?" asks George. "This way." And he walks up the broad sandstone steps that lead to the main entrance. I stare, amazed, as he turns a freshly polished brass knob and throws open the huge white door.

I follow him into a magnificent hallway. Doors open off left and right. A grand staircase curls upwards, lit from above by a heavenly shaft of sunlight.

"Oh George," I say.

He grins.

"Wait till you see your room," he says, and heads for the stairs. We ascend past paintings of proud-looking old men from centuries past. Each picture has a title card bearing some form of the name Wentworth. George sings and pokes a few of them on the nose as he passes.

He leads me across a landing and opens a door towards the back of the house. I stare into a newly decorated room with views north over the sea to Fife.

Impeccably chosen antiques stand beside bright modern paintings. Bookshelves fill one wall.

"You like it?"

"It's wonderful," I say.

"There's something else I want you to see," he says, and walks out and across the landing. I follow him into a grand old drawing room which occupies the whole front of the house and boasts three floor-to-ceiling windows, a marble fireplace and a huge chandelier. DJ decks sit on the hearth and either side of the fireplace columns are the biggest speaker towers I have ever seen.

But the most striking thing about the room isn't the furnishings or the sound system, it's the blonde-haired and very handsome man cabling up the decks.

"This is Fangio," says George, "The chap I was telling you about. From the pub."

Fangio moves across the room like a young lion.

"Fangio, this is my good friend Tom."

"Pleased to meet you," I say.

"No no no, the pleasure it is all mine," says Fangio, passionately grasping my hand. "I cannot thank you enough."

"What for?"

"If it hadn't been for you, I would never have met this wonderful man."

They both smile at each other then look sheepishly at me.

I point to the sound system.

"That's going to give the New Town Preservation Society something to think about," I say, and I smile back, so happy for them.

"We're having some friends round tonight," says George. "Perhaps you would like to join us? Celebrate your new freedom." And he reaches for a magnum of Moët which sits in an ice bucket.

"I would love to, gentlemen," I reply, "but I have a date that I've been waiting six months to keep. I was hoping to borrow your car, George."

"Perhaps you could both drop round later," he suggests, handing me his keys.

"Perhaps," I smile, and take them.

★

The flat Judy and I shared is in a modern development on a corner of Craiglockhart hill. There are trees and space here, and the view over the city is nice.

For a long while I sit in the Daimler, looking up the neat tarmac path that leads to the ground floor front door.

I get out of the car. Above me, the boughs of an old horse chestnut tree sway and heave in the rising wind. I walk as forcefully as I can up the path, but my legs are still weak and my knees wobble in a less than impressive way.

I reach her front door and am about to press the buzzer when, above the sighing of the trees, I hear raised voices. They're coming from a far room in the flat, but the sound of them is clear. A man and a woman are disagreeing. Loudly.

I reach for the buzzer and again my finger hovers short.

What am I actually doing here? Should I have called? What if this new guy answers the door?

This is pointless. I turn and walk back to the car. Soon as I get to the Daimler I grab its roof to steady myself. Then I open the car door and get in. I look back up the path for the last time.

The plain little door could be a castle portcullis.

I sigh and put the key in the ignition.

Then the wind blows the horse chestnut branches and again I hear them creak. For a long, long moment I just sit there, listening to the noise of the wood.

Then I get out of the car and walk hard back up the path. I can hear the voices again through the door. Even angrier than before.

I dig my finger into the buzzer, holding it there for a long time. Like the doctor said, it's good to surprise people.

When I let go, the voices have stopped. For a second there's total silence. Then I hear the clip-clop of hard-soled shoes on laminate and the front door flies open and she's standing there.

"Yes?" she barks. Then she sees it's me. "Tom!" she gasps. Tears streak her face. She swipes a hand at her cheeks. Spreads the moisture over their redness. "What are you doing here?"

I suppress an urge to reach out and wipe the tears from her cheeks.

"You said we'd talk," I say quietly.

She looks over her shoulder. A shadow passes through the hall. A man's shadow.

"This isn't a good time-" she starts, and pulls the door a little more closed behind her.

"There never will be a good time," I say. "And what I have to say won't take long."

She opens her mouth to speak. I silence her with a single raised finger and say:

"Judy, what happened to us was more terrible than we realise. Death came into our lives when we least expected it. Clamped a vast, icy hand over our whole world. Froze us so solid we couldn't even talk to each other. We drifted apart like icebergs in the night.

"And since Rowan was taken, I've done nothing but search, trying to find a reason for death coming. I looked in Wentworth's basement... I tried to find it on the walk... nothing came. And then, lying in a gully two thousand feet up, broken and bleeding and one breath from death myself, I suddenly realised... the cold is natural. You can rage against it all you like, but you can't tell the sky not to snow on the mountain. You just have to remember that spring will come again. One day the snow will melt. And so the journey never ends."

I look up at the budding chestnut and take a breath.

"Judy, I'm going to buy a little tree," I say. "I'm going to drive north and plant it. Somewhere sheltered where it can grow in peace. Then I'm going to say some words, come back home and start enjoying spring."

And I look at her.

"That's it," I add, "told you it wouldn't take long."

A rough male voice from the other side of the door says:

"Who are you talking to, Judith?"

She drops her head and that unruly lock of hair flops forward, casting her face into shadow.

"Tom," she whispers, "I really can't-"

I nod.

"Goodbye, Judy," I say, and turn towards the car.

I hear the door close completely as I walk down the path.

It's a few minutes before my eyes are clear enough to drive.

A fabulous party is in full swing back at the house. George is doing a great job of laying down the tunes. Fangio is dancing on an ottoman to the delight of a selection of very cool-looking men and a few women. Champagne buckets and trays of nibbles fill every polished walnut surface.

All this joy in the house makes it even more magnificent. And part of me is so happy for George. But I simply can't be around this much cheerfulness right now. I don't fit in here any more.

Despite my friend and all he's done for me, I know I will never spend another night here.

I walk into my beautiful room and get my tent.

★

The tree I bought from the garden centre lies on the passenger seat beside me, its pot in the footwell, its young branches leaning against the headrest. It looks like the world's skinniest hitchhiker.

The drive north passes in a dull blink, like an afternoon on co-proxamol. It's funny – the route that the boys and I spent a whole week walking I drive in a couple of hours.

I return to the same campsite I stayed at before my accident. The manager is only just opening it for the year. He seems pleased to see me.

The beautiful old car looks out of place on the muddy grass of the campsite, but I rather like its oddness.

I pitch my tent, crawl into my sleeping bag and lie like a grub once more, looking out at the glen.

The highlands are very different to the last time I was here. The snow has gone from everywhere but the very tops of the highest hills. There may be no leaves on the trees, but the buds are swelling. And there's a colour to the light that says a warmer season is just one high pressure away.

I am on my own amid the beauty of the hills.

But I don't feel alone.

I take out my notebook and write down my last rhymes.

*

I'm up with the sun at half past six. I fry some sausages and make some coffee.

Then I walk over to the Daimler and gently remove the tree. It stands neatly on the muddy grass in its pot. Now I get out my rucksack and open it up. I try to hold the top of this open while I insert the tree's pot. But the nylon keeps flopping closed at the crucial moment.

I curse and throw the rucksack to the ground.

"You want a hand with that?"

I whip my head up.

She's standing there, right above me, and the light behind her eyes is burning like June's glorious sun. I'm going blind with the power of it, but I can't stop staring. I stare and stare and stare.

"Well," says at last Judy, "do you?"

I drop my eyes to the ground.

"I have to ask," I say. "Do you love him?"

And I raise my head, hope screaming from my every pore.

She sighs. Then she looks around the campsite.

"We came here once before, didn't we?" she asks.

"Our first camping trip," I say. "Bunked off a mediaeval history seminar and hitched north."

"I couldn't believe anyone would be so irresponsible," she says.

"And I couldn't believe I'd found a girl who actually liked sitting in tents in the rain," I say.

She smiles.

"Makes you feel so cosy," she says. "So close."

I nod.

"Hold the rucksack open," I say. "I'll lower the tree in."

We get it in first time.

*

We walk out of the campsite and start up the glen. The tree is surprisingly heavy, and it's awkward the way it sticks out of the top of my rucksack.

"You okay walking with that?" Judy asks.

"I could tap dance with it," I reply.

She smiles and we walk on.

"Where you thinking?" she asks after a while. "Up by the waterfall at the end of the glen?"

"Yeah," I say. "As long as we're up beyond the plantation. We don't want them chopping it down in a few years."

She nods. And when the road reaches the car park at the far end of the glen we branch to the right and take the narrow track that leads up the side of the rocky ravine.

The heavy stream crashes over rocks and into dark pools beside us. It's wildly beautiful, but none of the places we walk through are quite right. They're either too rocky or too exposed.

After an hour of hard climbing we sit down to rest. The view of the Aonach hills opposite is stunning, but I'm too exhausted to enjoy the sight. Sweat pours down my face and spots zip in front of my eyes.

"Maybe we should go back down," Judy says. "Find somewhere on the glen floor..."

And then I see it.

"There!" I say, and jump to my feet and lead the way laterally across the hillside.

It's a smaller ravine, whose stream joins the main one further down. There's a rocky waterfall, maybe ten feet high. After this gentle cascade, the water flows calmly through a small pool dotted with moss-heavy stones. The heathery banks are flat here for a few feet before they rise up more steeply to protect the little pool from the winds.

It's clearly a good spot, because two rowan trees have already set up home here.

Judy nods at them.

"They'll keep an eye on her," she says.

★

I put my rucksack down and gently remove the sapling, still in its pot, and place it upright on the ground. Then I take the trowel I brought from the side pocket. Judy holds the tree steady as I start to dig.

It's slower going than I thought it would be. After a while I sit back and wipe the sweat from my forehead.

Judy drops to her haunches. Holds her hand out for the trowel. I watch her hack at the ground for a while, then I lean forward and start tearing at the heather roots with my hands.

We scrabble like dogs at the rough soil. The stream chatters its approval as we work. Half an hour later we have a foot-deep hole.

I ease the tree root ball from its plastic pot and lower it into the hole. Then I hold it steady as Judy packs stones and earth into the gap around its base.

We stand back, panting, and look at what we've done.

The tree stands calmly in its new home. The water is by its side, the older trees are just above. Across the glen are the broad flanks of Ben Nevis and, higher up, its snow-dusted crown.

For a long time we just stand there, unable to add anything to the beauty of the scene.

"What now?" whispers Judy at last.

"Now I read my poem," I say. And I do:

The Shooting Star
By Tom Fitch

I stood upon a hill and stared
At the heart of a winter's night
So cold and dark that no life dared
Spot the black with humble light.

And then you came – free and wild
You lit the dark and world about
Your power was life – inside I smiled
And as I did, your light went out.

So bright, so brief, you passed me by
I frowned. It seemed to me unfair
That you should burn across the sky
And leave no trace of living there.

How many other unjust suns
Still sparkle smugly in the night?
Confident that they're the ones
Certain that they have that right.

I yearned to scream and shout and cry
"My star was here, it did exist!"
And write your name across the sky
To show the world that you are missed.

Saddened, I looked back to earth
- and stopped. I saw I had been wrong
This was not death, it was a birth
A happy, everlasting song -

Another presence showed me how
It would live on, the star that fell,
My smile returned. I'm better now.
My love, you saw the star as well.

★

My notepad is soaked. Rain, tears, who knows.
It crumples now too as Judy crushes herself into me.
I hold her little body as it bucks with sobs.
"That was so beautiful," she says into my chest.
Then she pulls away. Looks up at me. And her burning light is softened now.
I can look right back at it with peace.
"I'm sorry, Tom," she says. "You were right. It was cold and dark, and I was

251

so scared. But now-"

And she throws herself into me once more.

As we finally clamber out of the ravine, Judy takes my hand to steady herself. She leaves it there as walk down the slope.

A gentle rain is falling when we finally reach my little tent.

"You got any room in there?" she asks.

"All the room you want," I smile.

And we climb inside.

We start to do the things you need to do in a tent to be comfy – undoing boots off, unrolling sleeping bags, taking things out of pockets.

Then we stop-

-stare at each other for a split second-

-and kiss.

After we make love we both drift off.

It is the sweetest sleep of my life.

★

Many, many hours later – I don't know what time it is, but the darkness is fading into dawn – I wake up. As quietly as I can, pick up my notebook and pencil.

"What are you doing?"

I turn round, and for a second I think I must still be asleep and dreaming because Judy is lying beside me, soft light flooding from her eyes.

"Finishing my book," I say. And then I snap the pencil in two and stuff the notebook back deep into the rucksack.

"No more poetry?" she asks.

I shake my head.

252

"There must be somewhere that would take me back as a teacher," I say.

"Lots of places would love to have you," she smiles. "If you're ready."

"I am," I nod, and truly mean it, and I reach to hug her when suddenly she stiffens and her eyes go wide.

"You hear that?" she asks.

"Yes," I say, "I do."

"What is it?"

"Sounded like some sort of creature," I say. "I think it's just outside the tent."

Judy gasps and shrinks behind me as I ever-so-slowly unzip the flysheet. We peer nervously out into the half-light as I pull back the flap, inch by nervous inch.

And we recoil together in astonishment.

Sitting outside on the grass is the fluffiest kitten I have ever seen. A sort of tortoiseshell tabby with ginger patches. It is so young it can hardly stand, and sways from side to side in newborn confusion.

"Oh!" gasps Judy. "He's so beautiful!"

Judy reaches out and gently rubs the kitten's ear. It looks up at her with huge eyes, cocks his furry head on one side and mews once, pathetically.

"You think he's lost?" she says.

That's when I see the movement in the corner of my vision. I strain my eyes and look further out into the pre-dawn haze. I can't be sure, but I think I see a couple of shapes out there at the edge of the woods.

Shapes about the size of cats.

"No," I smile, "I think he's a gift."

The shapes watch us for a second, then disappear into the wilds, taking their twisting cat tails with them.

"Or maybe a sign of something to come," I add, and I pick the kitten up and bring him into the tent.

Judy stares at the tiny creature, her face molten with love.

"Can we keep him?" she sniffs, smearing tears across her cheeks.

"Of course," I say. "We can call him JJ."

She looks at me.

"Jones Junior," I explain. "George and I had a cat. He was called Jones and… it's a long story."

"JJ is lovely," she smiles, and she starts stroking the kitten.

I watch her fingers moving gently on its fur.

The kitten begins to purr. Its golden eyes shine like tiny suns as the first light of dawn glows on the tent around us.

I say:

"Will you marry me, Judy?"

"You silly idiot, of course I will."

Now the tears are flowing down my face too. And I give her the biggest hug I ever remember giving. So big it goes on for a lifetime.

And Jones Junior just sits there in the tent between us, licking his bum and loving it.

DIARY CONCLUDES.